PALM BEACH PRETENDERS

A CHARLIE CRAWFORD MYSTERY (BOOK 5)

TOM TURNER

TRIBECA PRESS

Published by Tribeca Press.

www.tomturnerbooks.com

Palm Beach Pretenders/Tom Turner – 1st ed.

ALSO BY TOM TURNER

CHARLIE CRAWFORD MYSTERIES

Palm Beach Nasty

Palm Beach Poison

Palm Beach Deadly

Palm Beach Bones

Palm Beach Pretenders

STANDALONES

Broken House

JOIN TOM'S AUTHOR NEWLETTER

Get the latest news on Tom's upcoming novels when you sign up for his free author newsletter at **tomturnerbooks.com/news**.

ACKNOWLEDGMENTS

As always, to my beautiful and talented daughters, Serena and Georgie, who I never get to see enough. I would also like to thank my friends, Tim Pitts and Rob Shaw (known affectionately as Rude Rob to his friends) for their critiques, comments and generous reviews.

ONE

If you go to the Mar-a-Lago website, you will see photos of catered weddings, which take place at the club. One shows an exterior pathway leading to an ornate, white arch, where men and women are united in holy matrimony. A profusion of palm trees sway in the breeze over rows of white wooden chairs on either side of the path. The wedding in the photos appears to be fairly small, seating a hundred or so guests.

Today's wedding party was much larger, and the white wooden chairs looked tiny because the average guest weighed between two hundred fifty and three hundred pounds. It was the wedding of the son of legendary college football coach Paul Pawlichuk, who'd recently signed a five-year contract for nine million dollars per year. Rich, the bridegroom, was a linebacker for the Miami Dolphins and made even more than his father, though it was Paul who was the member of the Mar-a-Lago Club. Rich was marrying Addison, the younger sister of Carla Carton, the lead actress in the hugely successful Netflix series *Bad Karma*. Not much was known about the bride except that she'd recently been a Miss Universe runner-up and was a woman who demanded things be done her way.

Rich's Miami Dolphin teammates and friends were sitting in the fragile-looking white chairs, along with a number of former college football players who had remained friendly with their coach, Paul. Fortunately, and somewhat surprisingly, as the ceremony came to a close and all rose to watch and photograph the ring exchange and protracted kiss between Addison and Rich, it appeared that all the white chairs had survived intact. The only casualty was the well-tended and recently mown lawn, into which countless chair legs had sunk three or four inches below the dark-green zoysia grass.

The ceremony concluded, the bride and groom were walking down the aisle, followed by the wedding party. As they headed to the area where the reception would be held, three waves of white-jacketed waiters made their way into the crowd with trays of fluted glasses filled with champagne.

"Thanks," Paul Pawlichuk said as he reached for a glass, then proceeded to drain it in one long gulp.

His wife Mindy, aware of her husband's prodigious appetites in so many areas, thought nothing of it when Paul grabbed a second flute off another waiter's tray on the fly.

"Beautiful ceremony, didn't you think?" Mindy asked her husband as their daughter Janice approached them with her husband George Figueroa and young son in tow.

"Very nice," Paul said, then under his breath, muttered, "But the padre kind of dragged it out a little."

The "padre" was a renowned monsignor from Miami who spoke too slow and flowery for Paul's taste.

"Hey, hon," Paul said, kissing his daughter Janice and ignoring his son-in-law the way he always did.

Janice shook her head. "You do see George standing next to me, Dad...and your grandson?"

Paul nodded. "Hey, Jorge, how's it goin', bro?"

Paul called everyone 'bro' except his brother.

Janice looked furious. "It's not Jorge, for God's sake."

Paul refrained from saying what he was thinking, *Well, it used to be*, and instead gave his four-year-old grandson a pat on his undersized head.

Janice turned to her mother and whispered under her breath. "You believe that tramp?" she said, flicking her head in the direction of the TV star and bride's sister. "Decked out like some Las Vegas hooker."

"Hey, hey," her mother said. "A little reverence on your brother's wedding day."

"Well, it's true," Janice said, as she caught her father sneaking a glance at Carla.

ACROSS THE ROOM, CARLA HAD WALKED UP TO ONE OF THE two outside bars and was talking to an older man who had followed her there. He was Robert Polk, the billionaire owner of Polk Global.

Carla leaned close to Polk and asked under her breath, "When was the last time you spoke to Alex?"

Polk glanced around to make sure no one was within hearing distance. "I went up to Deerfield and saw him play in a soccer match," he said, "Took him out for dinner afterward."

Carla frowned. "That was way back in the fall, for God's sake," she said. "It's spring now."

"Well, you had him for Thanksgiving and Christmas," Polk said.

"Yes, but there was a lot of time in between."

"What can I tell you, I've been busy as hell lately," Polk said. "When does he hear from Yale?"

"In a couple of weeks," Carla looked concerned. "It's a sure thing, right?"

Polk nodded and took a sip of his champagne.

Carla's sister Addison, clad in her twenty-thousand-dollar Zac Posen wedding dress, walked up to them.

"There she is," Carla said, giving her sister a big hug and kiss.

"Such a beautiful ceremony. And, oh my God, your flowers are *so* gorgeous—"then turning to Polk—"you remember Robert?"

"Of course, hello, Robert," Addison Pawlichuk said, then turned to her sister. "Well, it's official, I just married into the Polish royal family of football."

"Mazel tov," Carla said, raising her drink.

Addison laughed. "That's Jewish, not Polish."

"Close enough," Carla said. "You got a real mixed bag of people here. Which makes for the best weddings, they tell me."

"We'll see about that," Addison said.

Carla, looking over her sister's shoulder, zeroed in on her husband, Duane Truax. "Which one of your bridesmaids is Duane impressing with his race-track heroics now?"

Addison turned around and looked. "Oh, that's Chelsea."

"Is she the Prada model?" Carla asked.

"Yes, exactly, living with a chef at Nobu," Addison said.

"Where's he?"

"Working."

Carla nodded knowingly. "While the cat's away, I guess."

Addison laughed.

Robert Polk took a step closer to hear better.

Carla, still looking at her husband and the young model, shook her head disdainfully. "I've seen that look in his eye. I bet he just told her he was Driver of the Year."

Addison turned to her sister. "He was?"

"Yeah, back in 2005."

Addison glanced over at the six-piece band, which had segued into something slow after having just finished a bouncy number.

"Would you like to dance?" Polk asked Carla, sounding very formal.

Carla rolled her eyes and raised her eyebrows at her sister. "You mean, would I like you to tromp all over my toes?"

Addison tried to suppress a laugh. Polk looked stung.

Carla couldn't care less. "No, thanks," she said, looking away from Polk. "I'm going to go talk to my old friend, the movie director. It's been a while."

Addison glanced to where her sister was looking. A short man in his fifties with slicked-back blond hair and a ring in his ear was talking to a young woman.

"Movie director?" Addison said with a knowing smile. "I'd say you just gave him a promotion."

Carla laughed. "Okay, how about...director of short features where none of the actors wear clothes."

Addison patted her sister's shoulder and smiled. "Yeah, exactly, the kind that never have much of a plot."

"But plenty of skin," Carla whispered, then gave Robert Polk a kiss that barely grazed his cheek. "Bye, Robert, nice to see you."

"I'll give you a call," Polk said.

"Go ahead, but I'm going to be busy as hell," Carla zinged him.

Carla walked over to the man with the slicked-back blond hair. He was talking to a woman—late teens or early twenties—who had boobs so tightly packed into her dress that they looked like they were struggling to come out for air.

"Hello, Xavier," Carla said.

The short man swung around and came eye level with Carla's expensive Bvlgari diamond necklace.

"Well, hello, Carla," Xavier Duke said.

Carla glanced at the young woman. "Hi, I'm Carla."

The woman's baby blues lit up at having been addressed by the well-known actress.

"And this is my friend, Taylor Whitcomb," Duke said.

"Hi, so nice to meet you," Taylor said. "I love your show."

"Well, thank you," Carla said. "Wait, are you related to Rennie and Wendy?"

Taylor laughed. "Daughter."

"Well, I'll be damned," Carla said. "I haven't seen them in such a long time. Do they still live in New York and have a house down here?"

"Yes," Taylor said. "Sure do."

"Well, please give them my best," Carla said.

"I definitely will," Taylor said.

Carla turned back to Duke and said flirtatiously, "So how 'bout a dance, big boy?"

Big boy he wasn't, but game he was. "I'd love to," Duke said, then to Taylor, "See you in a little bit."

Xavier Duke had no original parts left on his face. Two years ago, he'd had a major facelift to expunge the bags under his eyes, and the plastic surgeon had thrown in a complimentary Kirk Douglas cleft chin. All of his crow's feet, frown lines and smoker's lines had been lasered into oblivion. His teeth had been bleached to an extreme, almost unnatural white.

Duke and Carla made their way to the dance floor, then she dropped her voice...and her smile. "A hundred thousand dollars," she said, suddenly all business.

"Add a zero," Duke said.

"Fuck that."

"It's like a tip to you."

"Two hundred is the best I'm doing," she said.

"You've got until Monday," Duke said.

Carla pulled back from him. "And you've got until I make a phone call."

She didn't have some big *goombah* on speed-dial but figured there was no harm in implying she did. Carla walked away quickly, headed for the bar.

She watched Paul Pawlichuk walk across the room with a drink in his hand and decided to follow him. He seemed to be heading in the direction of Mar-a-Lago's living room. She looked around to see if anyone was watching and, seeing no one, walked faster until she was right behind him. As he got to the door, she reached between his legs and goosed him.

He swung around and, seeing her, broke into a wide smile.

"Hello, Paul," she said. "You weren't looking for me, by any chance?"

He touched her on the shoulder.

"I'm just going to take care of a little business with my son-in-law, then I plan to give you my complete, undivided attention."

TWO

"Guy's got to weigh close to three hundred pounds," Mort Ott said, looking down at a large, naked male body sprawled out in a white chaise longue.

Charlie Crawford nodded. He had his hand on his chin as he observed a woman's body, also naked, also dead, face-down on the pool deck ten feet away from the chaise. "Yeah," he said. "And I'm guessing she was on top."

"So, like 425 pounds of thrusting and grunting," Ott said. "Damn chaise must be pretty well made."

A row of eleven more chaise longues all faced the pool in a perfect symmetrical formation.

"I'm guessing she tried to run," Crawford said. "Shooter probably did her first, then him."

The man had been shot in the temple and chest and the woman three times in the back. The man—six-foot-five or so—had a Buddha-like paunch with slab-like arms and legs. He had a good tan, and, it appeared, based on the small triangular patch of slug-white skin from his hips to his mid-thighs, sunbathed in a bathing suit from the Speedo family. Crawford and Ott, both semi-knowledgeable about college football, had recognized the victim right away as Paul Pawlichuk, the legendary college coach.

The woman was shapely, had long blond hair and stunning good looks. She also had a nice tan, but without lines, so in their professional opinion she sunbathed nude.

It was 6:30 in the morning. Crawford and Ott were at the Mar-a-Lago pool on the ocean, which was across the street from where the Pawlichuk-Carton wedding had taken place. The actual address was 1100 South Ocean Boulevard, Palm Beach, Florida. With them was Bob Hawes, the local medical examiner, and two CSEUs—Crime Scene Evidence Unit techs—who were scouring the immediate area for hair follicles, DNA samples, and other useful forensic clues. Surrounding them, and watching them go about their methodical business, were two Palm Beach police officers, who had arrived first on scene, and another twelve unidentified men in civilian clothes, who may or may not have been Secret Service.

Ott, who was taking notes in an old, leather-bound notebook he'd had since his days as a homicide cop in Cleveland, lowered his voice. "She can't be the coach's wife. Why would he be banging her here instead of—"

"No way it's his wife," Crawford agreed.

Bob Hawes, who was crouching to examine the woman, looked up. "You boneheads don't recognize her?"

Ott shrugged. "Who is she?"

"Madeline in that Netflix show, *Bad Karma*," Hawes said. "I don't know her real name."

"Holy shit, you're right," Ott said. "The chick who plays the senator's mistress."

"What's your estimate of time of death?" Crawford asked the ME as he pulled out his iPad.

"Six and a half hours ago," Hawes said without hesitation.

One thing that always bugged Crawford about Hawes was how sure he always seemed to be about everything. He suppressed an instinct to ask how Hawes could peg the vics' time of death so precisely, but he let it go.

Crawford was six three with piercing blue eyes and dirty-blonde hair worn a little longer than his crew-cut boss liked. More than once, Crawford had been asked by people on the street whether he was that polo-playing Ralph Lauren model. Ott, shorter by seven inches, rounder by four belt-sizes, older by fifteen years, and balding, was an easy man to underestimate. That would be a mistake, because, at fifty-three years old, Ott could bench press his weight, outrun Crawford, and, thus far anyway, outthink any southern Florida mutt, miscreant or outlaw.

The detectives had already inspected the couple's clothes, which had clearly been hastily tossed onto a nearby chaise. They hadn't found a wallet or anything identifying either person.

Crawford took out his iPad. "So, Madeline's the character's name?" he asked Hawes.

Hawes nodded.

Crawford started scrolling on his iPad.

He found what he was looking for. "Says Carla Carton is the name of the actress who plays Madeline Larsen." He glanced down at the body again. "Thirty-nine years old, she was also in that show, *The Gloaming*. Before that, a bunch of soaps. Married to—I'll be damned—Duane Truax."

Ott spun around and his mouth dropped. "Get outta here."

"Yeah, for the past fourteen years," Crawford said.

"Who the hell is Duane Truax?" Hawes asked.

"Christ, what rock you been hiding under?" Ott said. "Guy's a big time NASCAR driver."

"Why the hell would I pay attention to that redneck sport?" Hawes shot back.

A man in gray pants and a starched long-sleeved white shirt walked between the two Palm Beach cops and beelined over to Crawford, Ott and Hawes.

"Who's in charge here?" he demanded.

Crawford stepped forward. "Sir, this is an active crime scene," he said. "I'm going to have to ask you—"

The man got so close it looked like he was going to kiss Crawford. He lowered his voice. "We don't need this," he said. "Is there any way you can keep this whole thing under wraps? We *really* don't need this."

"Sir, I don't know who you are, but this is the scene of a double homicide, and we don't keep homicides under wraps," Crawford said. "Not only that, I don't know if you noticed, but there are a bunch of reporters out on the street who know something's up."

Ott nodded. "Cat's gonna be out of the bag any minute."

The man sighed as his eyes darted around nervously. "Okay," he said, "but do you need to release the victim's names? This is a matter of national security."

"It is?" asked Crawford. "And how's that?"

The man had no answer. He sighed theatrically, turned, then cut through the cluster of onlookers.

"Well," said Ott, "at least we know what qualifies as national security: when a guy making millions drawing up X's and O's gets whacked ballin' a TV hottie."

THREE

THE MEDIA, OF COURSE, WAS HAVING A FIELD DAY. HOW COULD they possibly have asked for more? A famous, married man having a moonlight tryst with a famous, married actress at Mar-a-Lago, gunned down together point-blank. It didn't get any better than that.

Palm Beach Police Chief Norm Rutledge, on the other hand, was on the verge of a nervous breakdown. In his eleven-year stretch as chief, he had never faced anything quite like this. Yes, there had been the billionaire killer a few years back, and the murdering, then murdered, Russian brothers last year, not to mention the famous talk-show host who had bought it in his pool house with his skivvies down around his ankles.

But there had never been anything like this: a murder at the home-away-from-home of the most powerful man in the universe.

Rutledge was calling Crawford, who was still at the crime scene, every five minutes for a progress report. When Crawford had stopped answering, the chief had begun calling Ott, but Ott had a firm policy of avoiding Rutledge's calls altogether.

Bob Hawes and the two crime-scene techs had come up almost completely dry in their initial analysis. They concluded that the murder weapon had been fired from less than twenty feet away, but that was about all they had. Worse, none of the bullets had lodged in either body and not one of them had been recovered. Hawes reported that the three bullets that had passed through Paul Pawlichuk's body had ricocheted off the cement pool deck on a trajectory toward the ocean. The slugs that had gone through Carla Carton, he stated, could have gone anywhere.

* * *

So, Crawford and Ott had very little to work with. In the six hours since the bodies were found, they had been interviewing people who had attended the wedding, their hope, of course, being to find someone who might have been an eyewitness to the murders. It quickly became apparent that no one had.

What seemed clear was that the murdered couple had wandered away from the wedding reception—which was being held outside the main house at Mar-a-Lago—and, no doubt in search of privacy, crossed Ocean Boulevard to the beach club and pool on the other side of the road. Several witnesses had noticed the two talking, after which they hadn't been seen again.

Mindy Pawlichuk had called Palm Beach Police at 3:25 a.m. to report her husband missing, though judging from her tone, she hadn't been overly concerned. Two plainclothes cops had arrived at 3:39 and spent an hour looking for Pawlichuk, while at the same time discovering that Carla Carton was not in her room. Finally, at 6:15 a.m., they found the two bodies and contacted Crawford and Ott, who'd arrived at Mar-a-Lago within five minutes of each other—at around 6:30.

They had met with Mindy Pawlichuk after having spent an hour and a half at the crime scene. Mindy's reaction was odd: she didn't seem shocked, nor did she cry. In fact, she hadn't looked too broken up at all. She simply nodded and asked who her husband had been with before they even had a chance to tell her that Pawlichuk's body was discovered ten feet away from a naked woman. Crawford and Ott concluded that this was not the first time Paul Pawlichuk had wandered off with someone who was not his wife.

Mindy, a woman in her early fifties, was wearing a loose-fitting caftan, possibly to disguise the fact that she was twenty to thirty pounds overweight. She had a pretty face with nice bone structure, but wore her hair in an unflattering bun. She said she had been married to Paul for twenty-six years. Her flat tone while reciting the facts seemed to indicate that many of those twenty-six years had been less than idyllic.

She spoke to Crawford and Ott for more than an hour and never came close to shedding a tear. A good cry might have been expected of one whose husband had just been brutally murdered, but Crawford got the sense that her crying days were long past. And judging by the hour spent with her, her smiling days as well. Then again, what was there to smile about when you were married to an apparent serial cheater?

"In order to find your husband's killer," Crawford had started out, "we're going to need to ask you some pretty blunt questions. I hope that's okay?"

Mindy nodded automatically.

"To the best of your knowledge, do you happen to know whether there was any history between your husband and Ms. Carton?"

Mindy Pawlichuk looked weary. "I don't know," she said. "There could have been. I never met the woman before, but, obviously, there was the connection between my new daughter-in-law Addison and Carla Carton. Them being sisters, I mean."

"Right, of course,"

"Plus, Paul was away a lot, for his job," she added.

Like being away from home was synonymous for being on the prowl for women.

Ott, who had been uncharacteristically quiet up to that point, weighed in with the velvet hammer he often wielded. "Does the name Madison Ko mean anything to you, Mrs. Pawlichuk?"

Mindy rolled her eyes and leaned back in her chair. "You mean the woman who Paul bought a house for five minutes from the stadium?" It was not a question. "The woman Paul promised to marry after he divorced me?" Another non-question question.

Crawford shot a glance at Ott, then back at Mindy. "How do you know that?"

"She told me," Mindy said, dropping her eyes. "When I went and confronted her ten years ago. I guess Paul decided a divorce would cost him too much money—" then, as if reconsidering— "or maybe figured having lots of girlfriends on the side was better than just one."

Crawford glanced at Ott. He was always impressed at how fast Ott was at digging up relevant information. He wondered how he had heard about Madison Ko. Probably a quick Google search. That was his own initial go-to as well.

"On another subject, Mrs. Pawlichuk," Crawford continued, "your new daughter-in-law, Addison, and her sister, we haven't heard anything about their parents?"

Mindy bowed her head slightly. "They were killed in a car accident...together. About three years ago. I never met them."

"Oh, I'm sorry to hear that," Crawford said.

Mindy nodded. "Yes, it was a terrible tragedy."

He wondered whether she'd put her husband and Carla Carton's double homicide in that category.

They spent another twenty minutes questioning Mindy Pawlichuk, then thanked her and said they'd be in touch as soon as they had something to report. She nodded but didn't seem to be particularly interested in whatever they might come up with.

It was strange.

Next up was Carla Carton's husband Duane Truax, a mustached man who was waiting for them in the Mar-a-Lago living room.

Upon first seeing him, Crawford was surprised at how short Duane Truax was. Five-eight, max. He figured maybe the race-car driver's stature helped him squeeze into those cars with all the decals on them. Maybe a lighter bodyweight let the car go round and around a little faster too. Truax wore black Levis, a black cowboy hat and cowboy boots that he rested on an antique chair. Crawford wasn't sure Mar-a-Lago's owner would appreciate the racer's heels on his furniture but left it alone.

Far from being broken up with grief, Duane Truax answered their questions in short phrases and yawned a lot. It turned out that he lived full-time in Birmingham, Alabama. Carla, he explained, didn't spend much time there and had a house in the hills above Hollywood. When Ott asked him the address, Truax didn't know, only that it was near Mulholland Drive.

That was strange too.

Truax was scheduled to fly back to Birmingham that night. He wasn't sure what Carla's plans had been. A little voice was suggesting to Crawford that Duane Truax and Carla Carton, like Mindy and Paul Pawlichuk, had something less than a marriage made in heaven.

Despite the yawns, Truax struck Crawford as a man who maybe had ADD. His hooded blue eyes darted around constantly and he couldn't keep his hands still. He had dark hair that stuck up in front and yellow teeth that could have used a Crest Whitestrip or two.

"Look, man, let's cut to it," Truax said, after Crawford and Ott got through their intro remarks. "I didn't kill my wife, okay? She and I were separated, okay? Not legally, but in fact. What else do you need to know?"

Might as well just cut to it, too, Crawford figured. "Mr. Truax, at any point last night did you go down to the pool on the beach here at Mar-a-Lago?"

"Not hardly. I didn't even know there was one. Last thing I was doing was following Carla around..." A long pause, followed by a confiding lean-in and whisper: "See, I had a little thing going with one of the bridesmaids."

Ott eyed him, not trying to hide his disdain. "Oh, did you now?" he said. "And what was *her* name?"

"Chelsea...didn't catch her last name," Truax said.

"Course you didn't," Ott muttered.

Truax shot him the maximum stink-eye.

"So, keep going," Crawford said.

Truax wiped his nose with the back of his hand. "Me and her ended up taking off, going to a strip club."

"You and her, huh?" Ott hated grammar-butchers. "'Til what time?"

"'Til after it happened. The murders."

"Oh?" said Ott. "And how do you know when the murders took place?"

"I heard a guy say."

Ott, taking notes, glanced at Crawford.

"So, were you aware of there being a relationship between Pawlichuk and Carla?" Crawford asked.

"I had kind of an inkling," Truax said. "But like I said, me and Carla had both moved on."

"'An inkling?' Where'd you get that from?"

"You know, like a hunch."

Crawford figured it was time he and Ott moved on too. Duane Truax was almost certainly not their man.

But Ott wasn't done. "So, you two weren't staying in the same bedroom?"

"Not hardly. Like I told you—"

"I know...separated."

Truax suddenly looked like a thought had just snuck up and slapped him on the side of the head. "I did walk past the room where she was staying and saw the door open. I thought that was a little strange."

"Why?" Ott asked.

"'Cause she almost never went to bed later than ten, and this was way after that," Truax said. "Needed her beauty sleep, she always said. Plus her mask."

"Her mask?" Ott asked.

"Yeah, she'd always get into bed, then put on her mask," Truax said. "Damn thing cost a fortune. Golden Luminescence Infusion Mask, it was called."

"I see," Crawford said, imagining hopping into bed with someone wearing a Golden Luminescence Infusion Mask. Romantic didn't spring to mind.

"So what time was that?" Ott asked.

"'Round midnight, I'd say."

They thanked Truax. He yawned and walked away.

"Another idol bites the dust," Ott said.

"Him?" Crawford looked at the back of the race-car driver and shook his head. "Christ, man, you musta been really hard up for idols."

FOUR

CRAWFORD AND OTT DECIDED TO RETREAT TO THE RELATIVE normalcy of their office. Normal, that is, until Rutledge invariably barged in and began one of his rants.

Crawford had a whiteboard on the wall opposite his desk. Ott, who had by far the better penmanship, had written only five words, four of which were names.

The first word he wrote was SUSPECTS:

Then, the only obvious suspects:

1. Duane Truax.
2. Mindy Pawlichuk.

Next to Truax he wrote "Unlikely," then, next to Mindy, he wrote "more unlikely."

He glanced at Crawford. "By the way, what's with all these slimeballs?"

"What do you mean?"

"Not one of 'em we've come across so far had a normal relationship. Pawlichuk buying a house for a Japanese chick and banging a movie star who's married to a guy who doesn't know what his wife's address is and who's taking a bridesmaid half his age to a strip club. I mean, what the fuck, dude?"

"Korean," Crawford said.

"Huh?"

"That woman Pawlichuk bought the house for."

"Whatever."

"And does every other sentence or yours have to have the word 'banging' in it?"

Ott shook his head. "Sometimes I say 'bangin' and sometimes I say ballin'." He tilted his head and looked at Crawford. "What do you want me to say? Shtupping or boinking or—"

"Okay, okay, 'banging' just sounds so...late Elvis."

"Noted," Ott said. "So let me ask you this: do you think this was premeditated or spur-of-the-moment?"

Crawford leaned back in his chair. "That's a good question. My gut says pre-meditated but I've got absolutely no proof. If it's spur-of-the-moment that means it's got to be someone who was jealous of Pawlichuk doing Carla, or the other way around—"

"Oh, so that's your word for it?"

"What?"

"'Doing.'"

Crawford shook his head. "For Chrissakes, will you let me finish? And since the obvious choices, Mindy and Truax, are 'unlikely' and 'more unlikely'—"

"Yeah, but I guarantee we'll be adding some boyfriends and girl-friends to the list."

"But so far, we just have the Korean woman, and I got a feeling she wasn't on the guest list."

"Yeah, but just because she wasn't invited doesn't mean she couldn't sneak in—" He saw Crawford's skeptical look. "I know, long-shot department. But, I tell you what isn't...Hollywood Carla and boyfriends."

"Yeah, that could be a long list."

Ott nodded. "Bet your ass it is."

Crawford leaned back in his chair and thought for a second. "I think you're ruling out Truax a little too fast," he said. "I did a Google search and found out he has a long history of being a hothead."

"Yeah, well, as someone who's seen a bunch of his races, that's a fact," Ott said. "You're talking about going after other drivers in the pit after they cut him off and shit, right?"

Crawford nodded. "I guess. Like one time he dragged that guy Jeff Burton out of his car at a race and beat the shit out of him."

"So, tell you what: I'll put him down as 'still in the running' instead of 'unlikely.' That make you happy?"

Crawford nodded as Ott walked up to the white board and made the appropriate edit.

"Done," he said.

"So, we got Rich Pawlichuk and his new bride in ten minutes," Crawford said, looking at his watch and standing.

They left the station on South County Road and drove the short distance to Mar-a-Lago on South Ocean for the 2:30 p.m. interview. There were three men at the front entrance to Mar-a-Lago. Shaved heads, tight-fitting dark suits, ear buds, every stereotype of a fed there could ever be.

Crawford hit the button for his window and it rolled down.

One of the men bent down and looked in.

"Detectives Crawford and Ott, Palm Beach PD," he said. "Here to interview Rich Pawlichuk and his wife in the main living room."

"Okay, Detective, you know where it is, right?" the man said, friendly enough.

"Yeah, we were here this morning."

"How's it comin' so far?" the man asked.

"Nothing much yet," Crawford said. "You heard anything that might be helpful?"

The man shrugged. "Sorry." Then he stepped back and ushered them in.

Mar-a-Lago, a 126-room, 62,500-square-foot house, had been

built in 1924 by cereal heiress Marjorie Merriweather Post and her
husband E.F. Hutton. The forty-fifth president had purchased it in
1985 and converted it into a club, where members paid a $200,000
initiation fee and $14,000 a year in membership dues. The club
contained 58 bedrooms, 33 bathrooms, 12 fireplaces, and three bomb
shelters. It also had five clay tennis courts, two pools, a putting green,
and a croquet court. Michael Jackson and Lisa Marie Presley had
spent their honeymoon there in 1994 and were said to have been
quite pleased with the accommodations.

Crawford looked back in his rearview mirror as he approached
the house. "One of the shaved heads is behind us."

"I noticed," Ott said.

Crawford slowed to a stop and he and Ott exited the car. They
flashed their IDs to a few more plainclothes men, who directed them
inside to the club's living room. Cozy was not a word that came to
mind as they were ushered to a corner of the vast room.

A few minutes later, a couple in their mid-twenties walked in and
joined them. Rich Pawlichuk looked larger in person than he did
making open-field tackles on TV. His bride was tall, thin, striking,
and appeared to be more irritated than in mourning for her sister and
short-lived father-in-law.

Crawford and Ott got to their feet and shook hands with the
couple. Rich's handshake was predictably bone-crushing. Crawford
saw Ott try not to wince.

"Thanks for meeting with us," Crawford said as Rich and his
bride sat on a couch across from Ott and him. "We're sorry it had to
be under these circumstances."

"Yes, sorry for both your losses," Ott added.

The couple nodded

"I hope you don't mind if we ask you some difficult questions,"
Crawford said. "But in order to find out—"

"Yes, we understand," Addison Pawlichuk said. "So, if you could
get on with it, please? And would you mind if we sat out by the pool?
Instead of in here?"

"Aw, come on, hon," Rich said. "We just sat down."

Addison shrugged. "What's the big deal?"

Crawford looked at Ott. "Sure, that's fine."

The four walked outside, followed by two shaved heads ten feet behind them.

Addison, who was wearing a short skirt, sat in a chaise and immediately peeled off her collared shirt. She had a black bikini top underneath. She looked up and saw Ott glancing at her funny. "We're supposed to be on a beach 5,000 miles from here," she explained. "On our honeymoon."

"Gotcha," said Ott.

"So, Rich, our first question is, did your father know"—Crawford turned to Addison—"your sister before the wedding yesterday?"

Addison nodded. "Yes," she said. "Well, we assume they did, but we're not a hundred-percent sure. See, Carla was a cheerleader at Paul's college eighteen years ago—"

Rich took over. "My dad's been coaching there goin' on twenty-three years now."

"But that's going back a long way," Ott said. "You think they knew—"

Rich nodded. "Yeah, I'd bet on it," he said. "See, one thing you're going to find out is my dad had an eye for the ladies"—then he realized—"Well, obviously you already did."

Addison was nodding. "And my sister back then—and until today—was a stone-cold fox."

Crawford had read that phrase in a bad novel once and heard it on a few cheesy TV shows but didn't realize people actually said it in real life.

"But you don't know if they had seen each other since then?" Crawford asked.

Rich shrugged and glanced at Addison. "We don't know for a fact," he said, "but I wouldn't rule it out."

Since Rich had put it out there, Ott felt free to pursue it. "So you seem to be saying that your father had affairs with, I guess it's safe to say, more than a few women?"

"Yes, it's safe to say that," Rich said.

"Hundreds," Addison said, straight-faced. "Possibly thousands."

"She's exaggerating," Rich said.

"But not by much," she said.

It was time for Ott to take a few swings again with his velvet hammer. "So, what I infer from what you just said is there are maybe a lot of—you'll excuse the expression—pissed-off husbands and boyfriends out there."

"Good inferring, detective," Rich said. "To name just a few, my assistant coach at Miami, my best friend's older brother, my uncle Burt..."

"Not to mention me," Addison said.

Rich cocked his head. "What do you mean? What are you pissed off about?"

"The fact that because of your father and his...wandering dick, we're not at the Hotel du Cap right now."

"Where?" Ott asked.

Addison was shaking her head. "The Hotel du Cap Eden-Roc in Antibes, France," she said. "That's where we were supposed to be for the first three days of our honeymoon. Instead we have to hang around this glorified roach motel."

"Come on, hon," Rich said. "It's not so bad."

"The hell it isn't," Addison said. "Look at what Yelp had to say about it. Mostly 1-stars."

Ott glanced at Crawford, completely taken aback by what she was saying about the famed Mar-a-Lago.

"So, Rich," Crawford took over. "It's difficult to ask you, but could you provide us with a list of women you have reason to believe might have slept with your father?"

"Jesus," Addison said under her breath, "he's gonna need a couple of legal pads."

Rich sighed deeply. "Yeah, sure I'll do it," he said, "if it'll help find his killer." Then, to his wife: "Do you need to be so hard on the man? He was my father."

Addison kissed him on the cheek. "Sorry, hon."

"We wouldn't ask you to do it unless we thought it might help our investigation," Ott said.

"You might want to ask my mother, too," Rich said softly. "Though maybe you could wait a little."

Crawford nodded, not bothering to tell him they'd already spoken to her. "Of these men you mentioned, the Dolphins assistant coach, your best friend's brother, and your uncle, were any of them at the wedding yesterday?"

"Just Uncle Burt," Rich said. "But he and my Dad had patched things up."

"So it's safe to assume all three are innocent?" Crawford asked.

"Yes," Rich said. "Definitely."

"So, of the people who were here yesterday, it's obviously crossed your mind that one of them may have murdered your father and Carla. So, question is, who would you put on that list?" Crawford asked Rich.

Rich sighed again. "Well, I've actually thought about it a lot," he said. "But it's really hard to think of a friend or family member as being a murderer."

"What about that guy who crashed?" Addison asked.

This was news.

"Who was that?" Crawford asked.

Rich nodded a few times. "This guy who used to play for my Dad. A bad dude. Showed up drunk and started cursing him out at the wedding."

"What was the reason?"

"He thought Dad didn't put a good word in for him in the pro draft. He had a couple of pro teams interested but not when they found out about his two domestic abuse cases and showing up drunk for a game."

"And what's his name?"

"Joey Decker," Rich said.

Crawford thought he'd heard the name before. Lying on his couch one Saturday afternoon watching a game probably. "So what happened to him?"

"A bunch of us tossed him out. I don't really see him as a murderer."

Ott wrote the name down. "We'll check him out anyway."

Addison leaned forward in her chaise and shaded her eyes. "What about Duane?"

"I don't know," Rich said. "You know him. Is he the first one you thought of?"

Addison nodded. "He'd probably be my choice," she told the detectives. "Not that he really strikes me as a murderer, either."

"Then why'd you mention him, Ms. Pawlichuk?" Ott asked.

"'Cause my sister was going to divorce him," Addison said. "And 'cause now he's got a shot at getting her money."

Ott glanced at Crawford. "Keep going," he said. "We'd appreciate every detail you can give us about that."

"Well, Carla got paid a fortune for that TV show, something like a million an episode," Addison said. "And I don't know whether you follow NASCAR, but Duane isn't really cutting it anymore."

"I follow it," Ott said. "You mean, he hasn't won a race in a while?"

"Yes, that's what my sister told me. And he had a lot fewer sponsors putting those little thingies on his car," Addison said.

"So they were actually in the process of getting a divorce?" Crawford asked. "He just told us they were separated."

"Yes, well, I think he was fighting it. But I know she recently brought it up with him. Going through with it, that is," Addison said. "The reality is, I wasn't that close to my sister, so I don't know all the ins and outs. Mainly because of our age difference. I hardly remember her as a kid."

Ott nodded. "Understood. And did Carla have another man she was seeing that you know of?"

"She never went into that with me," Addison said. "But my impression was, she had several. And if you believe those supermarket rags...*quite a few.*"

Supermarket rags were pretty far out of Crawford's wheelhouse, so on that subject he deferred to Ott, who wasn't ashamed of sprinkling quotes from the *Star* and the *Globe* into his daily conversations.

"Did I read about your sister and a TV producer, I think it was?" Ott asked.

"Yeah, he was one of them," Addison said. "Maurice Littlefield."

"And what about, wasn't there a big Wall Street mogul who lives down here now?" Ott asked, making notes.

Rich chuckled. "You do your research in the check-out line at Publix, Detective?"

Ott nodded. "Close. I'm actually a Winn-Dixie guy," he said. "What's the name of the Wall Street man?"

"One of the Polk brothers," Rich said. "He was at the wedding yesterday."

"Oh, really? Which one?" Crawford asked.

"Robert?" Rich said.

His bride nodded. "What I heard is they had an on-again off-again thing over the years."

Crawford made a mental note to talk to Robert Polk.

"I also heard rumors about that writer, Rolf Richter," Addison said.

"Isn't he really old?" Ott said. "I remember reading a book of his in high school."

"I got news for you," Addison said. "Guys' libidos never die. Look at that place the Villages up north of here in Florida. People in their eighties goin' at it with a vengeance. Half of 'em got venereal disease, I read somewhere."

Crawford could see it was time to steer Ott and Addison back on course. "Anyone else?"

"'Anyone else' what?" Addison asked. "Oh, you mean, rumored to be having a thing with my sister? Yes, there were a few others, but I'd probably put them in the one-night-stand category."

Crawford glanced at Ott. Ott shrugged. They were out of questions.

"Well, thank you both for your time," Crawford said, as he noticed Addison stripping off her skirt, revealing a banana peel-sized black bikini bottom.

"You're welcome," Addison said with a smile. "Time to get my bottom half too."

Crawford and Ott tried not to stare.

FIVE

CRAWFORD AND OTT WERE ON THEIR WAY BACK TO THE station. Ott, as usual, was the designated driver, along with being the designated note-taker and whiteboard-scribbler.

"What's with that Addison? She acted like her hamster had died instead of her sister."

"I know," Crawford said. "Pretty tough on Pawlichuk, too."

"Yeah, no shit, making him out to be the world's biggest pussy-hound," Ott said. "Not to mention being in such a rush to get to that hotel and work on her tan some more."

Crawford nodded.

"You grew up with rich people, Charlie. Are these people typical?"

Crawford exhaled and shook his head. "That was a long time ago. I can't really remember, but I'd have to say no. Maybe it's just Addison. Rich seemed all right."

Ott flicked his blinker to turn into the station. "Yeah, I guess. What's next?"

"We gottta check out Joey Decker."

Ott nodded. "Aka, the wedding crasher."

✳ ✳ ✳

CRAWFORD HAD TWO GO-TOS WHEN IT CAME TO MURDER investigations in which he didn't have much physical evidence. The first one—Google—he had already gone to. The second one was Rose Clarke.

Rose was the most successful real-estate agent in Palm Beach and knew everything there was to know about practically everyone in town.

It was unlikely you'd go to a cocktail party in Palm Beach and not see Rose there. Sometimes she'd hop from one to the next, hitting three or four in a single night. And as far as the charity-ball circuit went, she hadn't missed one in years. Not that she particularly liked them. She'd told Crawford it was just where she got her real estate listings. And dirt on people that could turn out to be useful.

One thing about Rose was that she was incredibly well-disciplined and never had more than two chardonnays in a night, no matter how many parties she attended. An old boyfriend had once joked that she could listen to four conversations at once and have total recall of all four. There were few people in Palm Beach she didn't know at least something about, and part of her well-honed discipline was her ability to keep that knowledge all to herself.

With one exception, that is. Charlie Crawford.

They were both in the business of exercising absolute discretion at all times. Like Rose, Crawford had to listen carefully and be highly attentive. Sort out fact from fiction, discern lies from the truth. It wasn't so easy.

They also had a mutual understanding—a pact, really. Their unspoken arrangement was the following: Rose would answer three questions regarding people or events that factored into Crawford's investigations in return for lunch on him. Or five questions for dinner at a nice restaurant. Or unlimited questions at a *really* nice restaurant, followed by an overnight stay at either her luxurious Palm Beach house on the ocean or, less frequently, at his not-so-luxurious apartment in West Palm Beach overlooking the vast Publix parking lot.

Often, Rose would call Crawford and volunteer information she thought might be helpful to a specific case. As she put it, Charlie was her friend with benefits, and they were both quite happy with the arrangement.

It was five hours after Crawford and Ott's interview with Rich and Addison Pawlichuk. Crawford and Rose were at Amalfi, one of the nicer Italian restaurants in West Palm Beach. Crawford never took Rose to places in Palm Beach because he liked to put distance between his social life and where he worked.

"I've been there a few times," Rose was saying about Mar-a-Lago. "The architect was Marion Sims Wyeth, who did a lot of good houses around here, but I think he had an off-day when he designed that place."

"Why do you say that?"

"'Cause it's downright gaudy. All those Moorish, Gothic, baroque whatever-the-hell-they-are decorations. Didn't you think it's all a little bit over the top? Actually, now that I think about it, a man named Joseph Urban designed the interiors. A million frescoes, Venetian arches and Spanish tiles. Too damned busy for my taste. I do love that tower, though. I was up there once. What a killer view."

Crawford shrugged. "Can't say I know much about architecture. And less about interior decoration."

Rose shook her head. "Yeah, yeah, you know a lot more about that stuff than you let on," she said. "Once I went to a Celine Dion concert there that was pretty good"—Rose's eyes lit up—"but my favorite Mar-a-Lago story was when Jennifer Lopez and that guy Puff Daddy, later to become P. Diddy, showed up there one memorable Easter."

"What happened?"

"You never heard this story?"

Crawford shook his head.

"Oh, God, listen to this. So, J Lo and P were taking a stroll on the beach and, as you know, the Mar-a-Lago beach club is right next to that WASP bastion, the Bath & Racquet Club"—Crawford nodded and took a sip of his red wine, knowing this was sure to be entertaining—"And apparently one or both of them started feeling amorous all of a sudden. So, they went over to a chaise on the beach and, without a care in the world, started doing it."

"Come on. Really?"

"Swear to God. Hey, it was in the Glossy." Also known as the *Palm Beach Daily Reporter*. "Their ace society reporter, Sharon Donleavy, wrote about how Bath & Racquet grandmothers who were having lunch there with their grandchildren suddenly looked out the picture windows in horror as J Lo and P did the, quote-unquote, horizontal rhumba."

Crawford shook his head slowly. "You know, you should write a book about all the stuff that's happened here."

"Too late," Rose said. "Someone already did. It's called *Palm Beach Babylon*. A classic, which should be required reading in everyone's library."

"Maybe that's where Paul Pawlichuk and Carla Carton got the idea," Crawford said. "The chaise."

Rose nodded. "Hey, I never thought of that." She put her glass of chardonnay down. "That wedding, what a mutt convention." She put her hand over her mouth. Then more quietly, "Oops, I guess I should be a little more respectful of the dead."

Crawford smiled. "Tell me what you know about it."

Rose put her hand on Crawford's. "Okay, here's the skinny, from my vantage point. Ready?"

"Let 'er rip."

"Both Paul Pawlichuk and Carla Carton made it a habit of screwing everything within a twenty-mile radius."

"Said with typical Rose candor."

"Just tellin' it like it is." Then she seemed to have a sudden brainstorm. "Hey, I just noticed the alliteration thing."

Crawford thought for a second. Then it dawned on him "Oh, you mean, PP and CC."

Rose laughed.

"What?"

"You said pee-pee."

Crawford laughed. "Okay, Rose, we're devolving fast here," he said. "What else?"

"Well, what comes to mind is that Paul and Carla are perfect examples of the all-American success story."

"And what would that be?"

"How a person can become fabulously rich and famous starting out as a high-school cheerleader in pissant Arkansas or as a Neanderthal who makes large men run after other large men and jump on top of 'em."

"Only problem is the ending."

Rose nodded and frowned. "Well, yeah, there's that."

"Okay," Crawford said, "but come on, I need suspects."

Rose smiled. "That's ol' cut-to-the-chase Crawford I know and love."

"Hey, I can't help myself," Crawford said. "But I know damned well that in the ten hours or so since you heard about the murders, you've already got a long list of possible killers. Am I right?"

"Of course," Rose said. "So, here's what I can tell you so far. Carla was definitely doing that old skinflint, Robert Polk."

"He's a skinflint, the fifteenth richest man in America?" Crawford had checked.

"Oh, yeah, definitely, and I know from personal experience," Rose said. "He asked me out to lunch once on the pretext of possibly listing his house with me. Took me to Sonny's BBQ for wings."

"I love that place."

"Yes, but to take a date and get her in the mood?"

Crawford nodded. "Wouldn't be my first choice for that," he said. "Okay, he's already on my interview list. Who else?"

"Does it have to be someone at the wedding?"

Crawford put his hand on his chin. "That's a good question," he said. "Mort and I were talking about that—whether it could have been someone who planned to kill either Pawlichuk or Carla beforehand and found his best opportunity to be when they were—"

"Doin' the rhumba?"

Crawford laughed.

"Then, of course, there's Duane Truax," Rose said. "Who may have seemed like a catch when Carla was twenty and stupid, but not in her late thirties and a star."

"We have him on our short list, which, at the moment, is too damned short." Crawford reached into an inside pocket of his jacket. "I printed out a guest list of everyone who was at the wedding. I asked Addison Pawlichuk for it and she emailed it to me."

Rose rubbed her hands together. "Oh, goody," she said. "Guarantee you I'll find a few more suspects for you in here."

He handed Rose the list as his cell phone rang. He looked down at the display. It was Ott. "Gotta take this. It's Mort."

Rose barely heard him, already engrossed in the wedding list.

"Yeah, Mort, what's up?"

"You know what Norm is really good at?" Ott asked, referring to their boss.

Crawford thought for a second. "Uh, not really. Bocce maybe."

"Good guess," Ott said. "But the answer is college football. For a guy who don't know shit about shit, the guy's a freakin' encyclopedia when it comes to college ball. Figured out that Paul Pawlichuk, who never graduated from high school, is worth about a hundred mil."

SIX

THEIR DINNERS WERE GETTING COLD AS ROSE PORED OVER THE three-page wedding list and Crawford listened to Ott.

"So, when Pawlichuk started out back in 1995 as head coach, he was making a mere one-point-five. Flash forward to his most recent deal—"

"Nine mil a year, I read?" Crawford said.

"Yes, plus bonuses and extras, which puts it probably closer to ten."

Crawford paused for a second "Okay, but the question is, so what?"

The waiter returned and refilled their wine glasses.

"I don't know," Ott said. "Maybe nothing. But that old cliché 'follow the money' comes to mind."

"Yeah, I hear you," Crawford said.

"Where are you anyway?"

"At a restaurant, watching my food get cold."

"Okay, man, I won't keep you," Ott said. "Couple other football-related things that Norm came up with but they can wait. What time you gonna be in tomorrow?"

"Eight or so."

"Okay, see you then."

"Later." Crawford clicked off and looked up at Rose, who hadn't taken a bite of her soft-shelled crabs. "Come on, girl, you gotta eat or you'll waste away."

"Appetite like mine. Ain't gonna happen," Rose said, not looking up. "Pretty interesting list."

"Like who?"

"Like a guy named Arnie Stoller," she said. "He's a big money manager down in Miami. Handles a lot of high-net-worth individuals. Probably handled Paul."

Crawford pulled a pen out of his pocket and handed it to her. "Do me a favor, underline his name, will you, please?"

"Sure." Rose did it.

"How do you know him? Stoller?" Crawford asked.

"Another real-estate connection. At one point, he was looking for a house in PB," Rose said as Crawford flagged the waiter. "His plan was to commute by helicopter to Miami. I think he ended up in Manalpan instead."

The waiter approached their table. "Yes, sir?"

"Do me a favor, will you," Crawford said. "Would you heat up our plates, please."

"Absolutely," the waiter said, reaching for their plates.

"Thanks," Rose said, looking up and smiling.

"Who else of interest is on there?" Crawford asked.

"Well, we got the porn king, for one," Rose said, pointing at the name.

Crawford leaned closer. "Xavier Duke?"

"Yup," Rose said. "Apparently they shoot about as many here as in California. Word is, he does them all at his house." Rose looked up. "Is that legal?"

"Tell you the truth, I don't really know," Crawford said. "Not my department."

"You do dead people, not naked people. Right?"

"And sometimes naked, dead people." Crawford patted Rose's hand. "So, tell me about this guy Duke."

"I'm happy to say I've never had the pleasure. And if he wanted to go around and look at houses, I wouldn't allow him to stink up my car," Rose said. "I just know the guy is a sleaze. Supposedly has mafia connections. He used to have a house up on Jupiter Island until he moved down here. Somewhere near Tiger Woods, I heard."

"What? Staid old Jupiter Island?"

"Don't kid yourself," Rose said. "They've got a few dubious characters up there."

"But mostly bluebloods and Hall of Fame golfers, right?"

"Mostly, but a few rotten eggs slip through."

"Anybody else look interesting on that list?"

"I haven't gone through the whole thing yet," Rose said. "But I'll tell you something else."

"What's that?

"Your victim hit on me once."

"Paul?"

Rose nodded.

"Jesus, with all his skirt-chasing, when did the guy ever have time to coach?"

"I don't know, but I can assure you I was one skirt he chased but never caught."

"'Cause you've got good taste in men."

Rose nodded. "Yeah, that. But I'm also proud to say that I have never had sex with a married man."

SEVEN

CRAWFORD AND ROSE WERE IN HER KING-SIZE BED, CRAWFORD looking out the window at her killer view of the ocean. It was a view he never got tired of. He had fleetingly wondered what it would be like to be married to Rose. Probably not so terrible. Pretty good, in fact. She was stunning, funny, smart and independent, so they'd have a lot of time to do their own things. She was also rich and had this house with the amazing view.

But then there was Dominica McCarthy, the beautiful crime scene tech he occasionally worked with, and yes, slept with. And unless she was dead—what a horrible thought—or married to another guy—an almost equally horrible thought—she would always have a lock on Crawford's heart. He silently scolded himself for pining for Dominica in another woman's bed.

Rose was still sleeping, but Crawford had been up since five, going over the Pawlichuk-Carton case in his mind. He was eager to talk to Robert Polk, Arnie Stoller, and Xavier Duke. Duane Truax deserved another closer look, too. Particularly in light of the financial motive: If his wife died before she divorced him, he'd have a good shot at getting her money, which sounded like it was considerable. He wondered how it was possible to make a million dollars for *each* episode of a TV series. He did the math, knowing each season had twelve episodes or so. It was simple. Twelve million. Was that possible? Then he remembered reading somewhere how the main characters in *Game of Thrones* were paid two and a half million per episode in the seventh season. Poor Carla, a paltry millon-per...

All of a sudden, he felt a warm hand touch his hip, then start gently moving down his leg. Rose's breasts pressed up against his back.

"Don't think for a second you're going to get out of here without the breakfast special," Rose whispered. "And I don't mean bacon and eggs."

Crawford turned, put his arms around her and pulled her close to him. "Are you kidding?" he said, breathing in her luscious aromatic smell. "This is going to be the high point of my day."

"Day?"

"Week."

"Week?"

"Year."

"That's more like it."

* * *

CRAWFORD WALKED INTO OTT'S CUBICLE. OTT SMILED UP AT him, moved his head a little closer and sniffed a few times.

"I've smelled that a couple times before," Ott said, his smile getting bigger. "It's not that Irish Spring shit of yours."

Crawford shook his head. "Maybe if you spent less time sniffing me like a dog and more time on the case, we'd be getting somewhere."

"I am getting somewhere," Ott said glancing in the direction of Norm Rutledge's office. "Thanks to ol' dipshit over there."

"He came up with more football intel?" Crawford asked dubiously.

"Yeah, and it's not half bad." Ott put his hands behind his head and his feet up on his desk. "He tells me he read a while back that one of the NFL owners approached Pawlichuk and secretly negotiated a five-year guaranteed deal with him."

"For how much?"

"Fifty-nine million supposedly."

"So what happened?"

"So supposedly Pawlichuk agreed to it," Ott said, "and based on that—even though it wasn't signed—the owner fired his head coach. Had to eat something like ten million remaining on the guy's contract."

"Guess he figured it was worth it," Crawford said.

Ott shrugged. "Yeah, except the next day Pawlichuk changed his mind. And since all the owner had was a handshake—"

"The owner was screwed," Crawford said.

Ott nodded his head. "Big time. Ended up looking like a schmuck and had to go hire another guy."

"This is all from Norm?" Crawford said, cocking his head.

"Yeah, and don't sound so surprised." Ott smiled. "Every couple of years or so, the guy has a good idea."

"So, what was it?"

"His idea?"

"Yes."

"That the owner was so humiliated and pissed off he hired a guy to take out Pawlichuk. Carla was collateral damage."

Crawford shook his head and frowned. "You back on the crack again, Mort?"

"I think it could have happened." Ott held up his hands. "Hey, we gotta at least look into it."

Crawford shrugged. "Have at it. Go waste your time."

Ott looked like a spanked child. "He also told me about a guy named Sims Thaw. Ever hear of him?"

Crawford shook his head.

"Well, he's the head coach of a Canadian Football League team. I forget which one," Ott said. "So, according to Norm, Thaw used to be

Pawlichuk's assistant coach before he got the CFL job. A week ago, it comes out that Pawlichuk and Thaw are the two leading candidates to be head coach of another NFL team. Anyway, Thaw was at the wedding 'cause he and Pawlichuk stayed in touch. Went hunting and fishing and shit together—according to Norm."

Crawford locked eyes with Ott. "Gotta tell you, Mort, that's a whole pile of worthless bullshit. I mean, I get that we don't have anything, but we ain't that desperate."

"Why are you shooting it down before we look into it?"

Crawford shook his head slowly. "How many times have you heard about a guy killing a high-profile rival for a job? Or, in this case, a rival who's a friend."

Ott started tapping a pencil on his desk. "I'm sure it's happened," he said. "And don't forget, we're talking about a ten-million-dollar job here. That's per year."

Crawford slowly shook his head. "It's really thin, man. There's nothing there," Crawford tilted his head and looked into his partner's eyes. "And I think deep down you know it."

"We gotta humor Norm a little," Ott said.

Crawford shrugged. "Why? We never have before. But—what the hell—put the guy on our interview list. Even though it's a total waste of time. The football player we need to be speaking to is Joey Decker."

"I know. I've been trying."

"But nothing yet?"

Ott shook his head. "Not yet. I'm also lining up both Mindy Pawlichuk and Duane Truax for re-interviews," he said. "Figuring we've got new questions for both of 'em. What about Carla's billionaire boyfriend?"

"Robert Polk. He's been ducking my calls," Crawford said. "I've got two other guys we definitely need to talk to."

Crawford told him about the Miami money manager Arnie Stoller and porn king Xavier Duke. When he mentioned how Rose Clarke had clued him in about Stoller and Duke at dinner the night before, Ott smiled knowingly and said, "Aha...the soap mystery has been solved."

When it came to women, Ott was more of a traditionalist than his partner. He had a long-standing, exclusive relationship with a woman named Rebecca, whom he'd met on match.com. They'd been seeing each other for almost two years.

"I mean, call me old-fashioned, but I just find it all pretty lame." He was back on the people at the Pawlichuk wedding. "Everybody's screwing around on everybody else. I don't know whether it's a rich-guy thing, or maybe a *nouveau-riche*-guy thing?"

"For starters, it's not just a guy thing," Crawford said. "And second of all, don't let it get you so crazy."

Ott shook his head. "I'm trying not to. It's just...I don't know, man..." He snapped his fingers. "Now that I think about it, maybe it's a French thing?"

"A French thing?"

"Yeah, you know, how those frogs have mistresses all over gay Paree."

"Oh, yeah, is that a fact?"

Ott chuckled. "You know, Charlie, I wouldn't be surprised if you had a little French blood in you."

"What the hell are you talking about now?"

"All your women," Ott said. "Let's see there's Rose and Dominica...that reporter babe who works at the Post. Then there was Lil Fonseca, but of course, she's in the slammer up in North Carolina now."

Crawford flashed Ott his best exasperated look. "I'm not going out with Dominica," he said without much conviction.

"At the moment, you're not," Ott said. "But can you honestly tell me with a straight face that you've never gone out with two women at the same time?"

"Jesus, correct me if I'm wrong, but don't we have a murder to solve here?" Crawford sighed.

Ott smiled his 'gotcha' smile. "Okay, Charlie, go ahead change the subject, just when I got you by the short hairs."

Sims Thaw, the CFL football coach, was a dry well. He told Ott that right after the Pawlichuk wedding, he had skipped the reception and had gone with his family to have dinner with his sister up in Jupiter. He didn't get to see her much, he explained, living up in Toronto. He gave Ott her number in case he wanted confirmation. Ott called even though he was convinced Thaw was innocent. Sure enough, Thaw's sister said he was there and volunteered to send Ott photos of them together.

After Ott got off of the phone, he went in to Crawford's office to catch him up. Crawford was logged onto his computer.

"Whatcha doin'?" Ott asked.

"Checking out Mar-a-Lago."

"What about it?"

"Well, I just imagined it would be 5-star everything, but I remembered Addison Pawlichuk saying it was a 'roach motel.' And Rose said basically the same thing." Crawford clicked onto the website. "Pictures of the place look nice."

"What are you looking at?"

"The Mar-a-Lago website," Crawford said.

"Well, of course, they're gonna look good on that," Ott said. "You gotta check Yelp or something."

"Yelp?"

"Yeah, remember I told you, this site where people give reviews on restaurants, hotels and shit?"

Crawford started clicking. A few moments later, he leaned closer to his screen. "Holy shit," he said. "Listen to this: 'Absolutely horrible. Tremendous disappointment. Extremely tacky. Everything says "Made in China" on it. Roach-infested. Very, very poor quality towels and linens. Food was awful. Leaky faucet. Stained carpet. Sad.'"

"You're kidding," Ott said.

Crawford shook his head. "And here's another," he said. "'This place is a dump. I have been there several times and it is a clear failure. I have to say it folks, but they really need to drain the swamp there. Should be called MAL a Lago, it's so bad.'"

"Wow, that's unbelievable," Ott said. "The winter White House turns out to be the winter...shithole."

"I know...place seemed all right to me," Crawford said. "But what do I know?

They were scheduled for a meeting with Rutledge, something they looked forward to as much as getting a wisdom tooth pulled with pliers.

They walked into Rutledge's office at just past three. Rutledge was flossing his teeth. Always an attractive sight. Then Crawford noticed a snowy skim of dandruff on the shoulders of his long-sleeved blue shirt. To the side, a cockroach skittered across the floor.

All this in the first three seconds.

Rutledge tossed the floss into a trashcan next to him. He missed but left it on the floor. "So, you boys will be glad to know I got this sucker solved."

Crawford nodded. "So I heard."

"I'm serious," Rutledge said, opening up his MacBook Air. "Take a look at this. It's the Darlington 500 last year."

Crawford and Ott walked over and leaned over his computer. It was at the Darlington Raceway in North Carolina and showed Duane Truax climbing out of his race car, ripping off his white helmet, running up to another car and slamming his helmet on the car's front windshield repeatedly. Then it cut to another clip of a man in a racing uniform, whose pit crew seemed to be spraying him with bottles of champagne. Then Duane Truax came charging into the picture, again holding his white helmet and shouting:

"I'll kill you, you mother-fucking—"

At that point the sound cut out and several burly men quickly surrounded Truax, subduing him.

Rutledge looked up at Crawford and Ott with a proud grin. "Is it so hard to believe that this guy would go down to a pool and kill his cheating wife and the guy who was bangin' her?"

There it was again. Ott glanced at Crawford, then Rutledge, quizzically. "Wait a minute, Norm, what about the football guys—the owner and the coach?"

"They're off the hook," Rutledge said.

"Jesus, but you were so damned sure. Had me buyin' it," Ott said.

Rutledge tapped his desk a few times. "A murder case, Mort, is a fluid thing."

Ott shook his head. "And so I guess...the fluid leaked out of your football thing."

Rutledge eyed him funny. "I have no idea what that even means.'"

"You're saying they're no longer on your radar screen?" Crawford asked.

"I'm saying I dug a little deeper and got a better suspect," Rutledge said with an off-kilter smile. "Isn't that how you work, Crawford? New suspects replace old suspects? You find out shit and things change."

"We've talked to Truax," Crawford said. "He may have a solid alibi. We're still checking it out."

"I bet it's not as solid as you think."

"We'll see," Crawford said. "The alibi was one of the bridesmaids. Mort's trying to track her down."

Rutledge snickered. "This wedding was a real three-ring circus, wasn't it?"

Crawford nodded. "On that point, we agree."

"I've been playing telephone tag with the bridesmaid," Ott said. "She's already flown back to where she lives. Up in New York."

"Here's the thing, Norm, I definitely don't have the sense Truax was a jealous husband anymore," Crawford turned to Ott. "What about you?"

Ott nodded. "I agree."

"So that leaves the financial motive," Crawford said. "Him getting Carla Carton's money if she's dead. Not getting it if she's alive."

"See, there you go," Rutledge said. "That's why he's my suspect."

"Did you even know that?" Crawford asked.

"Well, not exactly, but I could have guessed."

Crawford glanced over at Ott, who shrugged.

"All right," Crawford said. "So the football players are out and Truax is in. You got anything else, Norm?"

"I'll tell you what I got"—Crawford knew he was about to be sorry he'd asked the question—"I got pressure coming at me from every direction to get this damn thing solved. The mayor, president of the town council, you name it, they've called me."

Crawford shrugged. "What's new? They're on your case, you're on ours."

"Yeah," Ott said. "Same old, same old."

"Yeah, yeah, I know, but not with the whole world watching," Rutledge said. "It *is* fucking Mar-a-Lago, you know. Illicit sex and murder aren't really the images we're trying to project in our little town."

Crawford nodded. "We've still got three guys we're eager to talk to," he said. "All of them were at the wedding. Pawlichuk's money-man, a guy supposedly in the porn business, and one of the Polk brothers."

Rutledge jerked his head back. "One of the Polk brothers? Which one?"

"Robert," Crawford said. "Word is he may have, or did have, something going with Carla Carton."

Rutledge nervously pulled on his tie. "That's a total waste of time," he said. "Robert Polk is worth twenty billion dollars, belongs to the Poinciana, and is a generous contributor to many worthwhile charities, including the Police Foundation."

Ott turned to Crawford and mumbled, "We've seen this movie before."

Rutledge frowned. "What's that, Ott?"

"Nothing."

"Don't gimme that shit. What did you say?"

"He said we've seen this movie before," Crawford said. "It's called, 'Same thing, different day.' Remember Ward Jaynes? How 'bout Sam Pratt? What did they have in common? I'll tell you. One, they were rich guys who belonged to the Poinciana. Two, they were generous contributors to charities, including the police foundation, and three, they killed people. And if I thought for a while, I might come up with a few more."

"All right, all right," Rutledge said. "But Robert Polk? That's like saying Bill Gates and Warren Buffett might be serial killers."

Crawford really didn't want to get sucked into a no-win debate like this. "Tell you what, Norm, we will be very gentle with your friend, Mr. Polk. If we can ever find the guy."

"He's not my friend and, in fact, I've never even met the man. As I've told you a million times, you just need to know where the bread's buttered in this town."

It was officially time to move on, so Crawford stood. "Well, thanks for your time, Norm. We'll keep you up to speed."

Ott got up and shot Crawford a quick smile—his, *Yeah, sure we will, Charlie, you betcha* smile.

EIGHT

BEFORE LEAVING THE OFFICE FOR THE NIGHT, CRAWFORD GOT IN touch with Paul Pawlichuk's money man Arnie Stoller and set up a meeting with him for the following morning at nine. It was nice to find a man who was immediately cooperative, as opposed to Robert Polk, whom Crawford had now called six times.

Driving down 95 at morning rush hour was the expected drive from hell and Crawford and Ott would have been late if Ott hadn't hit the car's siren and light at Pompano Beach. From that point on, it was pretty much clear sailing.

They parked and walked into the glass-clad, high-rise office building on Biscayne Boulevard a few minutes after nine. Stoller Financial occupied an entire floor. Crawford and Ott were directed into Stoller's glass-encased office by an assistant.

On seeing Stoller himself, Crawford guessed his wardrobe might have been influenced by Bobby Axelrod, the hedge-fund heavy and a main character on the TV show *Billions*. He was wearing tight black jeans and an equally tight black shirt, which had 3-buttons and no collar. Unlike Bobby Axelrod, though, Arnie Stoller had a substantial gut and a skimpy soul knob, which, together, killed the whole look.

"Thanks for seeing us, Mr. Stoller," Crawford said shaking his hand.

"Yes, we appreciate it," Ott said.

"No problem," Stoller said, directing Crawford and Ott to a conference table overlooking the ocean. "Nice of you to come all this way."

The three sat down and Stoller spoke first. "I'm going to really miss Paul," he said. "One of the best clients I ever had. Never called me in a panic, never second-guessed me. Even back in 2008, when the shit hit the fan. You getting anywhere on the case?"

Crawford shrugged. "Just a lot of interviews at this point."

Stoller nodded. "Don't they say that if a murder's not solved in the first forty-eight hours, there's only a ten-percent chance it will ever get solved?"

Crawford cocked his head to one side. "I don't really know where they come up with statistics like that." He refrained from telling Stoller that Ott and he were five for five with homicides and to this day had never solved one in the first forty-eight. "Because you were at Paul's son's wedding, I assume you were more than just a financial advisor to him?"

"Yeah, we were friends," Stoller said. "We'd shoot the breeze once a week or so. Start out talking about his investments, then about what was going on in our lives. Football, family stuff, politics, you name it."

Ott leaned forward. "In those conversations, did he ever talk about anyone who he had a problem with, maybe someone who threatened him or who he'd had a fight with?"

Stoller looked out at the ocean. "No, there really wasn't anybody he ever told me about like that," he said. "When I first heard about the murders, I was thinking the obvious...crime of passion. Someone who followed the two of 'em down to that pool. But the first ones I ruled out were the obvious suspects, Duane Truax and Mindy."

"Why?" Crawford asked.

"I'm sure you know by now," Stoller said.

"Tell us," Ott said.

"Because those two didn't much give a damn who their spouses were screwing anymore," Stoller said. "Truax was too busy chasing after a bridesmaid half his age, and Mindy, I think she had a drink or two at the reception, then headed up to her room. She was never very social. Besides, the idea of Mindy taking a gun down to the pool and killing her husband and Carla Carton is absurd."

"You can hire people to do that," Ott said.

"I know, but no way Mindy—"

"Yeah, we agree." Crawford leaned back in his chair. "Sounds like you're a good observer. So, if you had to pick someone who was there, who did do it, who do you think that might have been?"

Stoller shrugged. "I don't know. One thing that struck me was Robert Polk trailing along behind Carla like a little puppy dog. She'd be talking to someone, then he'd come up and insert himself into their conversation. Then she'd move on to someone else, almost like she was trying to ditch him. But he'd come up and be right there at her elbow again."

"So he'd be your pick?" Ott asked, taking notes in his old leather notebook.

Stoller shrugged. "I don't know," he said. "You don't really think of anyone that rich killing someone—" then he cocked his head— "but I did hear something about them having a history."

"Polk and Carla?"

Stoller nodded.

"What do you mean, a history?" Ott asked.

"Sorry, I don't remember anything more specific than that," Stoller said.

Ott scratched a few words on his notepad.

"Anybody else, Mr. Stoller?" Crawford asked,

"Well, there was that skeeve Xavier Duke," Stoller said. "He was sniffing around Carla, too."

"'Sniffing around?'" Crawford said. "What exactly do you mean by that?"

Stoller shrugged. "I don't know, maybe it's just that I know what the guy does for a living. Plus, people say he's hooked up with the mafia. He was talking to Carla and there was this young woman—a girl, really—with them. It just looked a little suspicious."

Crawford had told Ott what Rose had said about Xavier Duke on the way down.

"But do you have any reason to think Duke could have been the murderer?" Crawford asked.

Stoller shook his head. "No, I don't."

Ott looked up. "Did you see Carla leave, Mr. Stoller? And, if so, did you see her leave with Pawlichuk?"

Stoller shook his head. "No, I didn't see her leave. Actually, I never even saw her talking to Paul."

"When did you leave the reception?" Crawford asked.

"Ah, around nine-thirty, I think it was," Stoller said. "Me and my wife went up to our room then."

"And about how many people—out of the three hundred and six people at the wedding—would you say were still there then?" Crawford asked.

"Maybe a third. Or less. A hundred or so?"

"Do you remember if Robert Polk was one of them?"

Stoller thought for a second. "I'm almost certain he wasn't there then."

"Is there anyone else who you think might have had a possible motive?" Ott asked. "Based on how well you knew Paul and what he may have said to you?"

Stoller scratched the back of his head. "No, but I'd talk to Jaclyn Puckett," he said. "She knows where the bodies are buried...well, maybe that's not the right way to phrase it."

Ott wrote down the name, then looked up. "Who's she? We haven't heard that name before."

"Nobody's mentioned her?"

Crawford and Ott both shook their heads.

"She was Carla's...personal assistant," Stoller said. "Basically, organized her life. Made appointments for the nail girl, the masseuse, the personal trainer, the boyfriends, you know the drill."

Crawford and Ott actually didn't know the drill, but they nodded anyway.

"And she was at the wedding?" Ott asked.

"Oh, yeah," Stoller said. "I remember her going to get a plate of food for Carla at the reception. It had to be gluten-free. And a special kind of water, too. I mean, God forbid it be something so ordinary as Pellegrino or Perrier. I think she'd been with Carla for forever."

"How do you know so much about her?" Crawford asked.

"Because Rich Pawlichuk also had his money with me. And he'd tell me stuff," Stoller said. "I guess he heard about Jaclyn from Addison. Addison couldn't believe some of the stuff her sister had Jaclyn do."

"Like what else?"

"Like make her a Bloody Mary every morning at exactly eight o'clock," Stoller said. "And it had to be with V-8 juice, not tomato juice, and a lime, not a lemon."

"Pretty particular, huh?" Ott said.

"Ya think?" Stoller said.

"One last question," Crawford said.

"Go ahead."

"If you don't mind telling us, how much money did Paul have with you?" Crawford asked.

Stoller thought for a moment. "If Paul was alive, I would never disclose this...but let's just say, north of seventy-five million. Started out around fifty."

"We ballparked that he's made about a hundred million in his career as a coach," Crawford said.

"I didn't keep track of Paul's income," Stoller said. "I just invested what he gave me."

"Understand," Crawford said, "but assume we're right about that. That he's made a hundred million dollars. Do you know where Paul invested the rest of the money?"

"Yeah, sure. With his son-in-law George Figueroa," Stoller said. "He's a CPA. Paul had half with me, half with George—" Stoller looked around like someone was going to overhear and dropped his voice— "Off the record, Paul told me that he wanted to have it all with me, but his daughter Janice wore him out insisting that half be with her husband."

"Do you know why he wasn't happy with George?" Crawford asked.

"It wasn't so much that he wasn't happy," Stoller said. "Just that George put him into really conservative stuff. You know, where he'd make two percent a year."

"Well, thanks," Crawford said. "We'll put George and Janice on our interrogation list."

Ott looked up from taking notes. "You spell that F-i-g-u-e-r-o-a?"

"Yeah, that's it," Stoller said. "Figueroa & Associates. But he's got no associates that I know of. And, from what I hear, Paul is basically his only account. His office is just north of you. Up in Jupiter."

"Anything else you can think of?" Ott asked.

Stoller glanced out his window. "For what it's worth, in the last couple of years, Paul got pretty extravagant."

"How so?" Crawford asked.

"You know, the usual. Cars, boats—"

"Women," Ott added.

"Oh, yeah, definitely women. But you didn't hear that from me."

Ott nodded. "How 'bout drugs or gambling maybe?"

Stoller shook his head. "Oh, no, Paul was one of those 'my body is my temple' kind of guys. A few drinks and that was it. Gambling? Maybe he'd bet a few bucks on a game, but that's all."

Crawford got to his feet. "Well, thank you very much, Mr. Stoller. This has been worth the drive down."

Ott shook Stoller's hand and handed him a card. "If you think of anything else that might be helpful, please give us a call."

"I'm glad I could help," Stoller said. "I hope you catch the guy. Paul was a good man. Carla...I didn't know anything about her."

NINE

"What Stoller said, about Pawlichuk being a good man," Ott said, pulling out of the parking lot across from Arnie Stoller's building, "I ain't buyin' it. I mean, hosing everything in sight. Cheating on his wife on a daily basis."

"You know how it is," Crawford says. "Guys can overlook a lot that other guys do."

Ott chewed on that a while. "That Jaclyn Puckett could be a goldmine," he said, getting on to 95 north. "Wish I had someone to make me a Bloody Mary every morning at eight."

"Instead of that rotgut coffee at the station?" Crawford said.

"Exactly," Ott said as he glanced over and saw Crawford dialing his phone. "Who you calling?"

"Robert Polk."

This time someone answered.

"Mr. Polk?"

"Yes?"

"This is Detective Crawford, Palm Beach Police," he said. "I've left you several messages."

"Yes, what do you want?" Polk said curtly.

"To come talk to you," Crawford said as they waited at a stop sign. "About the murder of Carla Carton and Paul Pawlichuk."

A long pause. Finally. "I'll give you ten minutes," he said. "My office is at Phillips Point. Make it tomorrow morning at nine." He clicked off.

"What a dick," Crawford said.

"What did he say?" Ott asked.

"He's allowing us ten minutes of his precious time tomorrow morning at nine," Crawford said.

"What if we had something else scheduled for then?" Ott asked.

"Then we'd just have to change our schedule to fit his."

"What a dick."

Crawford smiled and nodded.

"I guess it's only fair to look at it from his point of view," Ott said.

"Which is?"

"That ten minutes he's wasting on us could be time he'd be making a million bucks on his fund."

"An even bigger dick," Crawford said, dialing his phone again.

"You calling him back to tell him that?"

"I wouldn't waste my time," Crawford said, putting the call on speaker.

A man answered. "Hello."

"Is this Rich?" Crawford asked.

"Yes. Hello, Detective. Got anything yet?"

"We've been talking to a lot of people," he said. "But nothing yet. Are you with your wife?"

"Yes, she's right here."

"Can you ask her if she has the cell number of Jaclyn Puckett, please?"

"Sure—" They heard Rich ask, "You got Jaclyn's number?"

Addison Pawlichuk called out a phone number in the background. It began with a 516 area code.

"Not 561?" Crawford asked.

"No," Rich said. "She was originally from Long Island. That's the Long Island area code."

"Okay, thanks a lot," Crawford said. "Also, while I have you, do you have your brother-in-law's office number?"

"I think so, hang on." Rich called out to Addison again: "How 'bout George's office number?"

"Just his cell," Crawford heard Addison say.

"Yeah, that's fine," Crawford said.

Addison called out the number and Ott wrote it down.

"Great, thanks a lot. I'll be in touch as soon as we have something to tell you." Crawford clicked off and dialed Jaclyn Puckett's number.

A woman answered.

"Is this Jaclyn Puckett?"

"Yes. Who's calling?"

"My name is Detective Crawford, Palm Beach Police Department. My partner and I are the detectives on the Carla Carton-Paul Pawlichuk murders and we'd like to come ask you some questions. How is ten tomorrow morning?"

"I figured someone would be contacting me," Puckett said. "Ten is fine."

"Would you mind coming to the police station?"

"Sure. What's the address?"

Crawford gave her the address. "Thanks, Ms. Puckett."

"See you then."

Ott glanced over. "Maybe she'll be kind enough to give us fifteen minutes of her time."

Finally, Crawford dialed George Figueroa and made an appointment to meet with him at his office the next morning after Robert Polk. He asked Figueroa to please have his wife Janice join them. Figueroa said no problem, he would.

＊ ＊ ＊

THEY GOT BACK TO THE STATION AND CRAWFORD WALKED INTO

his office and got on his computer. He wanted to do some homework on Robert Polk. With the help of Google, Crawford confirmed that the man was worth twenty-one billion dollars, but by tomorrow morning it would no doubt be five or ten million more. He was married to Lorinda Polk and had been for the past thirty-one years.

There were several articles about Polk in the *Daily Mail*, a UK publication that seemed to specialize in pictures of unusually large-breasted women and articles about instant-weight-loss diets. The flurry of Polk-related articles in the *Daily Mail* involved a lawsuit brought by a reporter for the financial channel CNBC, who alleged that Polk had sexually harassed her on several occasions five years ago. Crawford followed the thread, but it seemed the lawsuit was ultimately withdrawn—a settlement, no doubt, probably for millions of dollars, which would have only been a few days' work for Polk.

Needless to say, there were also many articles about Polk in financial publications like the *Wall Street Journal*, *The Financial Times*, and *Forbes* magazine.

Crawford decided that it would be better if Ott and he met with Jaclyn Puckett before Robert Polk. She might be able to shed some light on the relationship between Carla Carton and Polk, which could be useful when questioning the billionaire. Crawford called Puckett and asked if she would mind coming in at eight the next morning instead of ten and she agreed. He emailed Ott about the change.

It was going to be a busy morning.

TEN

Jaclyn Puckett looked to be in her early thirties and about thirty pounds overweight. She had a nice smile, curly blond hair, ice-blue eyes and a Starbucks coffee cup in hand.

"Thanks for coming in," Crawford said as he shook her hand in the reception area.

"Sure, no problem," she said with a smile.

"Just follow me back, please." He led her back to his office and introduced her to Ott, who was waiting there. She and Ott sat in the chairs facing Crawford's desk.

"So, we'll get right to it," Crawford said. "As I said, Detective Ott and I are the detectives on the Pawlichuk-Carton murders. Our first question is, do you remember seeing anything at all unusual or suspicious at the wedding?"

Jaclyn thought for a second. "Mm, not really. Just a lot of big football players in their twenties drinking a lot and getting a little rowdy. And then there were the rest of us, just talking, drinking, dancing, the usual stuff you do at a wedding."

Ott leaned forward in his chair. "Ms. Puckett, what specifically did you observe about the woman you worked for, Carla Carton?"

"Carla was just being Carla. She liked to flirt and be the center of attention. Men were buzzing around her the way they always do, women were giving her dirty looks...the way they always do."

"Who specifically?" Ott asked. "What men were buzzing around her? And what women were giving her dirty looks?"

Jaclyn exhaled slowly. "Xavier Duke talked to her, I noticed. I saw her talking to her sister and Robert Polk at one point. Then one of the football players, whose name I don't know. Lots of men."

"What about Paul Pawlichuk?" Crawford asked.

Jaclyn shook her head. "That's the funny thing, I didn't see them together at all."

"And the women...who were giving her dirty looks?" Ott asked.

"I was kind of kidding about that," Jaclyn said. "But a lot of women don't like Carla. Or I should rephrase that: they perceive her as a threat. And, you know what, they're not wrong. But I do remember Rich's sister Janice shooting daggers when Carla was talking to her husband. Not that Carla would ever have any interest in that slug George."

"George Figueroa, you mean?"

"Yeah, Mr. Excitement." Jaclyn covered her mouth. "Sorry, that was cruel."

"We won't tell," Crawford said. "What do you know about the history between Carla and Paul Pawlichuk?"

"Well, Carla didn't confide in me *that* much. I mean, about boyfriends and lovers," Jaclyn said. "But then again she didn't have to"—she chuckled—"All I needed were eyes and ears. But one thing I do remember her telling me, when we were flying down to the wedding, was that she and Paul had a thing way back when she was in college. She was a cheerleader, he was the football coach."

"But nothing since then?" Ott asked.

"I don't know for sure," Jaclyn said. "But my general observation would be that they didn't exactly travel in the same circles."

Crawford and Ott nodded.

"What about Xavier Duke?" Ott asked.

Jaclyn laughed. "Travel in the same circles, you mean?"

Ott smiled. "What I mean is, know each other."

Jaclyn glanced away. "Vaguely."

"I just thought...because they were *kind of* in the same business..."

Puckett laughed. "Hardly. Carla was in a hit series on Netflix and Duke made porn and supposedly was backed by the mafia."

"Tell us more about that?" Ott asked.

"Well, I didn't exactly read it in *Variety*, but you hear things."

"And what did you hear?" Crawford asked.

"That some mafia guys were the money behind Duke's porn movies."

"So, who was Duke friends with? Why was he at the wedding?"

"I don't know for sure, but my guess would be that he was a friend of Paul."

Crawford tapped his desk a few times, then leaned toward Jaclyn. "What about Robert Polk?" he asked. "There were rumors about...something between him and Carla."

Crawford knew that 'rumors' was pushing it. Just something Arnie Stoller had dropped.

Jaclyn's eyes fluttered and she quickly looked away. "I don't know what you're referring to. 'Something between them?'"

"You know, something in the past," Ott said. "Something they didn't want other people knowing about. Since they were both married."

Jaclyn scratched her arm nervously and glanced down at her shoes. "Sorry, can't help you with that."

By Crawford's count, Jaclyn Puckett had just exhibited three of the ten early-warning signs of someone who was lying. He glanced at Ott and saw he had picked up on it too.

"Ms. Puckett," Crawford said, going for his stern, school-principal voice. "We need to know exactly what you know about this."

"Yes, and the last thing we want to do," said Ott, "is ask you to take a polygraph test."

It was one of those Ottisms that had absolutely no teeth to it and would never happen. But Jaclyn Puckett looked unsettled, as if that was something she really wanted no part of.

She sighed deeply and spoke softly. "Well, I guess I don't officially work for her anymore. So, I don't need to be so confidential."

"The best way to look at it is," Crawford said, "whatever you tell us may help find her killer."

Jaclyn sighed again. "Well, this is a long story," she said. "You got a couple of hours?"

Crawford looked at his watch. "We've got twenty minutes."

"Well, that should be enough," she said. "If I talk fast."

* * *

OTT WAS GOING TO INTERVIEW THREE MEMBERS OF THE wedding party while Crawford was heading to meet with Robert Polk. Polk's office was in a modern glass building in Philips Point, just across the bridge in West Palm Beach.

It was only a five-minute ride from the station; Crawford parked in the building parking garage and took an elevator up to the penthouse. The reception area was unassuming. A lot of dark wood and functional furniture. Nothing in the least bit flashy, considering he was in the top twenty-five of the richest men in America. There was a small chrome sign that said, POLK GLOBAL LLC, then below it, even smaller, ESTABLISHED 1985.

A tall, well-dressed black woman who introduced herself as Jeanette came out into the reception area a few minutes after he got there. "Follow me, please, sir."

Crawford followed her back to Robert Polk's office, a space cluttered with papers, keepsakes, diplomas, and pictures on all four walls, the diametric opposite of Arnie Stoller's spartan office in Miami. It was like Polk had never thrown anything away. A billionaire hoarder. Crawford noticed three pictures of men dressed in football uniforms and recognized them as his old Ivy League rivals, the Yale Bulldogs.

Crawford introduced himself but Polk made no effort to shake his hand. Instead he made a show of holding out his arm, pulling up the sleeve of his white shirt and tapping his wristwatch. "Ten minutes," he said.

Not just a dick, but a colossal, prodigious monumental dick.

Polk wore a dark wool suit that looked way too hot for a day that was up to eighty degrees already. He was a short man, maybe five-six, and looked fit. He had black wavy hair that, Crawford guessed, had been professionally dyed and eyes that didn't seem to miss a trick.

"Okay, what is it you want to know?" Polk asked.

Crawford noticed several pictures of Polk behind him with a rifle in his hands and dead animals at his feet. A tiger. A lion. An elephant. If you'd never met Polk, you might get the idea he was a dangerous man.

Time was a-wasting, Crawford thought, might as well cut to the chase. "Okay, first question is, do you have any idea who killed Paul Pawlichuk and Carla Carton?"

Polk's expression did not change. "No. Next question."

"You and Ms. Carton," Crawford asked. "What was the relationship between you two?"

"Casual acquaintances," Polk said. "I met her once, then saw her again at her sister's wedding."

"That's surprising, Mr. Polk," Crawford said. "Because casual acquaintances who met once usually don't end up getting invited to family weddings." He let the silence stretch out between them. "You were family, were you not?"

A frown cut deep into Polk's face. "Family? What the hell are you talking about?"

"Meaning," Crawford said, "you and Carla Carton had a son together."

That was Jaclyn Puckett's bombshell and there was no denial from Polk.

The air seemed to start leaking out of Polk as he stared blankly at Crawford.

"The fact is, your relationship with Carla Carton is of absolutely no concern to me," Crawford said. "Except how it relates to her murder. These kind of...personal dynamics, as I'm sure you can appreciate, help fill out the picture."

Polk didn't respond.

"Okay, Mr. Polk, here's a question we've asked everyone: At the wedding, what did you see or hear that, in retrospect, might have given you a sense who might have killed Carla Carton and Paul Pawlichuk?"

Polk frowned. "You just asked me that."

"A little bit differently."

"I am not a detective and I have absolutely no idea."

Crawford nodded. "And did you at any point cross South Ocean Boulevard to the pool on the ocean?"

Polk shook his head. "No. Never been there in my life. Never been to Mar-a-Lago before, either."

"Even though you live in Palm Beach?"

"My politics are a little different from those of Mar-a-Lago's owner."

"I see," Crawford said. "Did you happen to see Carla Carton and Paul Pawlichuk walking in the direction of the beach?"

"No."

"Did you ever see them together at all?"

"No. I barely knew what Paul Pawlichuk looked like."

Crawford leaned forward in his chair. "Six-five. Roughly 270 pounds. Big man. Couldn't miss him."

"There were a lot of big men at the wedding."

"Yes, I know."

An irritating buzzing sound interrupted. Polk's wrist watch.

Polk stood. "Time's up. I told you ten minutes and I meant it. I don't know a damn thing about the death of Paul Pawlichuk or Carla Carton. I went home at nine o'clock and you can confirm that. Since they were both seen after that time, alive and well, you've been wasting my time here. Now if you would please leave my office."

"Who can verify that?" Crawford asked. "The time you got home."

Polk didn't hesitate. "My wife."

Crawford stood up. "Okay, Mr. Polk. Thank you for your time."

Polk looked down, clicked a key on his desktop computer and started typing.

Crawford walked out of Robert Polk's office, went down the elevator and got in his car.

Well, he thought, *that went well.*

ELEVEN

CRAWFORD AND OTT MET BACK AT THE STATION, HOPPED IN THE Crown Vic, and made the thirty-five-minute drive up to Jupiter.

Figueroa & Associates, LLC was located in a high-end strip mall on route A1A in Jupiter. Ott parked the Vic in front of the office and he and Crawford got out of the car and walked in. The reception area had light green wall paper, several leather chairs and a casually-dressed woman at the reception desk.

"One of you Detective Crawford?" the woman asked.

"I am," Crawford said and pointed to Ott, "and this is Detective Ott."

"Welcome," the woman said, "I'll show you in to Mr. Figueroa's office. Ms. Bartholomew is in there too."

"Ms. Bartholomew?"

"Oh, yes," the woman said. "Mr. Figueroa's wife. That's her professional name."

Crawford nodded as Ott and he followed the woman back.

She led them into a large office where a dark-haired man in a jacket and tie sat behind a desk and a woman in a tan suede skirt and blue top sat across from him. Crawford guessed the man was in his late thirties and the woman in her early thirties.

The man stood up. "Detective Crawford?"

Crawford shook his outstretched hand. "And my partner, Detective Ott."

"And this is my wife, Janice."

"Pleased to meet you," Janice said, and they all shook hands.

"Have a seat," Figueroa said to Crawford and Ott, and the four were seated.

Crawford looked at Figueroa, then Janice. "Thank you for seeing us," he said. "My partner and I would like to express our condolences about your loss."

"Thank you," said Janice.

Figueroa nodded solemnly.

"We're interviewing members of the family and others who were at your brother's wedding," Crawford said to Janice. "Our hope being, of course, to find out who killed your father and Carla Carton. So, our first question is, did either of you observe anything or notice anyone whose behavior made you suspicious?"

"It was either Robert Polk, Xavier Duke, Duane Truax, or Joey Decker," Janice blurted as if there was no doubt in her mind.

Ott nodded. "We're trying to track him down. Joey Decker, that is."

Ott had just found out that Decker went to high school in Boca Raton. Problem was there were six Deckers in the Boca Raton phone book.

"I can't believe he just showed up out of the blue," Janice said. "And how he even found out about the wedding."

"Good question," Ott said.

"Did you see him again, after he got thrown out?" Crawford asked.

Figueroa shook his head. "No, but who knows where he went from there?"

"You mean, like maybe he went down to the beach?" Ott asked.

"Could have."

"Did you hear him threaten Paul?" Ott asked.

"No, but I heard him call him a bunch of names."

"Do you have any idea how to get in touch with Decker?" Crawford asked. "Maybe Rich would know?"

"I doubt it," Janice said. "I don't think he knew the guy. They went to different schools, and Rich was older."

"Well, thank you," Crawford said. Then to Figueroa, "On another subject, Arnie Stoller told us that you and he split the management of Paul and Mindy's money. His sense was that you have around fifty million dollars under management. Is that about right?"

Figueroa shot a glance at Janice, then swung right back to Crawford. "Yes, that's about right, I'd say. Not that I check it every day."

"Understand," Crawford said, then to Janice. "So that's all your mother's money now?"

Janice shrugged. "I assume so," she said, her hand on her forehead. "I've never seen my father's will."

"As far as Robert Polk, Xavier Duke, and Duane Truax go, why do you suspect them, Ms....Bartholomew?"

"I'll tell you why: Duane, because he thought he was going to get Carla's money, though I bet Addison would fight that in court. Robert Polk, because he's been chasing Carla for years and she humiliated him a couple of times at the wedding—"

"Yeah, he was really furious, you could tell," Figueroa added.

Crawford shot a look at Ott, whose eyebrows were arched.

"And Xavier Duke because...because he's a lowlife," Janice said.

Crawford held up his hand. "One at a time, please. We know about Duane being the possible beneficiary of Carla's money, but how did Addison intend to block that?"

Janice fielded the question. "Because Carla had started a divorce action, I heard, which stated that Duane was not going to get a cent of hers. So, it was down on paper. His money from racing was his; her money from acting was hers."

"Okay, and you said Polk was 'furious?'" Crawford asked Figueroa. "How did you know that?"

"Addison told me," Janice answered for her husband. "She said Carla was really nasty to him. A rich guy like Polk isn't used to that."

Figueroa was nodding. "I noticed Carla treating him like a dog a couple of times. I kind of felt sorry for him."

"Except it's hard to feel sorry for a billionaire," Janice said. "I wondered why Carla wanted him at the wedding in the first place."

"So you're saying Carla asked her sister to invite Polk to the wedding?" Ott asked.

"As I understand it," Janice said. "Ever notice how he looks like a mole?"

Ott shrugged. "I don't know, I haven't had the privilege of meeting the man yet."

"Trust me," Janice said. "It's no privilege."

"But do you really think Polk might have followed your father and Carla down to the pool and shot them?" Crawford asked.

"Well, I think he could have. Absolutely," Janice said. "Have you done your homework on him?"

"You mean about being a hunter?" Crawford asked.

"Yeah, exactly. I mean most people think of him as just a rich businessman and that's all," Janice said. "But back when he was younger, I guess before it became unfashionable to kill animals in Africa, he was like this great white hunter. Someone told me he's got a trophy room full of lions and tigers and every other dead animal known to man."

"Yes, but we're talking about executing two human beings in cold blood," Ott said.

Janice raised an eyebrow at Ott. "You said you haven't met him yet, so I'll tell you, he's a cold-blooded man."

Crawford glanced at Ott, then back at Janice. "Okay, so tell us what you know about Xavier Duke, please."

Janice sighed and looked out the window. "To be honest, I don't know much about Xavier Duke. I just heard somewhere that his movies were financed by the mafia."

"But is it safe to say that falls more in the 'hearsay' department, Ms. Bartholomew?" Crawford asked.

"Yeah, I suppose it is," Janice said. "But I'm sure you're checking him out anyway."

Crawford nodded and glanced over at Ott, who gave him a look that said he was all out of questions.

"Well," Crawford said, getting to his feet and taking out his wallet, "we appreciate you taking time to meet with us." He handed Janice and Figueroa a card. "If you think of anything else, please give us a call."

Ott met Janice's eyes. "We'll let you know when we have something," he said. "By the way, just curious, but your receptionist mentioned that 'Bartholomew' was your professional name. What profession are you in?"

"I'm an interior decorator," Janice said, turning to her husband. "I didn't exactly think Pawlichuk or Figueroa were names that had the panache of, say, Sister Parish or Mario Buatta."

Ott laughed. "I'm guessing those are famous interior decorators," Ott said. "Football players are one thing, decorators...um, not so much."

CRAWFORD AND OTT WALKED BACK TO THE PARKING LOT. OFF in the distance, Crawford spotted a large, shiny, midnight-blue automobile with a license plate that caught his attention. It was noticeably larger and shinier than anything else in the lot. He walked over to it.

He turned to Ott a few feet behind him. "And who do you think JPF might be?"

Ott smiled. "I got a pretty good idea."

"You're a car guy," Crawford said. "How much does that thing go for?"

Ott walked up to it. "Well, that my friend is not just any old Bentley, but a Bentley Mulsanne." Ott licked his lips. "530-horsepower V8. Zero to sixty in four point one seconds. You could drive that sucker into your garage for a mere...three hundred thirty thousand. Oops, sorry I forgot, you don't have a garage."

"Get out of here! Three hundred thirty thousand?"

"Yeah. If you really hondled the dealer, maybe three twenty-five."

Crawford turned and walked back to the Crown Vic in a daze. He reached for the door handle. "And this. What could we get for this old beauty?"

"The Vic? Maybe eighteen K," Ott said. "If we detailed it first."

Crawford shook his head in amazement. "Ol' Janice has got *some* seriously expensive tastes."

"No shit," Ott said, turning the key. "By the way, has there ever been a more bullshit word than *panache?*"

"Yeah, *iconic,*" Crawford said, without hesitation.

"What's wrong with that?"

"Everything's iconic these days," Crawford said. "The iconic film director, the iconic vacuum cleaner, the iconic breakfast cereal...I mean, shit, enough."

Ott laughed. "So, what did you make of what they had to say?"

"I thought the thing about Polk was good info and everything else was shit we already knew. Or else, pure speculation."

Ott nodded. "Yeah, but sounds like Polk's definitely got a motive," he said. "What was your take on George?"

Crawford shrugged. "I don't know, man, if I had fifty mil to invest, I'm not sure I'd be breaking George's door down."

"Yeah, well, that's what family connections are for," Ott said. "And what was with that English accent of Janice's?"

Crawford nodded. "You mean the English accent that seemed to come and go. Like she had to remember to flip the switch," he said. "One thing's for damn sure, between those earrings, the necklace, and the rock on her finger, I guarantee you she was sporting at least three hundred K worth of jewelry."

"You think it was all real?" Ott asked as he stopped at a light.

"Yeah, definitely."

"How do you know?"

"I once had a girlfriend with very expensive tastes," Crawford said. "Which was maybe why it didn't last."

Ott was shaking his head. "So, between the Bentley and the jewelry...over six hundred K, you're saying."

"Yup," Crawford nodded. "Another thing about her: I got the sense that she was one of those whiner daughters."

"What do you mean?"

"You know, to get her way she whines and moans and complains. Wears you down until she gets what she wants," Crawford said. "I'm guessing Papa Paul got a big dose of that on a regular basis."

Ott nodded. "So, you thinking that's how George ended up with Paul's account."

Crawford nodded. "Could be," he said looking at his watch. "So next stop is Mindy again. Who, by the way, seems to be the exact opposite of her daughter."

"How so?"

"Well, my take is she keeps her whining and moaning and complaining pretty much to herself."

* * *

THEIR SECOND MEETING WITH MINDY PAWLICHUK TOOK PLACE in the library at Mar-a-Lago. Mindy was wearing a loose-fitting, blue pantsuit with her hair in a bun again. She was stoop-shouldered and looked even more weary than the first time they talked to her. Like life had worn her down.

Crawford scanned the room looking for some of the things he had read about in Yelp, but it just looked like a normal library with many shelves of books that probably hadn't been read in years. If ever.

"I hope you're feeling better, Mrs. Pawlichuk," Crawford said. "We won't take too much of your time."

"Thank you," she said. "I feel a little better."

"If you would, please," Ott jumped in, "can you tell us about Arnie Stoller, your family investment counselor?"

Mindy just shrugged. "I actually never met the man until the wedding." She let out a short sigh. "I'm *not* proud to say I had one of those old-fashioned marriages where the husband made all the financial decisions. At least Paul let me see the financial statements."

"So you did see them?"

Mindy nodded.

"And, if you remember," Crawford said, "how much money did you and Paul have with Mr. Stoller?"

"Last time I checked," Mindy said, "around seventy million, I think."

"And the rest of the money—fifty million, approximately— was with your son-in-law George Figueroa, right?"

Mindy sighed again. "Yes, that's right," almost like she didn't want to be reminded.

Crawford decided to probe it. "And they both had pretty good results?"

"Yes, well, George is an accountant," Mindy said. "Not a money manager."

"And, if you don't mind me asking, how do they get compensated?" Crawford asked. "Isn't it usually a percentage of the amount managed?"

"I think so, but I'm not really sure," Mindy said.

Crawford figured George had to get at least one percent, which worked out to $500,000 a year.

Crawford leaned closer to Mindy. "On another subject, what about Xavier Duke? He was at the wedding. What can you tell us about him?"

Mindy came close to shuddering. "I've said maybe ten words to that man in my entire life," she said. "He's one of Paul's...unsavory friends."

"Did Paul have a lot of 'unsavory' friends?" Ott asked.

Mindy didn't hesitate. "Too many."

"Do you know where Paul knew Xavier Duke from, by any chance?" asked Crawford.

"No, and I hate to think," Mindy said. "A couple years ago, I asked Paul what Duke did for a living and he smiled and said, 'Let's just say, he does movies for *mature audiences.*' I knew right away, I wasn't mature enough for them."

Crawford realized it was a joke. Not exactly a knee-slapper, but up until that time he had no idea Mindy Pawlichuk had any sense of humor at all.

"And do you know where Mr. Duke lives, by any chance?" Ott asked.

She shook her head. "No, I don't. But if I lived near him, I'd move." The ol' gal was positively on a roll now.

Ott thrummed his fingers on the coffee table next to him. "Mrs. Pawlichuk, another guest at the wedding was Robert Polk. Was he also a friend of Paul's?"

Mindy put her hand up to her chin. "No, he wasn't. I don't think they had ever even met before. Talk about traveling in different circles...I remember my son telling me that Carla asked if Polk could be invited. This was like six months ago. He was supposed to be her—what do they call it—plus-something...?"

"Oh, plus-one, you mean," Crawford said.

"Right," Mindy said. "But later on, I heard she asked that he be disinvited. But I guess by then it was too late because it was after the invitations went out."

"And you have no idea why she wanted to disinvite him, I take it?"

"No idea," Mindy said.

"And, Mrs. Pawlichuk, we heard about a football player by the name of Joey Decker who crashed the party and got into an argument with your husband. Did you happen to see that?"

"Yes, I did actually. It didn't last too long because Rich and some others broke it up."

"And what happened next?"

"He was told to leave and did. I asked Paul about it and he told me not to worry about it." She flashed a wan smile. "Good, old 'don't-worry-about-it' Paul."

Crawford looked at Ott. Ott gave a quick shrug.

"Well, I think that'll do it," Crawford said.

"We appreciate you seeing us again," Ott said.

Crawford nodded. "Yes, thank you very much for your cooperation." Normally he would have added, 'And again, sorry about your loss.' In this case, though, he felt that for Mindy Pawlichuk her husband's death might be more of a relief than a loss.

She'd probably do just fine with her hundred and twenty-five million and without the man who had earned it.

TWELVE

CRAWFORD AND OTT HAD A FEW MINUTES BEFORE DUANE Truax was scheduled to meet them at the station. They were in Crawford's office, Ott facing the whiteboard.

He had three lists: 'Suspects,' 'Family,' and '?' Under Family, he wrote 'Janice/George' and looked as though he were pondering what to do next.

Crawford raised an inquisitive eyebrow.

"I feel like Janice and George should also be in the question mark category too," Ott said.

"Okay, so put 'em there," Crawford said.

The question mark category was kind of a holding pen. A name could go from there to the 'Suspect' category. Or could disappear off the list altogether.

"There's just something hinky about those two, don't you think?" Ott asked. "I mean, I'd let George handle my paltry account, but fifty mil? NFW. And Janice...if she's an interior designer, you'd think she would have done something about George's office. Not exactly *Better Homes and Offices.*"

Crawford smiled. "Ah, I think it's *Gardens—*"

"Yeah, I know, Charlie. It was my little joke."

"Good one," Crawford said, checking his watch. "Hey, I'm thinking we could ask our friend Jaclyn Puckett what she knows about Janice and George."

"Good idea," Ott said as his cell phone rang. "Hello?"

"A guy to see you out front here," said the receptionist.

"We'll be right out."

* * *

Duane Truax had parked in front of the Palm Beach police station on County Road. The car he was driving was a Dodge Viper with an Alabama license plate that proudly proclaimed, FASTEST. He sat in Crawford's office wearing jeans and a Valvoline t-shirt.

"Thanks for coming in," Crawford said.

"Sure. What didn't we cover last time, boys?"

Ott leaned toward Truax. "I spoke to Chelsea, the bridesmaid you took to Rachel's"—the West Palm Beach strip club—"and she said you dropped her off at her hotel at 9:30."

"Yeah, around that time, I guess," Truax said.

"So what did you do then?" Ott asked.

"Went back to the bar at Mar-a-Lago." Truax scratched at his three-day growth.

"Straight back?" Ott asked.

"Yeah, why?" Then his expression changed. "You're not suggesting a detour by the pool on the beach, are you, Detective?"

Ott eyed him hard. "Just asking."

"I said I went straight back."

Crawford's turn. "And, Mr. Truax—"

"You can call me Duane. We're almost old friends by now."

"So, we know that you and Carla Carton were in the process of getting a divorce, correct?"

Truax rolled his eyes. "Yeah, man, we went through this last time."

"I know we did," Crawford said. "But speaking of your divorce, isn't it true that you would inherit quite a bit of money—actually millions of dollars—if you were married to Ms. Carton as opposed to getting none of her money if you were divorced?"

Truax groaned and shook his head. "So I guess that's your way of saying I had a motive to kill Carla?"

Crawford remained silent.

"Maybe you're unaware of the fact that I have a pretty damned good career on the NASCAR circuit. So why don't I just rattle off a few statistics, in case you boys aren't part of the seventy-five million NASCAR fans in America." Truax starting using his fingers to track his list: "Revenue last year was 3.1 billion dollars. The average number of fans at a NASCAR race is ninety-nine thousand. The average salary for a NASCAR driver, including endorsements, is 7.5 million..." Truax shook his head and closed his fingers into a fist. "You boys getting the picture here? If you don't believe me, you can look this shit up."

"Thanks. We believe you—"

"Not to mention, I was Driver of the Year."

Ott had done his usual thorough research. "As a matter of fact, I am one of the seventy-five million NASCAR fans in America, Mr. Truax, and am aware of everything you just said. I congratulate you on being Driver of the Year...back in 2005, I believe it was?"

Truax scowled.

"And, I think I've got my facts right, weren't you number thirty-seven on the money list last year?"

Truax looked like if he had a helmet handy he would have bashed it over Ott's head. He stood and Crawford saw what looked like a coffee stain at the bottom of his Valvoline T-shirt. "I don't need this shit from you two," he said. "Just a couple of fuckin' clowns who got absolutely no clue who shot Carla and Pawlichuk. Just throwing shit at the wall trying to get something to stick."

He was not altogether wrong about that.

Truax turned and walked toward the door. Just as he got to it, he turned back to Crawford and Ott. "So quit wasting my time harassing me. Go find the sombitch who killed my wife. Talk to that guy Duke, why dontcha?"

"Wait a minute," Crawford said, taking a step toward Truax. "Talk to him about what?"

"I don't know. Carla said he was trying to hold her up or some shit." He turned and put his hand on the door.

"Whoa, wait," Crawford said as he and Ott moved closer. "What do you mean, 'hold her up?'"

Truax shrugged. "That's all she said. Ask him."

He pushed open the door and walked out.

Crawford and Ott watched Truax walk out the door and, through the window, saw him get into his Dodge Viper.

"So *now* he's all concerned about his wife, after hitting the town with one of her sister's bridesmaids?"

Ott shook his head, watching Truax drive away. "That license plate worked back in 2005, not now that he's thirty-seven."

THIRTEEN

They were in Crawford's office.

Ott suggested Crawford be the one to call Jaclyn Puckett and set up a second interview, since—as Ott claimed—'she's got a sneaker for you.'

Crawford groaned in protest at Ott's charge but nodded.

Ott said he'd look into Joey Decker while Crawford talked to Jaclyn.

Crawford called her as Ott headed to his cubicle.

She answered. "Hello, Detective."

"Hi, Ms. Puckett, how are the arrangements going with Ms. Carton's funeral?"

"Oh, God, it's a bitch," Jaclyn said. "How's it going finding her killer?"

"Same," Crawford said. "So, I'm hoping you can give me some information about Janice and George Figueroa?"

"That glam duo?" Jaclyn chuckled. "All I really know about them is what I overheard when Carla talked to Addison. Like the day before the wedding Addison was telling her all about Janice's extravagant trips."

"How'd she know about them?"

"Rich always got an earful about big sis, then he told Addison. How Janice went to London all the time, stayed at Claridge's and the Connaught, supposedly for her business."

"Those are hotels, I'm guessing?"

Jaclyn nodded. "Very expensive hotels."

"And Janice is an interior decorator?"

"Yes, well, about the only interior she decorates is her own house. And to the nines, I heard. Again, this is from Addison by way of Rich."

Crawford flashed to all the jewelry dangling off of Janice's various body parts. "And what do you know about George? Does he go with her on her trips?"

"That was my impression. But to tell you the truth, I don't really know."

Crawford heard a phone ring. "Do you need to get that?"

"Nah, that's my land line. I can get back to them," Jaclyn said. "So, are you married, Charlie? I don't recall seeing a ring."

So now she's calling me Charlie? He was just glad Ott didn't hear that.

"No, but I'm seeing someone."

"I figured," Jaclyn said. "All the good guys are taken."

"I don't know about that." Back to business. "Well, I really appreciate your feedback on the Figueroas. Thank you so much."

"You're welcome," she said. "Call me anytime."

* * *

OTT HAD FINALLY TRACKED DOWN JOEY DECKER.

Online, he found a number of newspaper stories detailing Joey's troubled life off of the football field. The most creative headline was, *Joey Decked-Her.* Apparently, Decker had beaten up his girl-friend at a frat party in college. The article had mentioned that Decker had graduated from Boca Raton High School. Ott had called the six Deckers in the Boca Raton phone directory until he located Joey.

Now he was sitting in Decker's parents' living room while both his parents were at work. It was a nice, middle-class split level that had plastic on all the furniture, a look Ott had seen before but never in the pages of a magazine.

Ott was warming up with a little football talk.

Joey had just told him that he was going to get a try-out with Oakland and that the Atlanta Falcons and the Green Bay Packers were also interested.

"Well, I wish you luck," said Ott. "I'm sure you'll land somewhere good. My o and 16 Cleveland Browns could sure as hell use you."

Decker, who was taking up the better part of a 2-person loveseat, smiled, nodded and said thanks.

"As much as I'd like to talk football all day, you know why I'm here, right?"

Decker nodded listlessly. "That thing with Coach."

"Yeah, 'that thing with Coach,'" Ott said. "Joey, you can't show up drunk at Paul Pawlichuk's son's wedding and take a swing at him."

"Take a swing at him? Where the hell did you get that? I just got in his face. I mean, I busted my ass for four years for that guy and that's how he rewards me? Come on, man. How 'bout telling those teams how good a player I was, not the couple times I messed up."

"From what I could tell, it was more than a couple of times."

"Three, maybe."

"So after they told you to leave the wedding," Ott asked, "where'd you go?"

Decker sighed. "To a bar somewhere. In West Palm, I think."

"What was the name of the place?" Ott had a pretty good working knowledge of West Palm Beach bars.

"I don't know. It was on Clematis, I think."

"Well, there's the Grease Burger Bar?"

Decker shook his head.

"Roxy's?"

"No, an Irish place, I think."

"Oh, you mean, O'Shea's."

"Yeah, that's it."

"When did you get there?"

"Eight, maybe?"

"That early?"

"Yeah, I think so."

"I want you to think real hard, Joey. You sure it wasn't closer to ten?"

"No way," Decker said. "I was headed home before ten."

"Drunk, I assume."

Decker looked guilty. "Hey, man, it was better than what you thought I mighta did."

He was referring to killing Pawlichuk.

Ott nodded. "You got a point there, Joey."

FOURTEEN

Xavier Duke seemed to have a preconceived notion of how a famous director should dress. At best, his notion was antiquated. As antiquated as Hugh Hefner in silk pajamas, or Tom Wolfe in a white suit and spats or George Hamilton in Savile Row suits, pocket square and perpetual tan.

Xavier Duke wore Calvin Klein jeans, a loud Turnbull & Asser shirt complemented—he seemed to think anyway—with a dark silk ascot and a blue blazer with gold monogrammed buttons. The dandy look was topped off with a black cane with a silver knob which Duke was tapping on the black and white checkerboard marble floor in the large foyer of his Georgian white brick colonial on North Lake Way at the north end of Palm Beach.

He was talking to a man in his twenties who had just walked in with two women—girls, was probably more accurate, as they looked to be in their late teens. The young man, Jared, had introduced the girls to Xavier as Grace and Avery.

"So where are you ladies from?" Xavier asked.

Grace, tall, willowy, and drunk, answered. "Greenwich, Connecticut," which came out more like *Gren-ish, Connesh-icut.*

"Oh, are you?" Xavier said. "And your parents have a house down here?"

"Yes, on Clarke," Grace said.

Xavier turned to Avery. "And what about you, my dear?"

Avery, cute, short and high on MDMA, commonly known as ecstasy, said, "Lake Forest," then giggled. "Illinois."

"Oh, I know where it is," Xavier said. "I grew up in Winnetka." The wrong side of the tracks, he chose not to add.

"The girls are down here on spring break," Jared added to the conversation.

Xavier pointed in the direction of the bar and the rear of the house. "Well, hell, Jared, what are you waiting for? Go show the ladies a good time."

"You got it, dude," Jared said, then to Grace and Avery. "Come on, you guys aren't gonna believe this place. It's sick."

Xavier had bought the house from the estate of Vasily and Aleksandr Zinoviev, two Russian businessmen/thugs who had died violently the year before. The brothers had somehow gotten their hands on the plans of the Playboy Mansion in Los Angeles and copied it inch for inch.

First, Jared took Grace and Avery to a bar manned by a black man with a shaved head and two gold-hooped earrings. There were two other men and four women sitting at the bar, all of them in their early twenties. Jared said hello to two of the women, then turned to the bartender.

"This is my man Marsh," Jared said to Grace and Avery. "Makes the best drinks in Palm Beach. Possibly the whole Sunshine State."

Marsh shot Jared a look, like he didn't need compliments from this ofay honkey.

The girls ordered drinks. As he had been instructed, Marsh went extra heavy on the pour.

"What do you guys feel like doing first?" Jared said. "There's the game room with these cool, old pinball machines, arcade games, and a pool table. Or we could take a swim in the grotto. Or shoot hoops or play tennis. Bu-ut, that might be dangerous, considering our present conditions."

Grace laughed, glanced at Avery. "Yeah, I don't know 'bout you, but I'm way too messed up for anything that requires coordination." She struggled mightily with the last word.

Avery gave her a nod. "Yeah, but a swim would be awesome. Never swum in a grotto before," she said. "Is it swum or swam?"

"Swimmed," Grace chuckled.

"Whatev. Come on," Jared said, grabbing the girls' hands. "Only thing is, bathing suits aren't allowed."

Avery smiled and looked at Grace. "I don't have a problem with that. Do you?"

"Nah," Grace said. "Not the first time I ever skinny-dipped."

* * *

JARED, GRACE AND AVERY WERE TREADING WATER IN THE POOL, each with a glass of champagne in their hand. Another man named Ned, who kept unabashedly sneaking peeks at the girls naked bodies, had joined them. Jared was telling them about the aviary in back of the house.

"It's got cockatoos, peacocks, parrots...what else, Ned?"

Ned glanced away from Grace's breasts. "Like toucans and pelicans and shit."

Jared nodded. "Yeah, toucans and pelicans and *lots* of shit."

It was Jared's little joke, but the girls missed it.

The girls were increasingly becoming more drunk, stoned, and dysfunctional.

"I don't even know what a cockatoo is," Grace said. "Or a toucan."

Avery laughed and attempted the equivalent of patting her head and rubbing her belly: treading water, holding her champagne glass, and talking. "I think a toucan is the one with a big yellow and orange beak."

"'Zactly," Ned said.

"And what about the other," said Grace, laughing. "The cock-a-doodle-doo?"

Jared laughed so hard he spit out a mouthful of champagne.

* * *

NED WAS PASSED OUT IN THE SCREENING ROOM AS THE FOUR watched a Jessica Chastain movie that hadn't been released to theaters yet. He was sprawled on a couple of big suede cushions while Jared sat between Grace and Avery on a massive black leather couch. Jared had been necking, first with Grace, then Avery. The girls didn't seem to mind that after a long tongue session with one, he'd turn to the other and start in on her.

There were two other couples in the expansive room, but they seemed to be there to actually watch the movie rather than use the space for a pre-coital warm-up.

After their swim, Jared had told the girls that there was really no need to go to the bother of putting their clothes back on, but Grace and Avery, in a quasi-modest gesture, had both put their panties and bras on. Grace was in a black thong, Avery a not-so-shocking pink one.

About halfway through the movie and another bottle of bubbly, Jared suggested that the girls follow him to an adjacent bedroom and, without much hesitation, they agreed.

They walked in, not bothering to turn on the light. Jared put his arms around the two girls and led them to the bed. As he took the few steps to the big king, he looked up to a corner of the room above the elaborate molding and saw the tiny red flashing light he had seen many times before.

The three got into bed, and Jared turned to the girl on his right.

"Avery?" he asked.

"No, Grace."

Jared leaned toward her and kissed her passionately as he took off her panties, then climbed on top of her.

He felt a hand on his back. "And what am I supposed to do?" Avery asked.

"Here," said Jared. "I'll show you."

FIFTEEN

Rose Clark called Crawford as he was walking into the station at eight the next morning.

"Morning, Rose," he said into his cell.

"Hey, Charlie," she said. "So, I was looking at that guest list you gave me of the Pawlichuk wedding again and another name popped out at me."

"Who was that?"

"Her name is Taylor Whitcomb, and she's the daughter of these big socialites, Rennie and Wendy Whitcomb. I remember reading in the Glossy last summer that she just came out in New York."

Pause. "Of what?" Crawford asked, writing the Whitcombs' names in his notebook.

Rose howled. "Come on, Charlie, it was her debutante party. As in, she 'came out...in society." A brief pause. "Don't play dumb with me, you grew up in that world."

"It's all a distant memory," Crawford said.

"Anyway, the reason I brought it up is the rest of the people on the list were a far cry from the socialite/deb party crowd. I mean football players, racecar drivers, porn kings, know what I mean?"

"I do know what you mean," Crawford said. "And I appreciate you telling me about her."

"You're welcome and this time it's not going to cost you."

"A freebie?"

"Yeah, because I had such a good time with you the other night."

"Me too."

"Well, good," Rose said. "See you, Charlie."

"You will, Rose."

Having no appointments until later in the morning, Crawford went straight to his internet-telephone listing site. It was pretty reliable for providing landline numbers and often cell phone numbers as well. He typed in "Rennie Whitcomb," then wondered if that was a nickname for something like Renwick or Renchester or some fancy socialite name. But 'Rennie Whitcomb' came up, along with a number.

Crawford dialed it.

"Whitcomb residence," said the woman's voice.

"Hello," said a male voice simultaneously. "I've got it, Iris."

"Mr. Whitcomb?"

"Yes, who's calling?"

"My name is Charlie Crawford, Mr. Whitcomb, I'm a detective with the Palm Beach Police Depart—"

"Oh, Christ, what did she do this time?" Whitcomb asked.

"Who?"

"My wild-child daughter."

"Nothing that I know of," Crawford said. "But that's why I'm calling. I just wanted to ask her a few questions about the Pawlichuk wedding last Saturday."

"Where those two people got murdered, you mean? At Mar-a-Lago?"

"Yes."

Pause. "Well, why would she know anything about that?"

He apparently had no clue his daughter had gone to the wedding. "Because she was there, I think."

Long pause. "She told us she was going to a party up on Jupiter Island."

"All I know is she was on the guest list for the wedding," Crawford said. "Would you mind if I ask your daughter a few questions?"

Whitcomb laughed. "Now? It's 8:30 in the morning, detective. There's not an eighteen-year-old kid in the world who's awake at this hour. Especially one on spring break."

It was a good point. "Well, how about if I stop by your house, maybe, say, one o'clock this afternoon?"

Whitcomb laughed again. "You mean, prime sunbathing time? That's sacred. How about four o'clock? I'd like to find out about this, too."

"Four o'clock is good," Crawford said. "Where do you live, Mr. Whitcomb?"

Whitcomb gave him his address.

An hour later, Crawford grabbed his jacket and went out to Ott's cubicle. Ott was clad in his favorite color: brown. Dacron pants with a perma-crease, a polyester shirt with a wide-splayed collar and a tie of indeterminate material.

"Ready?" Crawford asked.

Crawford had called Xavier Duke and set up a ten o'clock meeting with him up at 1753 North Lake Way.

"I'm ready," Ott said.

Crawford and Ott went down the elevator, got in their car behind the station, and made the fifteen-minute ride.

On the way up, Ott told Crawford about meeting with Joey Decker. He had taken a picture of Decker on his iPhone, dropped by O'Shea's bar on Clematis Street, and shown it to the bartender. The bartender said he'd been on duty when Decker came in at around eight the night of the murders. He said he couldn't forget Decker because of his red hair and six-foot-six frame. So, although Decker had never really been in the running as the Mar-a-Lago killer, he'd now been officially eliminated.

Crawford dialed Rose Clarke.

"Hey, Charlie," Rose said. "Twice in one day."

"One morning, even."

"Such an honor. What did you forget?"

"The Russians' house on North Lake Way, now owned by Xavier Duke...do you know what Duke paid for it?"

"Fifteen point five million. Commission was a lousy four percent."

"Wow, that sounds low for such a big place."

"Yeah, it's over twenty thousand square feet. But it had two big problems. No, actually three. One, it was hideously decorated. Tacky. Tacky. Tacky. Two, the whole place had a lot of deferred maintenance. And three, it was the scene of multiple murders. Tends to make people a little squeamish to know people were carted out in body bags from a house they're thinking of buying."

"I get it," Crawford said.

"You going up there?"

"Yeah, we're on our way. Thank you, Rose."

"You're welcome," Rose said. "Say hi to Mort."

"I will," Crawford said, clicking off and turning to Ott. "Rose says 'hi.'"

Ott pulled into Duke's driveway. "Not, 'Send my love to that big stud, Mort?'"

Crawford laughed. "I'm sure that's what she was thinking."

SIXTEEN

As Crawford and Ott walked up the steps to Xavier Duke's house, a man in his twenties with two young women came out of the house.

"Hey, how ya doin'?" the man said, nodding at Crawford and Ott.

Crawford and Ott both nodded back as the threesome headed toward a black Jaguar.

Ott pressed the buzzer and turned to Crawford. "I might just throw a couple of curveballs at this guy."

And before Crawford could ask him what he meant, a man opened the door and smiled out at them. "A wild guess," he said with a smile. "Detectives Crawford and Ott?"

Crawford nodded. "Yes, I'm Detective Crawford, and this is my partner, Detective Ott."

They all shook hands. "Come on in," Duke said.

They walked into the black and white checkerboard floor lobby, then into the vast living room beyond. It was decorated with furniture and fabrics in soothing earth tones. The paintings were mostly landscapes—more English country pastoral than Palm Beach tropical.

Duke sat in a green wingback chair and Crawford and Ott on an upholstered sofa.

"I'd have never recognized the place," Ott said, looking around. "Last time we were here, everything was red, yellow and orange."

Duke laughed and nodded. "Yes, I know, including the Warhols, right?"

Ott nodded and took out his well-worn leather notebook.

"So, Mr. Duke, you know why we're here," Crawford said. "Question is, did you see or hear anything suspicious at the Pawlichuk wedding last Saturday? Anything at all that could be helpful to our investigation?"

Duke, wearing pressed jeans and a green shirt with a polo player on it, thought for a second. "I'm trying to think how best to answer the question...And I'm afraid the answer is 'no.' I mean, I've never seen so many big, strapping men in the same place before in my life. It was kind of intimidating, actually. Not that I'm implying one of them had anything to do with what happened there, but with all that testosterone mixed with alcohol, I just wondered. But please understand, I'm certainly not implying that I saw any one of them do anything threatening or hostile."

"Are you referring to an incident where one of these men got into a shouting match with Paul Pawlichuk?" Ott asked.

Duke shook his head. "No," he said. "I wasn't even aware of that. I just felt the potential for something violent to happen."

Crawford glanced at Ott who gave a quick shrug. Crawford hadn't given any thought at all to the fact that many of the men there worked at brutal, physical jobs. That inflicting pain was a big part of what they did. That injuring the competition was an unwritten and unspoken rule, no doubt encouraged.

He flashed back to playing halfback on the Dartmouth football team almost twenty years before. He remembered bone-crushing tackles by men who wanted to hit him so hard it would knock him out of the game. But, the reality was, Ivy League football was meek and genteel compared to the game played by colleges like Alabama and

Ohio State, which had programs designed expressly to make money for their colleges and catapult men into the NFL.

Yes, one of these men could have gotten drunk and, spur-of-the-moment, killed Paul Pawlichuk and Carla Carton. For whatever the reason. But it seemly unlikely, much like Mindy Pawlichuk being the murderer.

Crawford eyed Duke again and wondered why he had brought up the football players.

"Mr. Duke, did you hear or see anything involving one of the football players—maybe words exchanged between one of them and Paul Pawlichuk—or an argument possibly?"

Duke held up his hands. "I should have never brought it up," he said. "No, I didn't see or hear anything. It's just that when I thought afterward about what happened, I just couldn't picture anyone else there being capable of doing it."

Two women walked across the far end of the living room.

"When did you leave the reception, Mr. Duke?" Ott asked.

"I guess it was around nine-thirty or ten."

"Did you, by any chance, see Mr. Pawlichuk or Ms. Carton walking from the main house to the pool on the ocean when you were leaving?" Ott asked.

They had asked everyone that question, but so far no one had. In fact, no one had seen the pair together. Clearly, Pawlichuk and Carton had gone out of their way not to be seen. Crawford's theory was that they had not walked to the oceanfront pool together, but had planned to rendezvous there after making separate exits.

"No, sorry, I didn't see either one then," Duke said. "Last I saw of them, was Paul talking to his son and new daughter-in-law and Carla talking to that woman who worked for her."

"Jaclyn Puckett?" Ott asked.

Duke shrugged. "I guess that's her name."

Crawford glanced over at Ott and noticed his partner's eyes had gotten slitty and his mouth tight. He had seen it a thousand times before. It was Ott's look of impatience.

"Mr. Duke, what is it you do, again?" Ott asked.

"Again? I don't believe you asked me before," Duke said. "I'm in the film business, though not as active as I used to be."

Ott nodded his head slowly. "I actually knew the answer to my question, having taken the liberty of researching some of the films you've done over the years."

"Oh, did you?"

"Yes, and if I'm not mistaken, you did one called, *Tiger's Wood*, and another called, *On Golden Blonde*?" Ott asked his questions in the same measured tone.

Crawford choked off a laugh and tried to prevent his jaw from going into freefall after hearing Ott's "curveball."

Duke nodded. "Yes, but I did those a long time ago. *On Golden Blonde* was at least eight years back."

"And have you done any films similar to those in the last few years?"

"No, I have largely curtailed my activities in that field."

Two young couples walked through the living room. One of the women was a blonde wearing only a bra, panties and flip-flops.

Ott glanced over at them, then his eyes wandered back to Duke's. "*On Golden Blonde II*?"

"Very funny," Duke said. "Just friends of mine."

Ott nodded. "I see."

Crawford decided it was time to change the channel before Ott got too far afield. "So long story short, Mr. Duke, you didn't see or hear anything that looked unusual or out of the ordinary?"

Duke thrummed his fingers on a side table next to him. "No, sorry, I wish I could be more helpful, but it was just another wedding to me."

Crawford glanced at Ott, nervous, but also kind of hoping that his partner would go into his wind-up and fire another curveball. "Got anything else, Mort?"

"Nah, not that I can think of."

"Well, Mr. Duke," Crawford said standing and taking out his

wallet, "if there's anything else you can think of, give us a call, please." He handed Duke a card.

"I sure will," he said.

Crawford and Ott had decided on the way up to save their biggest question for last. Once Duke was good and relaxed.

"Oh, almost forgot, one last thing, Mr. Duke," Crawford said. "Someone mentioned that you had some information about Carla Carton that she didn't want anyone to find out about."

Duke frowned. "I have no idea what you're talking about."

Ott gave him a big smile. "Are you sure? A little secret between the two of you? Something you were holding over her?"

"I barely knew the woman," Duke protested.

Crawford and Ott stared at Duke until it was clear they weren't going to get an answer.

"Okay, Mr. Duke, thanks again," Crawford said and he and Ott walked out of the living room, through the foyer and down the steps.

"We gotta get to the bottom of that Carton thing," Crawford said to Ott.

"Jaclyn Puckett's the answer," Ott said.

"Just what I was thinking."

They walked up to the Crown Vic and got in.

Crawford turned to Ott with a smile. "Those were really the names of his skin flicks?"

Ott snickered as they got to their car. "You think I could make that shit up? He also had a couple of other beauties."

"Let's hear 'em?"

"Well, let's see. There was the unforgettable *Twin Cheeks—*" Crawford laughed— "and who could ever forget his classic, *Good Will Humping?*"

SEVENTEEN

It was a little past four when Crawford and Ott rolled over the tiny pebbles of the Chattahoochee driveway of a big, two-story Mediterranean house at 114 Hammon Avenue.

Ott's eyes scanned the house from top to bottom, then the guesthouse, the pool, the pool house, the tennis court and the lush landscaping of the property. "What does this guy Whitcomb do again?"

Crawford shrugged. "He's a socialite, according to Rose."

Ott looked bemused. "So, is that like a...paying job?"

"If it comes with a trust fund, it is."

Crawford parked their Crown Vic, on the back of which some wise-ass had written "wash me," between a top-of-the-line Lexus and a red Maserati convertible.

They walked across the crunchy driveway and Ott hit the buzzer. He was the designated buzzer-pusher, researcher, and curveball question asker.

A man wearing khakis, a sport shirt and a beige sweater draped around his neck answered the door.

"Mr. Whitcomb?" Crawford asked.

"Hey, guys," Whitcomb said, thrusting out his hand. "Rennie Whitcomb, come on in."

"Thanks," Crawford said, shaking his hand. "I'm Detective Crawford—"

"And I'm Detective Ott."

"Welcome," Whitcomb said. "My daughter's in the media room. Let's go join her."

"Sounds good," Crawford said, following Whitcomb into the house.

They went into a room that had six rows of plush leather chairs—eight across—facing a screen. In a bay window area were two more chairs across from each other with a backgammon board in between, and off to the side a bar and a refrigerator built into a wall.

A girl was pouring out a Coke into a glass with ice cubes.

"This is my daughter Taylor," Whitcomb said walking up to the girl. "This is Detective Crawford and Detective...sorry, tell me again?"

"Ott," said Ott.

They shook hands, then Taylor asked, "Can I get you gentlemen something to drink?"

"No, thanks, I'm good," Crawford said and Ott held up a hand and shook his head.

"So let's sit," Whitcomb said, and they did.

Crawford noticed that Taylor had a fresh sunburn on her nose and forehead. "So, you're down here for spring break, Taylor?"

"Yeah, I have to go back next Sunday," she said, then took a sip of her Coke.

"Where do you go to college?"

"I'm a freshman at Dartmouth, up in New Hamp—"

"I know where it is," Crawford said. "I went there a million years ago."

"Oh, wow, really," Taylor said, giving Crawford a thumbs-up. "Go Big Green!"

Rennie Whitcomb was eyeing Crawford. "No offense, but that's kind of unusual, a police detective going to an Ivy League college."

Ott smiled his big, dopey grin. "Whaddaya mean? I went to Harvard."

"Get out of here," Taylor said, eyeing his symphony of brown duds.

"Yeah, the Harvard of the Midwest," Ott said. "Cuyahoga Community College."

Taylor and Rennie Whitcomb laughed. Crawford had heard it before.

"So, Taylor, we saw your name on the guest list for the Pawlichuk wedding last Saturday. You went, I assume?" Crawford asked.

Taylor looked nervously at her father. "I, I—"

"It's okay," Rennie said, with a shrug. "You're old enough to go where you want. Within reason, of course. I just don't know why you told me you went to see friends up on Jupiter Island."

"I don't know," Taylor told her dad. "I just thought maybe you and Mom might have a problem with me going to the wedding with an older man."

"How old?" Rennie asked.

"Mm, in his forties," Taylor low-balled.

Rennie shook his head. "Matter-of-fact, I do have a problem with that. A twenty-five-year age difference, you bet I do"—Rennie looked at Crawford and Ott—"But we can talk about that later. You fellas go ahead and ask your questions."

Crawford nodded and leaned forward. "What was the name of the man you went with, Taylor?"

She smiled. "Xavier Duke. He's very nice."

Crawford did his best not to react.

Rennie shrugged. "Never heard of him," he said. "What's he do?"

"For a living, you mean?" Taylor asked.

"Yes, of course."

"He's a movie director," Taylor said.

"And what? Wants to make you a star?" Rennie said, shaking his head. "Like that creep Harvey Weinstein."

Taylor rolled her eyes. "No, Daddy."

Crawford held up a hand. "Okay, if we—"

"Sure, sure, Detective. Go ahead and ask your questions," Rennie said.

"When did you meet Mr. Duke?" Crawford asked.

"When I was down here at Christmas. We texted back and forth a little after that. He knew I was going to be here for spring vacation and asked me if I wanted to go to the wedding."

Crawford nodded. "And do you remember about what time you left the wedding?"

"Um, around ten. Xavier took me home." Then to her father: "A perfect gentleman."

Rennie nodded. "That's good."

"And while you were there," Ott asked, "did you happen to see any arguments, or confrontations, or fights involving either Paul Pawlichuk or Carla Carton with anyone else at the wedding?"

"Or, for that matter, between anybody at all?" Crawford added, and Ott nodded.

"Well, first of all, I didn't know who Paul Pawlichuk was until I got there," Taylor said, "then Xavier introduced me. But, no, I didn't see anything like that between him or anybody. Everybody acted pretty normal, I thought."

"What about Carla Carton?"

Taylor smiled. "I actually was a big fan of hers," she said. "Xavier knew her—from the business, I guess."

"So, there were no incidents of any kind that you might have observed?" Crawford asked.

"No, just a lot of football players doing shots of tequila," she said. "Getting a little rowdy."

"Rowdy football players. *Great.*" Rennie frowned at his daughter. "Just what kind of a wedding was this?"

Taylor chuckled. "Not your kind, that's for sure. There weren't a lot of society types." She looked over at Ott. "I do remember something that may have been nothing."

"What was that?" Ott asked.

"Well, I remember seeing Carla, after a dance with someone, go around the side of the house. Then, like thirty seconds later, a man went in the exact same direction."

"A man? Can you describe him?" Ott asked.

"Not too tall, maybe five-eight or -nine, had a Fu Manchu and I think a tattoo on one of his hands—"

Rennie rolled his eyes. "Oh, this sounds like a *very* charming bunch. Men with Fu Manchus and tattoos, football players doing shots. Were there any bikers or gangbangers?"

Taylor laughed. "I'm surprised you even know what a gangbanger is."

Ott took out his iPhone and handed it to Taylor. "Is this the man?"

Taylor looked at the photo and nodded. "That's him."

"That's Carla's husband," Ott said. "His name is Duane Truax. A NASCAR driver."

"Oh, my God," Rennie said, closing his eyes. "This line-up just keeps getting better and better."

Taylor sighed. "Maybe you understand now why I told you I was going to see friends on Jupiter Island."

Rennie flung his hands up in exasperation and stood.

"Where are you going?" Taylor asked.

"I've got a tennis game at five," Rennie said, patting his daughter on the shoulder. "In the future, honey, I'd prefer that you steer clear of weddings where people get killed."

It was Taylor's turn to roll her eyes.

"I'll leave you in the capable hands of the detectives." Rennie said good-bye to Crawford and Ott and walked out of the room.

Taylor waited until her father was out of earshot. "Does the word *snob* come to mind?"

Crawford and Ott smiled but didn't say anything.

Taylor shook her head. "My dad would rather stay home and twiddle his thumbs than go to a party that isn't the crème de la crème of Palm Beach society."

"I got that." Crawford smiled. "Taylor, how did you meet Xavier Duke in the first place?"

"You mean, 'cause it seems like we're from totally different universes?"

"Something like that," Crawford said.

"Well, he has these parties at his house," Taylor said. "Seems like they never end. Bar's always open and a million kids coming and going."

"Kids?"

"Yeah, I'd say anywhere from eighteen to mid-twenties, mainly."

Ott leaned forward. "And how did you find out about them?"

"This guy who's a friend of a friend," Taylor said. "He's always up there. One time a bunch of us were at the Poinciana having lunch. He stopped by our table and told us about the place. He went on and on about the grotto, the waterfall, all the games, so, of course, we all wanted to check it out."

"And so you went there with friends?"

Taylor nodded.

"And what was it like?"

For the first time, Taylor hesitated before giving an answer. "Um, when I first went there I thought it was totally awesome. It was kind of like this oasis in the middle of Palm Beach, with a lot of fun things to do. The second time, ah...not so much."

"What do you mean? What happened the second time?"

She hesitated again. Then. "Okay, I'll tell you 'cause you guys seem cool but you've got to promise not to tell my dad."

"Taylor, the reality is, we probably won't ever talk to your dad again. It was you we needed to talk to."

"And whatever you tell us is strictly confidential," Ott said.

"Absolutely," Crawford said.

"Okay, well, what I told my dad about Xavier dropping me off at ten was true. As far as it went, that is," Taylor said. "Then I went upstairs to my bedroom, snuck down the back stairway and out to Xavier's car on the street."

"I was doing that before you were born," Ott said with a wink.

Taylor laughed. "I know," she said. "So, we went up to Xavier's place and I had one drink with him, then he kind of disappeared. I ended up with this group who I knew a little bit. Actually, from up in New York. So, we were in the bar and one of the girls goes to the bathroom and I noticed this one guy put his hand into the pocket of his shirt and pull something out. Then put it in her drink."

"Really?" Crawford said.

Taylor nodded. "So, I got up and went into the bathroom and told the girl what I had just seen and told her not to drink her drink."

"What did she say?" Crawford asked.

"She thanked me, then when she went back to the table, she...had a little accident."

"What happened?"

"She knocked over the glass with her elbow."

"Oops," Ott said.

"Good move," Crawford said.

"So later on, a bunch of us went out to the pool and these two guys put heavy pressure on us to go skinny-dipping."

"What did you do?"

"I just took my shoes off and dangled my legs in the water. I'm kind of modest. Meantime, the guys brought bottles of champagne into the pool. I didn't touch a drop 'cause I just didn't trust them. Neither did the girl whose drink was spiked."

"Smart," Crawford said. "Then what?"

"We all went and played in this amazing game room. Everybody was good and ripped at that point. One of the guys pulled out an eight ball of coke and everyone was doing lines on this old Pong game. Not *this* girl, though," Taylor said, "'cause I didn't trust 'em at all. I don't really know why I even stuck around."

"So how many of you were there? In the game room," Ott asked.

"Ten of us, I think. Four guys and six girls."

"And what happened next?" Ott asked.

"At one point, 'cause I was totally sober, I saw this guy Jared leave with these two girls. And that was the last I saw of them."

"Did you know the girls?" Ott asked.

"Just one of them, but I don't want to get her in trouble," Taylor said.

"Don't worry," Ott said. "Nobody's ever going to know we had this conversation."

Taylor still seemed reluctant. "You promise?"

"Absolutely," Ott said, raising his right hand.

"Her name is Alexa Armistead," Taylor said.

"Wait," Crawford said. "Is her father Roger Armistead?"

"Yes, I think so." Taylor said. "I know she's really rich."

Crawford nodded. "So what happened?"

"So anyway, I tried to get one of the guys to give me a ride home, but they just kept putting pressure on me to hang around. Finally, I just called an Uber and left without a word."

"Wise decision," Ott said.

Taylor lowered her voice, like she was worried her mother or someone might be hiding behind the curtains. "That was after one of the other guys asked me and another girl if we wanted to go have a 'slumber party'"—she took a deep breath—"which sounded kind of innocent...until I saw the look in the sleazeball's eyes."

EIGHTEEN

"I don't get it," Ott said, as the Crown Vic drove over the crunchy Whitcomb driveway onto County Road.

"You mean, what Duke's racket is?"

"Yeah, exactly."

Crawford shrugged. "So, he disappears in his house and seems to have nothing to do with the floating party that's going on there. And he's obviously laying out a fair amount of money on drinks, champagne, bartender, cooks, and God-knows-what-else."

"Yeah, plus somebody's gotta clean the whole place up afterward."

"Except it seems like there is no 'afterward.' Like it's one long, continuous, never ending party."

They were back in Crawford's office. Ott was writing on the whiteboard. So far, under 'Suspects' it had the names Duane Truax and Robert Polk. They had taken Mindy Pawlichuk's name off the list. Under the "?" category Ott had now added Xavier Duke.

As Ott had explained to Crawford: "I don't know, he just seems like he's guilty of something." Below Duke, he'd added, 'Interview/re-interview.' He'd just written Jaclyn Puckett's name.

"I have an idea," Crawford said.

Ott turned to him. "Just by the way you said that tells me you're not sure it's a *good* idea."

"True," Crawford said. "But because I'm prepared to share it with you means it's cleared the first hurdle."

"Which is?"

"I'm not sure I've ever explained this to you before," Crawford said, "but I have a lot of thoughts that never make it to the spoken stage."

"O-kay."

"Meaning my self-censor kills them before I run them by you."

Ott thought for a second. "So, what you're saying is, I never have to hear your really shitty ideas."

Crawford nodded. "Yeah, basically."

"Well, lucky me."

"But this one, which you may think is a shitty idea, but which I kind of like, is one I've decided to share with you."

"I'm honored."

"So, the question is, how old do you think Dominica looks?"

"Shit, Charlie." Ott chuckled. "Isn't that your department?"

Crawford and Dominica McCarthy had an on-again, off-again relationship. When it was on it was very, very good and when it was off it was both uncomfortable and awkward. Which wasn't surprising, given that they shared the same employer.

"You're right," Crawford said. "And I know how old she is, but the question is how old does she *look*?"

Ott grabbed his chin and looked around the room. "I'm going to give you a range answer. How's that?"

"That's fine."

"Between, ah, twenty-six and thirty."

Crawford smiled. "I'm going to tell her you said that 'cause she's thirty."

Ott looked relieved. "Good. Means I'll score some points with her. By the way, I think I know where you're going with this."

Crawford smiled. "What took you so long?"

* * *

CRAWFORD WAS DOWN IN CSEU. DOMINICA McCARTHY, BIG brown eyes, high cheekbones, bouncy, full hair and a figure everyone agreed was way above average, had her espadrilles up on her white melamine desk.

"So, it's simple," Crawford said. "You just go to this party and observe what goes on."

"But you already know what goes on: a bunch of rich kids hang out, drink too much, do a bunch of lines, then some lowlife slips a girl a date rape drug and—"

"Yeah, I know, definitely not your idea of fun," Crawford said. "But the big question, and what I'm trying to find out, is what the owner of the house gets out of it."

Dominica shrugged. "Maybe he likes to watch," she said. "You know, a voyeur. He's got some two-way mirror in one of the bedrooms? Or peeps through the keyhole? There are plenty of creeps out there like that."

Crawford shrugged. "Yeah, I know."

"So what do you think it is?"

"The obvious. Duke's filming kids having sex and making money at it. We just gotta find out how it works."

Dominica thought for a second. "Did you run this by Norm? Bringing me in?"

Crawford shook his head. "Wasn't any point if you weren't on board."

"Let's just say, I've got one foot on board."

"That's a start."

"If I had two, would you run it by Norm?"

Crawford shifted from one leg to the other. "I already know what his reaction would be."

"What would it be?"

Crawford thought a second. "Well, as I don't need to tell you, Norm is a protector of the big fish of Palm Beach. Meaning anyone with money or juice. I think he might put Xavier Duke in one of those categories."

Dominica nodded. "Okay, here's how I look at it: We don't need to run it by Norm if it's got nothing to do with work. In other words, if it's personal. If it's just me going to a party because a friend told me about this place and I was dying to meet some new guys."

Crawford nodded. "There you go. Exactly."

Dominica wasn't done. "'Cause the guy I *was* going out with kind of...well, faded away. Too busy with his job maybe, or possibly just wasn't into me anymore."

Crawford folded his arms and shook his head. "That is *so, so* not true. It's nothing like that at all."

Dominica slipped into her surprised look. "Oh, Charlie," she said. "Did you think I was talking about *you?*"

NINETEEN

JACLYN PUCKETT HAD STAYED OVER AT THE CHESTERFIELD Hotel to handle all the details of transporting Carla Carton's body to its place of final rest, a cemetery called Westwood Village Memorial Park in Los Angeles. Not to mention make the funeral arrangements, which required a million logistical calls as well as back-and-forths between Duane Truax, Carla's sister Addison, and many other friends of Carla.

Ott had called Jaclyn and asked if she could meet with him and Crawford again, explaining that they had a few additional questions, which wouldn't take long. She told him how busy she was with all of Carla's business and said she couldn't do it until later in the week.

Ott, being by nature persistent and not disposed to take no for an answer, persuaded Jaclyn to meet with them later that afternoon. He volunteered to make it easy for her and meet in the lobby of the Chesterfield.

On the short drive over from the station, Ott urged Crawford to turn on the charm and give her that "big dazzler that melts chicks' hearts."

Crawford pretended to be lost in thought and ignored his partner. Besides, being accused of having a "big dazzler" was downright embarrassing.

When they met in the Chesterfield lobby, Jaclyn was wearing something in the muumuu family and had a harried look on her face. "Don't ever get stuck with the job of handling a celebrity funeral," she warned Crawford and Ott.

"I think it's safe to say that ain't gonna happen," Ott said, shaking Jaclyn's hand.

"Thanks for seeing us," Crawford said, motioning to a couch and some chairs across from the front reception desk. "Shall we?"

Jaclyn sat down and fanned her face with a hand. "A lot hotter down here than L.A.," she said.

"It's the humidity," Crawford said. "We want to thank you very much for all the help you've given us already. Our first question is, do you know anything about Xavier Duke having something on your old boss Carla Carton?"

Jaclyn looked puzzled. "Something on...?"

Ott nodded and smiled. "Come on, you know what he means."

Jaclyn sighed, then smiled. "I learned at our first meeting that if I play dumb with you two, you'll eventually browbeat me into submission, so I'm not gonna bother. Yes, I know all about Duke black-mailing Carla."

"We'd appreciate it if you tell us about it," Crawford said.

"Okay, but this is a little delicate," Jaclyn said. "And I'm going to have to choose my words very carefully."

"Take your time," Crawford said.

"*We-ll*, a year or two before Carla met Duane Truax—when she was still young and foolish—she auditioned for one of Xavier Duke's, ah, blue movies. Do they still use that phrase?"

Crawford shrugged.

"Well, you know what I mean." Crawford and Ott nodded. "It turns out she didn't get the part, thank God. But Xavier or one of his assistants took some very, um, explicit still shots. So, flash forward to three weeks ago: Duke called up Carla and, long story short, offered to burn the photos and the negatives if Carla paid him one million dollars. And if she didn't, he told her, the photos were going to somehow find their way into the hands of TMZ or one of those gossip rags."

"So, what happened?"

"Well, she stalled him and stalled him. Then finally at the wedding, she confronted him. She told me about it right after it happened. She offered Duke a hundred thousand and he laughed it off. Told her to add a zero. She told me she'd go up to half a million, but I bet she would have paid the million."

"Why do you say that?" Crawford asked.

"Because she had this thing in her contract—they used to call it a 'morals clause,' I think—where Netflix or any studio could cancel her contract if pictures like that were published. What would you do? Pay the man off and keep earning a million dollars per episode on *Bad Karma* or refuse and lose your job? I mean, *duh*?"

"I hear you," Crawford said. "Let me ask you a question on a slightly different subject: I Googled Xavier Duke and it said the last porn movie he made was five years ago. Do you have any idea, or maybe Ms. Carton mentioned something to you, why he stopped?"

Jaclyn laughed. "Well, I hope you don't think of me as an authority on porn movies, but it's probably just like everything else."

"What do you mean?"

"Simple. Some of them make money, some of them don't. I'm sure there's lot of competition, too. And probably there are directors who are hot one day, then cold the next. I think people figure they all make money, but if that was the case then everyone and his brother would be makin' 'em."

Crawford nodded. Made sense.

"Maybe Duke had a few duds in a row and got out of it. Who knows?" She shrugged.

Over Ott's shoulder, Crawford noticed a boy walk into the hotel wearing a black hoodie and aviators.

He glanced over at them and, seeing Jaclyn, waved, but kept walking toward the elevator.

Jaclyn smiled and waved back as the boy pushed the elevator button.

Ott turned and looked. "Who's that?" he asked, not able to make out his face at all.

"That's Alex," Jaclyn said. "Carla's son."

Of course, he'd be here, Crawford realized. His mother had just been brutally murdered. "He's staying here?" he asked.

"Yes," Jaclyn said with a sneer. "Let's just say that father Robert is less than welcoming at the moment."

"That sucks," Ott said.

"Yes, doesn't it?"

"How's he doing?" Crawford asked.

"Not great," Jaclyn said. "As you can imagine."

Crawford nodded. "Poor kid."

TWENTY

Dominica had a dress she never had the guts to wear in public. It had a slit all the way up to her right hip and more cleavage than she wanted anyone she knew to ever see. With its sequins and deep, whorehouse purple color, it would be perfect for Xavier Duke's ersatz Playboy mansion and a bunch of people she would probably never see again.

She had to admit as she looked into her full-length mirror that she looked fabulous in it. Although it was eighty degrees and clear outside when she left her apartment, she wore a raincoat so the neighbors wouldn't see her in the dress. She quickly took off the raincoat when she got into her car, then drove across the north bridge from West Palm to Palm Beach, careful not to speed or go through a light. The last thing she needed was to be pulled over by a cop she worked with.

She took a right into the long driveway on North Lake Way and had a flashback. She'd gone on a few dates with Aleksandr Zinoviev, one of the two Russian brothers who had once lived in the house now owned by Xavier Duke, though she had never actually been to the house. He usually took her out on his yacht, the biggest boat she'd ever been on by a couple hundred feet.

She left her Honda in a big parking court that looked like it could easily accommodate thirty or forty cars, walked up the steps to the massive front door, and pressed the buzzer.

A moment later, the door opened.

"Welcome to Windsong," a man said, ushering her in. "Please come in."

"Wait, I just want to make sure I'm at the right place," Dominica said. "Is this Mr. Duke's house?"

"It is," the man said. "And I am Mr. Duke."

Xavier Duke was wearing a burgundy velvet jacket and white ducks.

"Nice to meet you, Mr. Duke," Dominica said. "I'm Donatella Greer." The name came compliments of a girl in the sixth grade who Charlie Crawford had had a crush on. "A friend of mine told me there was a party here...well, like *all the time.*"

"Nice to meet you, too, Donatella, and your friend is correct," Duke said. "What is your friend's name, if I might ask?"

"Billy," Dominica said, then with a shrug, "Billy-with-gorgeous-blue-eyes-whose-last-name-I-don't-remember."

"Um, not sure I know who that is," Duke said. "Come on in. Would you like a drink?"

"I thought you'd never ask," Dominica said with a laugh as she followed Duke into the living room. "Oh, this is such an awesome place."

"Well, thank you," Duke said, as they went through the living room into a bar with mahogany paneling and large Audubon paintings of exotic birds on three walls.

A group of three young men and women sat in a booth, while a couple was perched on barstools.

"Oh, my God," Dominica said, looking around, "this is so fantastic."

One of the men sitting in the booth hadn't taken his eyes off her since she came into the room.

Dominica and Duke sat at the bar.

The bartender came right over. "Yes, sir," he said. "The usual, I presume?" Then to Dominica: "And the lady?"

"I'll just have a white wine, please. Do you have pinot grigio?"

"Coming right up," the bartender said.

Dominica turned to Duke. "So, what's your usual, Mr. Duke?"

"It's called a Pimm's Cup," Duke said, "and please don't call me Mister Duke. It's Xavier."

"Okay, Xavier." Dominica heard steps behind her.

She turned and the man who had been eyeing her from the booth joined them. He moved a foot inside her comfort zone and she leaned away.

"Oh, hello, Jared," Duke said. "This is Donatella."

"As in Donatella Versace?" Jared said.

"As in Donatella Greer," she answered.

"Well, welcome to Windsong," Jared said. "Your first time, right? Or I definitely would have remembered you."

Dominica nodded. "First time. My friends told me about the great parties here."

"And they weren't exaggerating," Jared said, sitting next to her. "I saw that incredible dress and told myself, I've *got* to meet that woman."

Xavier Duke had one Pimm's Cup and excused himself a little before nine, explaining that he wanted to go watch a show on TV.

Jared was intense. One of those men who asked a million questions but didn't seem to really listen to the answers. Who put his hand on Dominica's hand after having just met her. Who constantly looked at himself admiringly in the smoky mirror on the other side of the bar.

Half an hour after Duke left, a striking brunette who Dominica guessed was in her early twenties came up to Jared and they exchanged kisses on both cheeks. Dominica was strictly a single-cheeker. To her those who practiced the double-cheekers were either British or French or pretending to be.

Jared introduced the two women. "Claire, this is my new friend, Donatella."

"Hi," Claire said. "I love your dress. Michael Kors?"

"Lulus, fifty-percent-off sale," Dominica said because it was.

"Cool," Claire said, turning to Jared.

"Claire is a senior at Brown," Jared said. "Staying at her grand-parents' place"—dropping his voice to Dominica—"her grandfather is Terence Knowlton."

The name didn't mean a thing to her. "Oh, great."

She took a closer look at Claire's dress and knew that it was expensive. She could never keep all those Italian names straight: Dolce & Gabbana, Giorgio Armani, Prada, Fendi. She felt certain it was one of them.

Dominica had to pee but was worried Jared might drop something in her drink, so she held it. After a while, he suggested the three go take a swim in the grotto, "just like the one at the Playboy Mansion," he said. Perfect, thought Dominica, she could pee in the pool.

When the three got to the grotto, Jared took no time stripping naked and Claire did the same.

"Are there any bathing suits I can borrow?" Dominica asked.

Jared frowned. "It feels so much nicer wearing nothing," he said with a smarmy smile.

"I'm shy," Dominica said.

Jared patted her on the shoulder. "That's okay, I'll get you a suit," he said. "Xavier has one or two for you shy types."

It was a white one-piece that was a size too big but she didn't mind. She went into the girls' bathroom and killed two birds with one stone: changed into it and took a pee.

A swim in the grotto, along with some champagne that Dominica did not touch, led to them playing several games of pool in the game room. Dominica and Claire played against Jared and another man named Ned. Ned was drunk, stoned, or both. Several times he missed the cue ball altogether with his stick.

Claire joined Dominica as she was chalking her cue stick and said, "I've never even played before but I'm better than that bozo." Claire flicked her head in the direction of drunk Ned.

Dominica dropped her voice. "I know...we should play them for money."

Claire laughed as Ned proceeded to line up the cue ball, leaning on the pool table for support. He drew the stick back and thrust it forward. It slid off the bottom of the ball and his stick tore into the green felt.

Ned looked around, put his hand over his mouth. "Oops," he said, then caterwauled with laughter.

"You really suck, man," Jared said with a smile, "now you're gonna have to buy the X-man a new table."

"Seriously, dude?"

"No, but, Jesus, be careful."

Dominica high-fived Claire. "Guess we're the winners."

Jared looked over. "But we're not done yet."

"Maybe you're not." She pointed to wobbly Ned, who was knocking back a shot of Patron. "But your partner is."

Jared strolled over to Dominica and Claire with his pool stick resting on his shoulder. "So let's lose him"—he flicked his head toward Ned—"and go watch something in the screening room."

"Something?" Dominica asked.

"Yeah, Xavier's got that new movie with Tom Hardy and Issa Rae. S'posed to be killer."

Claire turned to Dominica. "What do you think?"

Dominica shrugged. "Sure, why not?"

* * *

DOMINICA, CLAIRE, AND JARED SAT ON A LEATHER COUCH, joining six others sitting elsewhere in the screening room.

It was a good movie until Jared put his arm around Dominica and tried to kiss her.

Dominica pushed him away. "I just met you five minutes ago."

That wasn't part of her deal with Crawford and Ott. She told them she'd play along and try to find out what went on at Duke's place—or Windsong, as it was now called—but she wasn't about to play kissy-face with some lame-o named Jared.

Turned out, Jared was not picky and a few moments later put his arm around Claire and was having a little more success with her.

The two of them necked for a while, then Jared got down to business. "Hey, how about the three of us go to the next room and have a slumber party?"

The more the guy had to drink, the worse his lines got.

Claire looked at Jared and said. "You mean, have sex?"

Jared's face lit up. "Oh, hey, what a great idea."

Claire turned to Dominica. "What do you think?"

Dominica was beginning to get the sense that Claire was more into her than Jared.

"Sure, why not?" Dominica said.

Dominica and Claire followed Jared into a bedroom. He hit a switch that was on a rheostat and turned it so it faintly illuminated the room.

"I'll be right back," Jared said and headed for bathroom.

Claire turned to Dominica and said in a seductive tone. "What do you say we lose him, too?"

"I like you Claire, but I'm not into girls any more than I'm into

Jared." She walked over to the bed, stepped up on top of it, and craned her neck around.

"What in God's name are you—" Claire started.

Dominica held up a hand. She found what she was looking for built into the crown molding and very well-disguised. She took out her iPhone and took four quick snaps.

She was halfway to the front door before Jared returned from the bathroom.

TWENTY-ONE

CRAWFORD, OTT, AND DOMINICA WERE AT THE STARBUCKS ON Worth Avenue in Palm Beach.

Crawford, being a dyed-in-the-wool Dunkin' Donuts man, was there under protest. He had already commented, "How can you stand this Kenny G shit?" about the CD that was playing.

"You mean, you're not a big fan of 'My Heart Will Go On?'" Ott asked.

Crawford shook his head. "No, it's right up there with 'You Light Up My Life.'"

"Are we going to talk shop or music?" Dominica took a sip of her latte.

Crawford leaned back. "You in a rush?"

"Yeah, well, I'm kind of eager to tell you what happened last night."

"Let's hear it."

Dominica took out four photos. "So I'm going to spare you the lurid details—which I'm sure you boys would love to hear—and just get right to the bottom line: I took these shots in a bedroom." She handed two to Crawford and two to Ott. "As you can see, there are two video cameras built into the molding in those two corners."

"So that's his gig," Crawford said, nodding.

"Look like state-of-the-art equipment," Ott said, taking a closer look.

"I wouldn't know about that," Dominica said. "But, long story short, I ended up in this bedroom with this college girl named Claire and this dope Jared. Who no doubt, works for Duke."

"Jared, you mean?" Crawford asked

Dominica nodded. "I took these shots and got the hell out of there with Claire. But I'm sure all kinds of *ménage a trois* and every other combination in the Kama Sutra have been recorded on those cameras."

"Recordings that Duke planned to sell," Crawford asked.

Dominica nodded.

Ott put his coffee down. "So Duke retired from making classics like *Finding Ryan's Privates* or *The Well-Hung Mr. Ripley* and got into this."

Dominica laughed. "Are those real names?"

Ott nodded.

"Guess you must've missed Oscar night five years ago," Ott said.

"What do you know about Claire?" Crawford asked.

She shrugged. "She's a senior at Brown, staying down here with her grandparents. Jared said her grandfather was named Terence Knowlton, like that was supposed to impress me."

"Oh, yeah," Crawford said. "Terry Knowlton, he was CEO of J.P. Morgan for a long time."

"How do you know that?" Dominica asked.

"My dad worked on Wall Street, remember?"

"Oh, right."

"So, that's how it works," Crawford said. "Rich party girls invited to Xavier Duke's house. And being videotaped having sex."

She nodded. "So Duke can put the bite on somebody."

"Exactly," Crawford said, "Like he tried to do with Carla Carton. But someone came along and messed up that plan."

"Which would have paid the bills at 'Windsong' for a long, long time," Ott said.

"Yeah, but he already had another plan in motion." Crawford started tapping his fingers on the table. "Just imagine if Duke taped Taylor Whitcomb or Terry Knowlton's granddaughter Claire on that camera with that guy Jared."

Dominica and Ott nodded.

"He goes to Rennie Whitcomb or Terry Knowlton and says, 'I've got a graphic video of your daughter,' or in Knowlton's case, grand-daughter, 'and I'd be happy to sell it to you for...pick a number...'"

"A hundred grand," Ott said.

"I think you're low," Crawford said. "And if Whitcomb or Knowlton balks, Duke says, 'Fine, I'm sure TMZ or the *Daily Mail* will pay me handsomely for it.'"

Ott took a long pull on his coffee. "Think you nailed it, man."

"But hold on, it's not like Taylor or Claire are celebrities," Dominica said. "Why would the public give a damn about sex tapes of some unknown, random women?"

"Good question, and I'll tell you why," Crawford said. "Let's say I'm the gossip editor at the *Daily Mail* and I dig up a picture of Claire in a virginal white dress at her debutante party, at, say, the Waldorf Astoria hotel." He silently thanked Rose for the idea. "I put that shot side by side with a blurry one of Claire and Jared having sex. Better yet, in a three-way with another woman they recruited. Then I come up with a headline, I don't know something like: 'New York Society Girl in Sex Triangle!"

"Oh, nice, Charlie," Dominica said. "Very subtle."

"Well, hell, I'm not a writer, but you get the idea."

"You think that would sell a lot of newspapers?" Ott asked.

"It might or it might not," Crawford said, "but if I'm Knowlton, and I'm worth, say, five hundred mil, I'd pay it."

"Just to keep the kid out of the spotlight?" Ott said.

"Not just to protect the kid but Knowlton's name as well," Crawford said. "How do you think he'd like it if the word got around down at the Poinciana about his slutty granddaughter?"

"Good point," Ott said. "So you're saying Knowlton would pay it to avoid the blowback on him."

"He'd sure as hell give it a lot of thought," Crawford said. "And by now, we can be pretty sure Duke has shot plenty of compromising videos."

Ott put his coffee down. "Jesus," he said, "what a racket."

Crawford nodded. "Yeah, well, problem is at this point it's just hypothetical. It's not like we know of someone it's actually happened to. I mean, we can speculate all day long."

"Yeah, but I have no doubt it's happened in real life," Dominca said, as Crawford's cell phone rang.

Crawford looked down at caller ID. It was the main Palm Beach PD number.

"Hang on," Crawford said to Dominica and Ott, clicking the number. "Crawford."

"Hey, Charlie, it's Jill in dispatch. We got a homicide at a vacant lot up on Reef Road."

Crawford got to his feet, signaled Ott, and asked the dispatcher. "How do you know it was a homicide?"

"'Cause the vic's got two shots to the face and one in the chest," Jill said. "White male between forty and fifty."

"Me and Ott are on our way," Crawford said, clicking off. Then he turned to Dominica. "Got a homicide up on the North End. Thanks for all your help last night. We're gonna need a CSEU at this scene, in case you're up next."

Dominica shook her head. "I'm not," she said, then frowned. "I thought I was going to get a little more than a lousy cup of coffee for my sterling undercover work last night."

"You are," Crawford said, headed toward the door. "Dinner this week?"

"You're on."

TWENTY-TWO

THE DEAD MAN LAY ON HIS BACK, ARMS OUTSTRETCHED, IN A vacant lot on Reef Road.

The vacant lot measured 100 by 125 feet and was densely landscaped on all four sides, with just a fifteen-foot-wide opening for a driveway coming off of the road. The body was not visible from the road, but lay in a corner, where it apparently had been dragged fifty yards or so by the killer. They knew that because there was a pool of dried blood near the entrance of the lot. The victim had been shot at close range, where no one could miss. One bullet hole in the chin and the other just below the right eye.

The one in the chest was unnecessary as the first two had clearly done the job.

"Holy shit," Ott said looking down at the barely recognizable face. "You believe this shit?"

It was none other than the man they had just been talking about. Xavier Duke.

Crawford was shaking his head. "Shooter couldn't have been more than ten feet away," he said. "Must have been someone he knew."

"Yeah," Ott said. "And if Carla Carton was still with us, she'd be my first choice."

Crawford pulled a pair of white vinyl gloves out of his jacket pocket and put them on. Ott did the same.

It turned out a woman walking her dog had discovered the body. The dog, not on a leash, had scampered into the lot and not come back right away. The woman had gone in to find it sniffing the corpse. She had quickly called 911 and, eight minutes later, a uniform arrived, first on scene, followed by Crawford and Ott, then two female CSEU techs. The CSEUs, Jan Kislak and Sheila Stallings, knelt near the body, looking for hair, fibers, or any kind of DNA-bearing material, but so far had come up short.

Crawford scratched the back of his head and looked around. "The question is, what the hell would Duke and the killer be doing here?"

Ott shifted his weight from one foot to the other. "Okay, this might seem a little bit out there," he said, "but when I first met Duke, I got the gay vibe. Just something about him."

Crawford nodded. "Like maybe when he said, 'big, strapping men' about the football players?"

"Yeah, maybe. Couple of other things he said too."

"So, what are you thinking? They met here for..."

Ott shrugged. "Hey, man, you never know."

One of the CSEUs glanced up at Crawford.

Crawford shook his head. "Not exactly a romantic hideaway," he said, looking around. "Nothing but a bunch of dirt and weeds."

"Just puttin' it out there," Ott said noticing the CSEU looking at them. "What do you think, Stallings?"

"I don't know," she said. "Sounds like you know the guy—" she glanced at Kislak— "but we haven't seen any signs of, ah, sexual congress."

Ott smiled. "That is so classy, Stallings. 'Sexual congress.' I love it. Well, keep digging."

Ott turned back to Crawford, who had dropped into a crouch to examine the shoeprints near the body.

"Got any ideas?" Ott asked.

"Just that the gun probably had a silencer," Crawford said, looking around. "There are houses on either side, plus behind and across the street, all on small lots. Nobody phoned in anything about shots fired."

Ott nodded. "And whoever did it, we can safely assume, was not someone he knew too well. Or they would have met at Duke's house or a bar or something."

Crawford nodded. "So it seems like it was two guys meeting and not wanting to be seen together. Or your gay theory."

Ott got down in a crouch, too. "Speaking of theories, what we were talking about at Starbucks might fit here."

Crawford nodded. "I was thinking of that. Duke meeting a rich father who he thought was going to pay him for a video of his daughter?"

"But instead, daddy had a gun?"

"Yeah, or maybe it was a hired gun."

"Possible," said Ott. His expression suddenly changed. "Aw, fuck, here he is."

Crawford didn't need to turn around to know that Bob Hawes, the ME, had just arrived.

"What's he wearing this time?" Crawford whispered.

Bob Hawes had a wardrobe that made Ott look chic.

"That red cardigan," Ott said.

"The one with the deer on it?"

"Yup. Fuckin' Bill Cosby wouldn't get caught dead in that," Ott muttered as Hawes approached them.

"My two favorite Palm Beach homicide detectives," Hawes said.

That was Hawes's little joke, since they were the only two homicide detectives in Palm Beach.

"Hello again, Bob," Ott said and Crawford nodded.

"Vic's name is Xavier Duke," Crawford said. "If that rings a bell it's because he was at the Pawlichuk wedding last week."

"Can't say it does," Hawes said.

"Anyway, he lives within a short walk. That house the Russian brothers used to live in on North Lake Way," Crawford said.

"Jesus, what's with that place? You buy it and end up tits up." Hawes caught Sheila Stallings's eye. "Oops, sorry, Stallings." He glanced down at Duke's body. "Wow, someone really didn't like this guy."

Crawford had the sense that Hawes felt it was part of his job description to be a wise-ass in the face of even the grimmest murders. Like he had seen a movie once where a wise, old ME had acted less than solemn in the face of death. Whatever the reason, that had become the MO of the ME.

Hawes got down in a crouch, and both knees cracked. "How ya doin', ladies," Hawes said to Kislak and Stallings.

"Hi, Bob," Kislak said with a nod as Stallings pretended to be preoccupied with a soil sample.

"I said, 'Hello, Stallings,'" Hawes said.

"Hello, Bob," Stallings said, looking up and seemingly suppressing a frown at the sight of Hawes' sweater.

"Found anything good?"

"I got a rusty bottle cap and an old lighter," Stallings said. "No wallet, but we didn't need one since Charlie and Mort knew the guy."

Hawes nodded. "What about you, Kis?"

"Nothin'," Kislak said.

"Question is, is it the same shooter as Pawlichuk?" Crawford said. "I mean, three shots apiece there, three shots apiece here. Close range in both cases. Entry wounds look similar."

Hawes looked up at Crawford and shaded his eyes. "I don't know, Charlie, I just got here."

"The good news is we got a slug," Kislak said.

"That is good news," Hawes said. "Unlike Pawlichuk."

"You'll let us know as soon as you got something, right?" Ott said.

Crawford knew what Hawes's next line would be. *All in due course.*

Hawes nodded. "All in due time."

Close enough.

Hawes turned and took pictures of the three bullet holes with his iPhone. Crawford signaled to Ott, and they walked away.

"No point in us hanging around here," Crawford said. "Let's go to Duke's house. See what we come up with there."

Ott nodded.

They walked back to Hawes and the CSEUs. "We're going to Duke's house," Crawford said.

"Okay," Hawes said. "But be careful, for Christ's sake. That place definitely has a hex on it."

CRAWFORD AND OTT GOT TO THE HOUSE ON NORTH LAKE WAY at just past ten a.m. They had no idea whether Xavier Duke was married and had kids but suspected he didn't. Their hunch was he was single and lived alone in the ten-bedroom house on the ocean and probably had a few freeloaders and hangers-on who tended to overstay their welcomes.

No one answered when Ott pushed the doorbell. He pushed it again, and they waited a full three minutes.

The man who finally answered was in his twenties and wearing short boxers and a tattoo above his right bicep.

"Hey, what's up?" he said, rubbing his eyes.

Crawford recognized him as the man they had seen leaving the house with two women.

"I'm Detective Crawford and this is my partner Detective Ott, Palm Beach Police Department," Crawford said, flashing his ID. "Are there any members of Xavier Duke's family living here?"

"No," the man said, "I don't think he has any. Wait a minute, 'cept for his mother up in Illinois, I'm pretty sure."

"And who are you?" Ott asked, taking his notebook out.

"Jared," the man said. "A friend of the X-man's."

"Your last name please?"

"Ford." Jared said. "What's this about?"

"Sorry to tell you, but Mr. Duke was killed," Crawford said.

Jared put a hand up to his mouth. "Oh, my God, you're kidding," he said slowly.

"He was shot several times," Ott said. "Not far from here."

A young woman in a bathrobe appeared behind Jared. "What's wrong?" she asked.

"Xavier was murdered," Jared said. "This is so terrible. I can't believe it."

The girl put her hand up to her mouth. "Oh my God," she said, putting an arm on Jared's shoulder.

"What's your name, please?" Ott asked.

"Ellie," she said. "Ellie Ferraro."

"When did you both last see Mr. Duke?" Crawford asked.

"Last night," Jared said. "I had a drink with him in the bar. Then he went upstairs."

"And you?" Crawford asked Ellie.

"I only met him once. About three or four days ago," she said. "I didn't see him last night 'cause I got here after he went up to his room."

Crawford turned back to Jared. "He went upstairs alone?"

Jared nodded. "Yeah, he wanted to see something on the tube. He isn't much into the parties here. Or, wasn't, I mean."

"Well, then, the obvious question is," Ott said, "why'd he have them so often?"

"I don't know exactly." Jared looked up at Ott and shrugged. "I- I guess 'cause he liked to have people around. Being a single guy, maybe he got lonely."

Ott eyed Crawford but Crawford decided not to press it. "Who else is in the house now?"

Another shrug. "I'm not sure," Jared said. "But my guess is there're a few others here."

"What's a few?" Ott asked.

"I don't know exactly."

"Two to four? Five to ten? Ballpark?" Ott asked.

"I'd say two to four."

Ott turned to Crawford. "Let's go find out."

Crawford nodded. "Don't go anywhere," he said to Jared, then to the Ellie, "You too. We might need to ask you some more questions."

They both nodded.

"Are all the bedrooms upstairs?" Ott asked Jared.

"There're actually two down here," Jared said, pointing. "At the end of that hall."

* * *

IT TURNED OUT THERE WERE THREE OTHER COUPLES AND A threesome at the house, so Jared had been low on his estimate. Ott took all their names, but he and Crawford were almost certain that none of them knew anything about the death of Xavier Duke. In fact, four of the nine claimed that they had never even met the man. They had come to Windsong for the famous parties and ended up spending the night there with, in two out of three cases, people they'd never met before.

None of the nine, including Jared and Ellie, had seen Duke leave the house. Crawford and Ott spent an hour checking the home's four security cameras—one at the front door, a second at the back door, and two exterior ones—and didn't see Duke leave the house.

Then they went to Xavier Duke's bedroom, which was large but not as large as they expected. It had a room off of it, which had been turned into a neatly organized office. The bedroom furnishings were a tasteful but dated Victorian style dominated by burgundy and deep blue colors. The most surprising feature was a simple, queen-sized brass bed. Or maybe it was just that Crawford expected that the bed would be the dominant feature of the room. Like it had been in Hugh Hefner's original.

There was an iPhone on a nightstand next to the bed. Crawford reached in his pocket, pulled out his vinyl gloves, put them on, and picked up the iPhone. Unlocked, fortunately. He scrolled down the recent calls. It looked as if Duke had called a man named Danny at least three times a day. Then Crawford saw one that said 'Mom' and recognized the 312 Chicago area code.

He looked at Ott across the room. "I found a number for his mother."

Ott glanced back. "You're up, bro. I did the last one."

Crawford nodded and dialed the mother of Xavier Duke.

Death notifications were a bitch.

* * *

Duke's mother didn't answer, so Crawford left a message on her voicemail for her to call him back. He was secretly relieved not to have to break the news about her son. For now, anyway.

Next Crawford and Ott went into Duke's office. It was a fine line between needing a warrant and conducting a simple search, so they went a few inches over the line. In the middle drawer of a desk Crawford found Duke's checkbook. It was one of those three-to-a-page, three-ring-binder kinds. He went through the check stubs from the account at PNC Bank on Royal Palm Way and didn't find anything that looked unusual. The checks were all for mundane things like water, electric, gas and telephone bills. Then there were large weekly checks made out to ABC Wine & Spirits in West Palm. He found no sign of what he was really looking for: deposit slips.

Meanwhile, Ott was rifling through the other drawers of the desk. One had various warranties for kitchen appliances and TVs, another one had brochures for expensive-looking resorts in Asia and Australia, and a third was catalogs for luxury boats. The others were empty.

"Anything?" Crawford asked Ott.

"Guy was apparently looking into expensive vacations and buying a boat."

Crawford looked up from the checkbook. "A boat, huh?"

"Yeah, million-dollar boats."

"But you couldn't tell whether he bought one or not?"

Ott shook his head. "Tell you what I would have liked to have found: a drawer full of DVDs."

"Yeah, no kidding," Crawford said. "I'm gonna get a crew of techs to get a warrant and go through this place. Let's go find those cameras Dominica spotted."

The bedroom with the cameras in it was three bedrooms down from the master. The cameras had been painstakingly embedded in the elaborate molding; you had to be looking for them to see them. They did a quick search of two bureaus in that room for DVDs, but found nothing. They decided to get a crew of CSEUs to search the entire house.

Then they walked back to Reef Road and canvassed the neighbors on all sides of the empty lot where Duke's body had been found. Turned out none of the homeowners they spoke to had heard gunfire, supporting Crawford's theory that a silencer had been used.

Four hours after arriving at the crime scene, Crawford and Ott had little more than when they'd begun. They went back to Crawford's office at the station and talked about what to do next, their conversation punctuated by long stretches of silence.

"They gotta find something," Crawford said, referring to the three CSEUs who were on their way to get a search warrant then head up to Duke's house. Their express purpose was to find DVDs but they'd take whatever they could get.

"You'd think they would have been in his office," Ott said. "Assuming they exist."

"They exist," Crawford said. "Remember with Pawlichuk how you said 'follow the money?'"

"Yeah."

"That's exactly what we need to do now. Look into Duke's bank accounts and see where the money came from. Or, rather, *who* the money came from."

THEY DROVE DOWN TO THE PNC BRANCH AND ASKED TO SPEAK to the manager.

He was a man in his forties named Randy Connors who, upon learning they were detectives, greeted them with something less than open arms.

"How can I help you?" he asked, facing them in his small office.

"Mr. Connors, we're investigating the death of one of your customers, Xavier Duke," Crawford said.

Connors looked appropriately shocked. "Oh, no, what happened? The poor man."

"He was found shot to death near his house on the north end," Crawford said. "And in order for us to try to find his killer, we would appreciate your cooperation."

"Of course. I'll help if I can."

"We'd like to examine all his accounts with your bank," Crawford said. "We're particularly interested in deposits he made."

Connors thought for a second. "I'm sorry, but as I'm sure you can appreciate, our customers expect confidentiality from us. I can't allow you access to his accounts."

Ott frowned. "Mr. Connors," he said. "Your customer is dead. Your cooperation might help us find his killer."

"I understand what you're saying, but that's bank policy, and I'm not allowed to act contrary to it."

"All we need to see are his bank deposits for the last year," Crawford said. "Specifically, who they were from."

Connors shook his head. "I can't do that."

Crawford stood up. He had seen plenty of minor functionaries dig their heels in before—a way of taking full advantage of those rare occasions when they could exert power over others.

"Okay," Crawford said. "We'll be back."

"Sorry, I—"

"We'll be back," Ott echoed his partner.

* * *

CRAWFORD AND OTT HAD A GOOD RELATIONSHIP WITH THE judge who they'd need to get the court order from. It would be pretty easy to demonstrate to the judge why they needed Xavier Duke's financials. The real problem was tracking the judge down. One time, they'd had him sign the paperwork they needed on the eighteenth hole of his country club's golf course. Another time, it was on his boat. The judge seemed to have plenty of time for recreation.

Today, he was actually at the courthouse. They met in his chambers and told him what they needed and why.

"You boys have been pretty busy lately." Judge Shanahan took a sip from a water bottle. "You getting anywhere on Paul Pawlichuk and that actress?"

"Slowly," Crawford said. "We've got a couple of leads, but nothing solid."

"Someone told me you guys have solved every case you've been on since you came down from New York," Shanahan said. "Is that right?"

Crawford gave Ott a pat on the shoulder. "In Mort's case, Cleveland," he said. "My partner's a dog with a bone."

"That's Charlie's way of being modest," Ott said.

"All right, well, I'll sign it," Shanahan said. "And maybe you can wrap it up by the end of the day."

"Something tells me it's gonna take a little longer than that," Crawford said.

* * *

THEY WERE BACK AT THE BANK AT 3:30. SITTING IN THE manager's office again.

"You fellas work pretty fast," Connors said.

Ott shot him another frown. "When we said we'll be back, what did you think we meant? In a year?"

Connors gave him a perfunctory smile. "So, what exactly is it you want?"

"First of all, how many accounts did Xavier Duke have?" Ott asked.

"A regular checking account and a money market," Connors said.

"Do you know what his balances are in both?"

"I took the liberty of looking them up," Connors said. "He's got about ten thousand in the regular checking account and just over three million in the money market."

"Whoa?" Crawford said. "Three million in a money market?"

Connors nodded.

"And what interest rate does that pay?"

"One point one percent," Connors said.

"Why would anyone keep that much money in an account paying so little?" Crawford asked

"Can't help you there, detective," Connors said. "He made most of his deposits fairly recently, so maybe he just hadn't decided yet what to do with the money. I had actually suggested that he meet with our people in the investment-advisory department who have instruments that perform much better than that."

"I mean, won't some CDs pay twice that much?" Crawford asked.

"Yes, they will," Connors said.

"We'd like to take a look at all the activity in Mr. Duke's account for the last two years, the emphasis being on his deposits. Those deposits will show who wrote checks to him or wired money into his accounts, correct?"

"Yes, that's correct," Connors said. "Would you like to come in tomorrow morning? I'll have it all set up for you."

Ott frowned. "Why can't we do it now?"

Connors looked at his watch. "We close in fifteen minutes."

Ott looked at his watch. It was 3:45. "Guess that's why they call 'em bankers' hours, huh, Mr. C?"

TWENTY-THREE

AFTER THE BANK, CRAWFORD WENT STRAIGHT DOWN TO THE CSEU cubicles. For business...and pleasure. The business part was to see if any DVDs had been found at Xavier Duke's house, but it turned out that the three who had gone up there hadn't returned yet. The pleasure part was to ask a certain CSEU out to dinner that night.

He sat down in the spare chair in Dominica McCarthy's cubicle, lowered his voice, apologized for it being last-minute and asked her.

"You know," said Dominica, "there was a time in my dating life—not so long ago—when I would have immediately said, 'Sorry, I'm busy,' just so you wouldn't think I was too available—"

"But hopefully that's not your answer this time?"

"It's 'yes' if you promise me you're not asking me out just for sex."

"That wasn't even in the equation."

"Oh, bullshit, Charlie."

"Well, maybe just a little."

"We'll discuss this in greater detail," Dominica said. "Where do you want to go?"

"I'm thinking Lentini's or Dos Caminos," Crawford said, "but I'm open to anything."

"I could do a margarita or two."

"So, Dos Caminos," Crawford said. "Pick you up at seven?"

"See you then."

* * *

Dominica looked like a million bucks. But then, she always did.

They sat in a back-corner table at the Mexican restaurant in West Palm Beach. They ordered Texas margaritas and Crawford caught her up on the murder of Xavier Duke. It didn't take long, since he had so little on the case.

"What's your gut say about whether Duke and Pawlichuk are linked?" Dominica asked.

"My gut hasn't really weighed in yet," Crawford said. "Kind of depends on what Hawes comes up with."

Dominica nodded, took a pull on her margarita and gave him a thumbs-up.

"But," Crawford said, sipping his margarita after licking a little salt around the edge of the glass, "Hawes being Hawes, he's gonna take his sweet time."

"You still think he likes to piss you off just to piss you off?" she asked.

"Yeah, 'cause I always used to ride him to get his reports done faster," Crawford said. "One time he gave me this big lecture. Said, 'Unlike how you probably did shit up in New York, we do things slow and deliberate down here.'"

"Implication being you did things fast and sloppy up there."

"Exactly. So nowadays I don't say anything," Crawford said. "Just get Ott to buddy up to him, give him a little nudge. So, what are you working on?"

"That string of burglaries in the estate section."

"Oh, yeah. That's got to be an inside job, right?"

"That's what we thought at first. Now we're not so sure."

"Who's we? You and Cato?"

Dominica nodded. "Yeah. I like working with her," she said. "Girl can spend five straight hours at a scene crawling around on her hands and knees."

"I know, I've seen her in action."

Dominica leaned forward and put her hand on Crawford's. "So, Charlie, we need to have a talk."

"We do?" Gulp.

Dominica nodded.

"O-kay," Crawford said, the word laden with apprehension.

"If I were my father, I might start this conversation by asking, 'So, Charlie, what are your intentions with my daughter?'"

"Is this going to get heavy? Because, if so, I'm going to order two more of these bad boys right now," Crawford said, hefting his glass.

"Two more and you'll need assistance walking out of here."

"I know, my cut-off is two," Crawford said. "The one time I had three, I had to call Uber."

"Are you filibustering to avoid my conversation?"

"Ah, I guess maybe a little," he said. "But, go ahead, what's the question?"

"I'll get around to the question in a second, but, first, here's a scenario: There's this handsome cop, who's kind of funny and, for the most part, fun to be around. Every once in a while, he'll call up one of two women, though there may be more, and ask them out to dinner. And because he's handsome, and kind of funny, and, for the most part, fun to be around, they'll end up in bed with him. Even though the two women are friends and know everything about what the other one does."

"Wait a second, there's something bothering me about this scenario of yours."

"And what would that be?"

"You said—twice—this guy is 'for the most part, fun to be around.' What's that all about, the 'for the most part' part?"

"Well, 'cause sometimes he drones on about his cases a little too much. I suspect to get help from those two women who, by the way, are both extremely intelligent."

"And there's another thing you said," Crawford said. "You mentioned there were two women, then said 'though there may be more...'"

"Yes."

"Well, there aren't."

"Oh, well, that's reassuring," Dominica said. "So, to go on, one of the two women, who shall go nameless at the moment though I think you know who she is, thinks that the handsome cop just asks her out when he's, well, horny—"

"Hold it, hold it, hold it," Crawford said, trying to stifle a laugh. "That woman must be smokin' something to come to that conclusion."

The waiter came to their table. "Can I take your orders, folks?"

They ordered their usual and he walked away.

"So you don't think the 'horny' conclusion is an accurate one, Charlie?"

"Put it this way, it's way down the list."

"Oh, but, so it is somewhere on the list?"

Crawford's face got red. "Near the bottom."

"But maybe you can understand why this woman might think that?"

"No, why?"

"Because this woman and the other woman...oh, what the hell, let's give them names, Rose and Dominica, didn't feel that these relationships were really going anywhere."

"What do you mean by that?"

"What do you think I mean? That it was always a nice dinner, nice conversation, followed by nice sex. No, that's not fair, great sex, but the relationship itself was never building to anything."

"Dominica, that is so not true. At one point last year—and you can't deny this—we had a full-blown relationship complete with *I love yous*, spending lots of days in a row together, and me even thinking about proposing to you."

Dominica's head jerked back. "Well, that's the first I heard of that."

Crawford bowed his head and nodded. "Yeah, well, I guess I got busy and chickened out or something."

"Then what happened?"

Crawford tapped the table nervously. "Well, it sort of lost a little steam."

"And the *I love yous*?"

"Ah, not as many as before."

"That's half true," Dominica said. "I didn't run out of steam and I was still saying those words." She picked up her margarita and took a sip. "You have to admit, it's a pretty strange relationship all around. Rose and me—good friends—both quasi-going out with you and there being no attempt on anybody's part to keep it quiet or hide anything."

Crawford smiled. "I guess strange is as good a word as any," he said. "But, let's be fair, there's no lack of exclusivity with either of you two."

Dominica cocked her head. "What are you referring to?"

"Well, there was that Russian guy you went out with."

"Which never went anywhere."

"You mean, 'cause he got killed."

Dominica shook her head. "No, 'cause it was never gonna go anywhere."

"Well, Rose has gone out with quite a few guys."

"Who were mainly men who had something to do with her business. Men whose houses she was hoping to list, stuff like that," Dominica said. "What if Rose and I were to make a pact and cut you off? No more nice dinners, nice conversation and nice sex 'cause we decide that good ol' Charlie just reeks of non-commitment."

Crawford shrugged. "That would, of course, be totally your call," he said. "But...if you're going to do that, would you mind starting tomorrow?"

Dominica burst out laughing. "This was supposed to be a serious conversation."

"Hey, I'm dead serious."

* * *

When dinner came, they were still talking about sex.

"Back when I was in college, I always thought that guys liked it and girls just put up with it," Crawford said. "You know, just to make the guy happy."

"Now who's smoking something?" Dominica said. "How'd you come up with that?"

"I don't know, I guess 'cause it was always the women who said no," Crawford said. "The guy never said no, he was always up for it."

"I would have figured that guys at a nice Ivy League school like Dartmouth would have been much better behaved than the dudes at hormone-raged University of Miami," Dominica said, taking a bite of her quesadilla.

"Well, then, you would have been sadly mistaken. If you ever had the misfortune of showing up for a weekend in Hanover, New Hampshire, good luck trying to find just one 'well-behaved' guy. Oh my God, we were the worst. That old movie, *Animal House*? That was based on a Dartmouth frat house. And it was pretty damned accurate."

"See, for some reason, I equate smart Ivy League guys as having better discipline. You know, they work harder, don't drink as much—"

"That would be your second misconception," Crawford said. "Because if you showed up for a weekend—say on a Friday—there'd be about a fifty-fifty chance your date would have already passed out."

"Really?"

"Really."

"Boy, was I mistaken."

Crawford got a faraway look in his eye. "Did I ever tell you about my first college girlfriend?"

"No. Let's hear."

"Miriam Wexley, the love goddess of Bennington College."

"A hot number?"

"I don't know if I'd go that far," Crawford said. "Just willing. And willing. And more willing. Every hour on the hour."

"Maybe you shouldn't have let her get away, Charlie."

"If I hadn't, I'd be dead of a heart attack," he said. Then, as an afterthought, "If I was going to die of a heart attack, I'd rather it be in your arms."

TWENTY-FOUR

They were waiting in front of Dos Caminos for the valet to bring Crawford's car up to them.

Crawford's brain was working so hard he was surprised his head hadn't started to smoke. He had no idea how to play it with Dominica after the sex conversations they had just had. He could be totally phony and say, 'Maybe it's best if I just drop you off at your place tonight based on what we talked about.' But if he did that, she might actually take him up on it. Which was the last thing he wanted. Or he could say, 'I just want you to know I listened very carefully to you tonight and would like it if we got things back to where they were before. When we were seeing each other for days in a row, and said 'I love- I love—' But he was worried that the three-word phrase might not roll off his tongue as it had not so long ago.

He decided instead to go with a line that he'd had success with in the past. "I got fresh sheets."

Dominica turned to him and shook her head. "You're just incorrigible, aren't you?"

He smiled. "I can't think of anything better than having that hot, tempestuous, Irish-Italian-Spanish body next to me between those nice clean sheets that I ironed myself."

"Get outta here. You ironed them yourself?"

"Absolutely," he said. "Slowly and carefully, so there were no creases. I've got a lot of domestic talents you probably weren't aware of."

"I am so impressed," Dominica said, as the valet drove up.

Crawford went around and opened her door.

"And always the gentleman," she said as she slipped into the passenger seat.

"Yup," he said, going around, giving the valet a fiver, then getting into the driver's seat.

"You know, Charlie," Dominica said, "there *were* a few times when we went out for dinner when I didn't sleep with you."

"I remember," he said, nodding. "Back in 1986, I think it was. Right before the Cuban Missile crisis."

Dominica laughed. "Your history sucks."

Crawford shrugged. "Must have been Miriam Wexley then."

"You mean the girl who *never* said no?" Dominica said. "Just more, more, more?"

"Yeah, the eager little beaver."

"Watch it." Dominica shook her head and sighed like she was dealing with a misbehaving twelve-year-old.

"Oh, in case you were wondering, this overnight package comes with eggs, toast and Nueske's triple-thick-cut bacon."

"I was expecting nothing less," Dominica said. "That one time you tried to take me to Dunkin' Donuts"—she shook her head and grimaced—"Tryin' to cheap out on me."

The kissing began just inside the door and they were naked from the waist up before they even got into the living room.

* * *

OTT WAS SNIFFING FOR A SOAP SCENT AS HE WALKED INTO Crawford's office at eight the next morning.

"Smells like your Irish Spring," he said, "but with a strong hint of—"

"Okay, knock it off."

Ott laughed, wondering who it was this time.

Crawford leaned back in his chair and rubbed his chin. "So, we got our favorite banker in an hour. You got anything new?"

"Aside from the CSEUs coming up empty?"

"I know. I stopped by there first thing," Crawford said. Still no DVDs had been found anywhere.

"We get the ballistics report from Hawes in three days if I push, but not too hard."

"It's a fine line, right?" Crawford said.

"Yeah, which you suck at."

"No argument there."

Ott sat down in his favorite chair opposite Crawford and put his feet up on his desk. "Speaking of ballistics, did Hawes ever give you his full-metal-jacket discourse?"

Crawford shook his head.

"I guess he just gives it to his buddies," Ott said. "So anyway, you know what full metal jacket is, right?"

"Yeah," Crawford said. "You know, I *have* been in this business for a while."

"Yeah, I know, so tell me."

"Where a lead bullet is covered in another metal, usually copper. Doesn't break up or change shape when it hits a body."

"Correct. You get an A," Ott said. "And a semi-jacketed bullet?"

"Where the tip is left uncovered," Crawford said. "It hits the target and flattens out and gets wider. A lot tougher on a body. And a hollow-point's even worse. It peels back into a mushroom shape with nasty jagged edges."

"Very good, Charlie," Ott said. "Guess you don't need to sit in on Professor Hawes's lecture. Okay, now for extra credit, here's the final question: 'Does a low-velocity round—defined as traveling less than 1,000 feet per second— cause more or less damage than a high-velocity round *and why?*"

"Sounds like a trick question," Crawford said. "I'm going to go with a low-velocity bullet causes more damage and I don't have any clue why."

Ott pressed an imaginary buzzer on Crawford's desk. "*EEHHHH!* Sorry, no extra credit," he said. "And here's the explanation. When a low-velocity bullet passes through tissue, it tends to crush everything in its path. This is referred to as "crushing" or creating a "permanent cavity." In high-velocity gunshot wounds, shock waves may precede the bullet deep in the tissue, causing injuries to organs and tissues a greater distance from the permanent cavity." Ott rapped Crawford's desk authoritatively. "Aren't you glad you asked?"

"Ah, can't say I remember asking, Mort," Crawford said. "And just how is that relevant to our case?"

"It's totally irrelevant," Ott said, looking at his watch. "Just a damned good way to kill a few minutes before our banker friend opens his doors."

* * *

TWENTY MINUTES LATER, THEY ROLLED UP IN FRONT OF THE PNC Bank on Royal Poinciana Way. They were the bank's first customers and Crawford saw Randy Connors through a glass window in what looked like a conference room.

They walked in, said Connors was expecting them, and a short woman in a blue sundress led them into the conference room. Connors had several rows of documents laid out on a big wooden conference table.

"Welcome, gentlemen," he said shaking Crawford and Ott's hands. "Got everything you need right here."

"Thanks," Crawford said as Ott nodded to Connors. "As we

mentioned, we're most interested in deposits made to Mr. Duke's accounts in the last year."

"I know you are," Connors said, "And what you'll see is there aren't that many deposits, but they're big."

Crawford nodded. "We assumed they would be since he had over three million in the money market."

Connors walked over to the front and back copies of four checks laid out side by side on the center of the conference table and pointed. "Here they are."

The first one was made out in the amount of one million dollars. It was check number 2123 from Carlton Kramer and his address was on the check: 208 Pendleton Avenue, Palm Beach.

Ott took his notebook out and wrote down the name and address. "Do you know who Carlton Kramer is, Mr. Connors?"

"No idea," Connors said. "I'd probably only know him if he banked here. But as you can see, he's at U.S. Trust."

When he saw the second check for a million dollars, Crawford did a double-take. It was from someone he actually knew. The year before he had asked his friend, David Balfour, to set up a golf game at the Poinciana Club. His ulterior motive had been to learn more about certain members who were on his suspect list for the murder of the talk show host, Knight Mulcahy.

The man who had signed the second check was named Tommy Sullivan and he lived in a modern British Colonial on Emerald Lane that Crawford had once visited.

Crawford leaned close to Ott and pointed at Sullivan's check. "I met with that guy about Knight Mulcahy last year."

Ott nodded. "I knew the name sounded familiar."

"Nice enough guy," Crawford said. "I'll give him a call and go see him."

Ott nodded and they both moved to the next check. It was made out to Xavier Duke and was for two cents.

The name on the check said:

EG, LLC

P.O. Box 335

West Palm Beach, FL. 33409

Crawford laughed. "What the hell's that?"

Ott looked at him blankly. "Some kind of joke?"

Crawford shrugged. "I don't know. But I think we better find out."

"How?"

"Get a court order to find out whose box that is."

"I'm on it."

Crawford examined the fourth and final check. "Know what we're not seeing?"

"What's that?"

"Any checks that seem to be related to the porn business. Which confirms our thinking that he's out of that."

"Yeah, whatever he made in the last year seems to be from individuals. Though we don't know what EG, LLC is yet."

The name and the address on the fourth check, also for a million dollars, was:

Tuck Drummond

1920 South Ocean Boulevard

Manalapan, FL 33462

That was it. Only the four deposits, which they took photos of with their iPhones. They skimmed the checks that Xavier Duke had written out but saw there was nothing of interest there. Utilities, Comcast bill, AT&T, all the usual expenses.

"So let's split 'em up," Crawford said. "How 'bout I do Carlton Kramer and Tommy Sullivan, the guy I met. You do Tuck Drummond and get going on the court order to find out the name behind the LLC."

"Sounds good," Ott said.

Randy Connors was over in a corner of the room texting.

"Mr. Connors," Crawford said, "we appreciate your help and taking the time to lay this all out."

"No problem," he said. "Happy to help out. You need anything more, just give me a call."

Ott just nodded at Connors, as they walked out of the bank.

Outside, Ott turned to Crawford. "Amazing how a guy can go from being a total pain in the ass to your new best friend in less than twelve hours."

Crawford shrugged. "Maybe the guy just needed a little project to give his life purpose."

TWENTY-FIVE

CRAWFORD CALLED IT A DAY AT 7:30 AND HEADED HOME TO HIS apartment. He had spent the last hour calling marinas in Palm Beach and West Palm asking if they had a boat owned by Xavier Duke moored there. As with the DVDs, he struck out. Now he was looking forward to reading a book he had just gotten from Amazon, taking a break from the 15-hour workdays. The book was called *Robicheaux* by James Lee Burke. The eponymous Dave Robicheaux was a recovering alcoholic and haunted Vietnam vet who was a sheriff's deputy in New Iberia, Louisiana. He was also a character who seemed to be one of the forerunners of the concept of operating outside the bounds of normal police behavior. Since that was where Crawford and Ott frequently went, Crawford was hoping that he might be able to get a few pointers from author Burke and his maverick hero Robicheaux.

Just as he finished chapter one, Crawford's cell phone rang.

"Hello."

"Charlie?"

He didn't recognize the voice. "Yeah?"

"Hey, it's Wayne Percy." Percy was a Palm Beach Police uniform.

"Thought you'd want to know, I just busted Duane Truax for drunk driving and possession of marijuana."

"No shit," Crawford said getting to his feet and setting the book down.

"Yeah. Heard you were looking at him in the Pawlichuk murder and thought you'd want to know."

"Yeah, thanks," Crawford said, grabbing his jacket and heading for his door. "Where is he now?"

"In a cell at the station," Percy said. "The guy reeked of booze and pot so I searched his car looking for the pot. Found a Ruger SR 9 instead. Guy had it hidden like he didn't want anybody to ever find it."

"Thanks, man, I'll be right down," Crawford said, clicking off, then speed-dialing Ott. He looked at his watch: 10:05.

Dave Robicheaux would have to wait.

* * *

DUANE TRUAX WAS STILL DRUNK.

He, Ott, and Crawford were in the hard room, which consisted of nothing but four chairs, a table, and for some inexplicable reason the famous picture of Albert Einstein with long white hair, sticking his tongue out.

"You have a carry permit for that, Thirty-Seven?" Ott asked.

"The fuck's 'Thirty-Seven?'" Truax slurred. Then he got it. Ott's way of reminding him that he was no longer number one—or anywhere close—on the NASCAR money list. "No, I ain't. Never got around to it."

Crawford could see Truax was just as arrogant drunk as sober. Like being Driver of the Year back in 2005 allowed him to ignore certain laws.

"So, you got drunk driving, marijuana possession, and unlicensed gun possession. Maybe you ought to think about being nice and cooperative with us," Ott said. "Otherwise, it's gonna be a while 'til you get back home to Birmingham."

Crawford was pacing. "Never, if you killed your wife and Paul Pawlichuk."

"Yeah, good point," Ott said.

"So, you hid that Ruger in your tackle box," Crawford said. "Under that false bottom. You really didn't want anyone to find it, did you?"

Truax eyed Crawford contemptuously and didn't answer. He was sweaty and smelled like a locker room at half-time.

"Didn't you tell us you were headed up to Birmingham a few days ago?" Ott asked.

"Shit came up. I had to meet a sponsor," Truax said. "Plus a bunch of stuff with lawyers."

"You want to tell us about what happened down at that pool at Mar-a-Lago?" Ott asked.

Crawford caught his partner's eye, flicked his head toward the hard room door, and started walking.

They both went outside.

"I know what you're gonna say," Ott said. "Whatever comes out in there will be inadmissible"—he laughed— "due to the suspect being humongously shit-faced."

"Yeah," Crawford said. "The worst lawyer in the world could get him off. We might as well get out of here. Start hammering away at him tomorrow morning."

"I agree. Nothing to be gained now."

They didn't bother going back into the hard room to say good night to Truax. They got in their cars and went home.

Crawford was glad to get back to his book.

* * *

RIGHT AFTER THEY HAD THEIR ROTGUT JOE AT THE STATION THE

next morning, Crawford and Ott planned to head back down and see their prisoner again.

"Hope he sobered up," Ott said, following Crawford out of his office. "What's your morning line look like?"

"You mean on Pawlichuk?"

Ott nodded.

"Polk by a couple of lengths. Unless something comes up on ballistics for Truax's gun," Crawford said.

"Yeah, I'm not ruling him out, though," Ott said, as he and Crawford got into the elevator.

Crawford pushed the elevator button for the basement.

"Maybe you can give your buddy Hawes a nudge on it."

Ott nodded. "What works best on him is to tell him how great an ME he is."

"No kidding. Man's a huge fan of himself," Crawford said, as they approached Duane Truax's jail cell.

They stopped and looked through the bars. Truax glanced out, his hair going in at least eleven directions and his eyes bloodshot.

"Top of the morning to you, Thirty-Seven," Ott said.

Truax sat up straight. "Will you quit fuckin' calling me that?"

Ott examined Truax's rumpled shirt. "You puke on that shirt?"

"Yeah, and you're next."

"All right, Duane, first question is, what were you doing with a fully-loaded unlicensed firearm?"

"What every other guy in the south has one for...protection," Truax said, rubbing his face with both hands.

"From what?" Crawford asked.

"From what-the-fuck-ever. Muslims, guys who shoot up churches, maniacs who want to kill someone famous, wackos, Muslims—"

"You already said that," Ott said.

"What about a wife who was about to become an ex-wife and make sure you didn't get any of her money?" Crawford asked.

"We been through this before," Truax said. "I didn't need her fuckin' money."

"That's your story," Crawford said.

"Yup. And I'm stickin' to it," Truax ran his hands through his greasy hair.

"You seem pretty casual about all this," Ott said. "How well do you know Florida law?"

"I'm a few credits short of a law degree."

Ott chuckled. "You're a real funny fucker, aren't you? Let me enlighten you," he said. "Possession of a concealed firearm is a third-degree felony and you can get up to five years in prison. Drunk driving, up to six months plus suspension of your license for between three months and a year"—Ott raised his hands and smiled broadly —"You don't see any problem, bro?"

"The hell you talkin' about?"

"You drivin' in NASCAR races if your license gets suspended for a year?"

Truax looked blank.

"Guess you were too drunk to think of that, huh?"

"Did you go to your car and get that Ruger at any point during the wedding?" Crawford asked. "There are cameras all over that parking lot."

Truax still had a blank look on his face. Like the reality of having his license suspended had really knocked him for a loop.

"Did you hear what my partner asked you?" Ott asked.

Truax turned to Crawford. "Look, man, I'm telling you again, I had nothing to do with what happened to Carla and Pawlichuk and your ballistic report is gonna clear me"—he shook his head and dropped his voice—"Wish I had never gone to that goddamn wedding."

"Lot of people probably feel that way." Crawford glanced over at Ott.

Ott shrugged. "Okay, we're gonna leave you then," Ott said. "You got anybody to post bail for you?"

Truax nodded. "Yeah, Jaclyn Puckett's takin' care of that."

"Well, good." Ott sounded as if he was actually feeling a little sorry for Truax.

"We may need to ask you some more questions after we get the report," Crawford said.

Truax just nodded as Crawford and Ott walked away and went toward the elevator.

"What do you think?" Ott asked as he hit the elevator button.

"My gut still says distant second," Crawford said, as the elevator door opened. "But you know as well as I, there are some really good liars out there."

Crawford went back to his office and looked up the names of marinas north and south of Palm Beach. He wasn't all that hopeful about finding anything. He figured if Duke owned a boat, why dock it a half an hour away from where he lived? But on his eleventh call, he hit pay dirt. Xavier Duke had a Mangusta 108 moored at a marina in North Palm Beach. This according to the marina manager, who explained that Duke had bought the boat from a man who'd kept it at that same marina and had spoken highly of how well they cared for it. Given that, Duke had decided to keep the boat there.

Crawford went straight to Ott's cubicle. "I found a boat owned by Xavier."

Ott looked up with a big grin. "No shit."

"Yup, and I'm putting you in charge of getting a warrant to search it stem to stern."

"Hey, I'm from the Midwest. Does that mean from front to back?"

Crawford nodded. "Attaboy."

TWENTY-SIX

ONE OF CRAWFORD'S FIRST DISCOVERIES WHEN HE CAME DOWN from New York to Palm Beach was how little time people had for him. The good folks of Palm Beach always had a golf or tennis game, lunch at the club, the latest exhibit at the Norton museum, a lecture at the Four Arts, a charity ball, or even a nap that interfered with his request to interview them. He was like a minor nuisance who was to be avoided altogether or, at the very least, put off for a few days. His questions were not high priorities on people's lists. Their attitude seemed to be: The detective can wait, my nap cannot.

But, surprisingly, Carlton Kramer agreed to see him right away and Crawford was on his way to Kramer's house on Pendleton Avenue. He parked in front of number 208, an imposing white, brick colonial, walked up to the house, and pressed the doorbell.

A bald man wearing madras shorts came to the door. Crawford thought that madras shorts had gone the way of top hats and dickeys.

"Hi, I'm Detective Crawford."

The man's eyes lit up as if Crawford had just said, 'and I'm here to give you a two-hundred-million-dollar check for winning the Florida state lottery.'

Kramer stepped closer to Crawford and looked at him expectantly. "Any luck?"

"Any luck with what, Mr. Kramer?"

"My wallet," Kramer said. "Did you find it?"

"Sorry, I don't know anything about your wallet."

Kramer looked hugely disappointed. "I got pickpocketed at the Kravis Center. *The Book of Mormon* matinee."

"I'm actually a homicide detective investigating the murder of Xavier Duke," Crawford said. "I'd like to ask you a few questions related to that."

Kramer frowned. "Oh, yeah, I heard about that," he said. "But you're sure you don't know anything about my wallet?"

"No, that would be someone in burglary," Crawford said, still standing on the houses front stoop. "Would it be okay if we went inside, Mr. Kramer?"

Kramer sighed. "Sorry, we can't. My wife has her bridge group in the living room."

Crawford wanted to get on with it. "Okay, this is fine right here," he said, "So my first question is, why did you write a check for a million dollars three months ago to Xavier Duke?"

Kramer's frown deepened. "What do you want to know for?"

"As I said, I'm investigating the murder of Duke and that's one of the questions I have."

"I don't have to answer the question."

"No, you don't," Crawford said. "But why would you not, unless you've got something to hide?"

Kramer wiped his mouth with his hand and looked away. Then his eyes met Crawford's. "I've got absolutely nothing to hide," he said. "It was an investment."

"An investment in what?"

"Xavier Duke was a filmmaker," Kramer said. "We have a mutual friend who introduced us. Duke told me about a movie he wanted to make and I decided I wanted to invest in it."

"So presumably for the million dollars you kicked in, you end up making a certain percentage of the profits? Something like that, right?"

"Yes, something like that," Kramer said.

"And just out of curiosity, where was the movie being shot?"

Kramer looked stumped. "I'm not a hundred-percent sure. Hollywood, I guess."

Maybe he was a guy rich enough to take million-dollar flyers on a regular basis, but Crawford wasn't getting that vibe. The only vibe he was getting—loud and clear—was that Kramer was winging it.

"So, if you don't mind me asking, Mr. Kramer, what was the movie about?"

The frown that had gone away for a few moments came surging back. "Well, it basically was about this sorority house, ah, back in the sixties. Then, ten years later they, the girls, that is, have a, ah, reunion..."

"I see."

Kramer smiled nervously. "It's a character-driven vehicle."

"Oh, is it?" Crawford tilted his head skeptically.

He had the sense Kramer was saying whatever floated into his head. "Had they picked a title for the movie?"

Kramer looked blank for a second. "Well, let's see, *Sorority* was the working title. They tell me things like that sometimes change."

Crawford nodded, looking for a way to trip up Kramer. "I see," he said. "What might be really helpful is if I could see the screenplay."

"Unfortunately, I never saw one. You see, Detective, I made my decision about investing in the project based on Duke's track record."

"I understand," Crawford said. Now it was zinger time: "Didn't Mr. Duke make porn movies?"

The frown slowly turned to a smile. "Well, yes, and my impression was that this movie might fall into the category of soft porn. I mean, when you think about it, a sorority house is rife with possibilities."

Crawford nodded. "Okay," he said, "I just never think of any porn movies—soft, hard or whatever—as being character-driven."

Kramer shrugged. "I don't know. That's just what Xavier told me."

Crawford was running out of questions. "Was there anything like a prospectus that laid out for investors how the finances worked?"

"Not that I recall," Kramer said. "As I said, I was going on the recommendation of a friend who had done pretty well financially in one of Duke's movies."

"And what is your friend's name?"

"Dale Marston. He's got a house down on the ocean."

Crawford wondered if he just made the name up. "Okay, well, I guess that'll do it then." Crawford looked around. "Beautiful house you have here. You have kids living here with you?"

"Nah, I live up on Long Island most of the year. Got two boys working in the city. And a daughter in college."

"Does she come down on Christmas and spring break?"

Kramer nodded. "Yes, she does."

"Well, okay," Crawford reached out for Kramer's hand. "Thanks for your help."

"No problem," Kramer said. "Hey, do me a favor, give the guys in burglary a kick in the ass, will you? Tell 'em to try to find my wallet. Damn thing cost me over two grand. Bottega Venata."

"I'll tell 'em," Crawford said, as he turned and walked down the steps.

He was pretty sure he'd never spent more than twenty-five bucks for a wallet.

TWENTY-SEVEN

"I didn't buy a word of it," Crawford said to Ott who was sitting opposite him in Crawford's office. "You know what it seemed like to me?"

"What?"

"That Xavier Duke and Carlton Kramer spent fifteen minutes concocting a cover story, just in case they ever needed one. Same with your guy, Tuck Drummond?"

Ott nodded. He and Crawford were comparing notes after having just returned from their respective interviews.

"Yeah, except maybe they spent a half hour on Drummond's. It was a little more detailed," Ott said.

Drummond had told Ott that his million-dollar check to Xavier Duke was to finance a travel movie set in the Galapagos Islands. Duke had told Drummond—so Drummond said, anyway—that he was going in a whole new creative direction and that he and the National Geographic channel were combining to do a joint venture about exotic birds, mammals and fish indigenous to the Galapagos.

"It was pretty convincing and I was buying it at first," Ott said. "The guy was telling me all about Galapagos fur seals, marine iguanas and blue-footed boobies, not to be confused with red-footed boobies." Ott paused. "Nothing he said sounded suspicious except when I asked him where the Galapagos Islands were. He looked kind of blank for a second, then said off of Chile somewhere. Well, the only thing I was good at in high school was geography, so I knew they were off of Ecuador, which is like two thousand miles away."

"And we're supposed to believe that the porn king suddenly changed his stripes and hooked up with the National Geographic channel." Crawford said. "National Enquirer channel, now that I might believe."

"Like I said, I was buying it for a while with all his goddamn boobies."

"Did you ask him about his kids?"

"Oh, yeah, I was just getting to that," Ott said. "Gotta hand it to you, Charlie, that was a good idea. So, turns out, he's got a daughter —" Ott checked his notes— "at some place called the College of Charleston. She's a junior there."

"Isn't that interesting?" Crawford said. "So that's what they have in common. Daughters in their late teens or early twenties. Investing in the movies is just one elaborate smokescreen. But to make sure, we need to go through every inch of Duke's boat. See if we find any DVDs."

Ott nodded. "I've got a meeting with the judge at 2:00 to get that court order. I'll get a search warrant like we talked about."

"Perfect," Crawford said. "We gotta get this thing wrapped up before Norm weighs in with another one of his half-assed theories."

* * *

OTT WAS BACK AT THE STATION AT 2:30 WITH A LOOK IN HIS EYE that Crawford hadn't seen much lately. The most recent time he remembered seeing the look was after Ott had his first date with Rebecca, a woman on match.com who he was still going strong with. The first time Crawford remembered noticing it was right after Ott tackled hedge-fund billionaire/murderer Wardwell Jaynes on the beach behind Jaynes's house as a camera from CBS Action News 12 was capturing the momentous event live.

"So, I see you got something," Crawford said.

"Yeah, I do, I'm just not totally sure what it's worth," he said. "The identity of EG LLC, the owner of that P.O. Box."

"Good going. The two-cent-check guy?"

Ott nodded

"Who is it?

"A guy named Ellis Gorman."

Crawford shot up straight in his chair. "No shit!"

Ott nodded. "You know who that is?"

Crawford nodded. "I'm guessing there aren't a whole lot of Ellis Gormans in the world, but the one I know is from up in New York. The Bronx, or one of the boroughs anyway. He's a guy who, I'm guessing, started out with nothing but ended up a U.S. congressman. A congressman who was for sale. Like, if you were in the real estate business and wanted to build a skyscraper that exceeded the number of stories the building code allowed, you'd go to Ellis. If you were a company and wanted to do a merger with another company which violated anti-trust laws, you'd go to Ellis. So let me try to fill in some blanks here—"

Ott spread his hands. "Be my guest."

"So, Xavier Duke, not knowing a lot about Ellis Gorman except he's rich, finds out his daughter is hanging out at Windsong." Ott nodded. "Duke gets Jared to put the moves on her and, fast-forward, they end up in bed and on film together. Then Xavier calls up Ellis and tries to put the bite on him. But Ellis, who's used to having his hand out—not the other way around—basically tells Duke to go fuck himself and, just to make sure Duke got the message, literally gives him his two cents' worth."

"That makes sense," Ott said, patting his jacket pocket. "Oh, I also got the search warrant for Duke's boat."

Crawford stood up. "Well, shit, what are we waiting for?" he said.

"Let's go. I'll start at the stem, you start at the stern, meet in the middle."

* * *

DUKE'S BOAT WAS A 110-FOOT MANGUSTA, ITALIAN-MADE AND built in 2000, though a man at the marina said it had undergone a major refit in 2015. It was sleek and elegant both outside and inside, with polished mahogany interiors in all five cabins. Similar to Duke's house, it featured an office abutting the ample master stateroom. Crawford guessed that it had once been another cabin, as it had a small bathroom off of it. The centerpiece of the office was a built-in desk that looked like it was the product of a master woodworker. On either side were thin drawers and, above it, three rows of built-in bookshelves.

Crawford found a Day-Timer in the top drawer on the left, along with a passport and a birth certificate. He skimmed through the calendar and, based on the entries, concluded that Xavier Duke behaved like many other rich, retired men in Palm Beach. He played tennis and croquet almost every day at the Royal & Alien club, just down the street from his house. Those activities alone seemed to consume between two and three hours per day.

It appeared that he used the boat quite frequently, hosting dinners and lunches for friends.

His calendar also made regular mentions of meetings with a man named Danny. However, there was absolutely no mention of any movie-making endeavors, whether they featured naked sex partners, red-footed boobies, or others.

Crawford put the Day-Timer down and looked at the bookshelves above the desk. On the top shelf to the far left was a book entitled, *100 Books to Read in a Lifetime*, then to right, *Pride and Prejudice*, *1984*, *To Kill a Mockingbird*, *The Great Gatsby*, *The Catcher in the Rye*...Crawford scanned to the end of the shelf, then down to the two shelves below and, sure enough, it looked as if Duke had bought and shelved all 100 of the recommended books.

Crawford sighed, realizing he had a fair amount of reading to do before he even got halfway through the list.

He started to look away, but then noticed a space between *Ulysesses* and *Of Mice and Men*. Something metallic and silver in color was behind the tomes. He pulled the two books out to get a better look and saw that it was a wall safe with an electronic keypad.

"Mort," he said to Ott, who was going through built-in drawers on the other side of the master stateroom. "Check this out."

Ott walked over. "Well, well," was all he said.

The safe looked much like the ones you'd find in certain hotels to keep your valuables in.

"You any good at safe-cracking?" Crawford asked.

"One skill I never acquired." Ott shrugged. "We just need four numbers."

Crawford reached back into the drawer and took out Duke's birth certificate.

"Why don't you do the honors," Crawford said, and Ott moved closer to the safe. "Try 1-0-1-4."

"What's that?" Ott asked, punching in the numbers into the safe.

"October fourteenth. His birthday."

Ott shook his head.

Crawford put the birth certificate back in the drawer, picked up the Day-Timer and started turning its pages. "Try 1-2-2-1," he said to Ott.

Ott tried the numbers and shook his head. "What was that?"

"A guy named Danny's birthday. Who I'm guessing might have been his significant other."

Crawford turned several pages of the Day-Timer. "How about this one: 0-3-1-0?"

Ott tried the number on the safe and it opened. "Bingo. What was that?"

"His mother's birthday."

"Of course."

Crawford leaned down to the open safe. "So what's he got in there?"

Ott slipped on his vinyl gloves and pulled out the only thing that was in the safe: a dark, wooden box that looked to be about ten inches long and half that wide and high.

"Open it," Crawford said eagerly.

Ott opened it and saw five DVDs.

He took one out. It had a simple white label on the side that said, "Samantha Kramer."

"No shit," Ott said with a smile.

Then he picked up the next one, which read. "Jennifer Sullivan."

The third one read, "Natalie Drummond."

"Olivia Gorman" was the fourth.

The fifth one read simply: "AC."

TWENTY-EIGHT

THE FIRST FOUR DVDs WERE BETWEEN FIFTEEN AND TWENTY minutes long. Crawford and Ott didn't feel it necessary to watch them all the way through. They got the idea in the first minute or two after playing one in a DVD player on Xavier Duke's boat. Jared was the male lead in all four. Crawford wondered whether the man knew he was being filmed. He guessed he did but made a mental note to ask Dominica what she thought.

"What do you think?" Ott asked. "Jared along with a buddy or two got them up to the house, then Duke figured out who they were—"

"More importantly who their fathers were—"

Ott nodded. "Then Duke told Jared to go put the moves on 'em."

"Yeah," Crawford said. "Sic loverboy on 'em, then press record. They tried it on Taylor Whitcomb, but no sale."

"But Duke thought she was worth another shot," Ott said. "So after she blew off Jared at Christmas, Duke invited her as his plus-one to the wedding so he could lure her up to his house a second time. I'm guessing it was another time, another guy, same outcome."

Crawford shook his head long and slow. "I've got two observations. One, Taylor's got a good head on her shoulders. And two, this whole set-up is really sick."

"Yeah, no shit," Ott said, loading the fifth DVD in the machine. "Wonder why Duke just put initials on this one instead of the whole name?"

Crawford shrugged. "No clue."

The film started out with a young guy—not Jared—taking his clothes off, then panned to a girl under the covers of a bed.

"Holy shit," Ott said, his eyes wide. "She looks about fifteen."

Crawford was thinking even younger. "Turn that thing off."

Ott hit the DVD switch and looked at Crawford. "Like you said: sick, man."

Neither said anything for a few moments.

"We've gotta track down Jared," Crawford said finally. "Find out who that couple is."

Ott nodded. "This thing's really ugly, Charlie."

Crawford nodded.

Ott turned the DVD player back on and took out his iPhone.

"What are you doing?"

"Gotta get some screenshots of those two."

Crawford nodded, looking away from the images.

Ott took a few quick shots then turned off the DVD player again.

"There's another reason to track down Jared," Crawford said.

"What's that?"

"As a potential murder suspect."

Ott turned and met Crawford's eyes. "How do you figure that?"

"So, imagine Jared finds out Duke is making millions. And he thinks, 'Wait a minute, I'm the star of the show.'"

"You mean, getting the girls on tape so Duke can shake down their fathers?"

"Yeah, and just assume Duke's paying his star actor peanuts, so Jared starts thinking he deserves a bigger slice of the pie."

"So he goes to Duke and hits him up?"

"Exactly, like, 'Come on, Xavier, for all I'm doin' for you,'" Crawford said. "But Xavier goes, 'Sorry, there're a million pretty faces out there,' and one thing leads to another and Jared gets pissed off and kills him."

Ott thought for a few moments. "I ain't buyin' it."

"Why not?"

"Mainly 'cause Jared doesn't strike me as the type. Kind of passive."

Crawford nodded and thought for a second. "I think you're probably right. But we gotta check it out anyway."

"Agreed," said Ott. "So, who else we need to find?"

"First, AC, whoever he may be. And I keep going back to Ellis Gorman."

"Why?"

"'Cause basically that two-cent check, as I said, was his way of telling Duke to go fuck himself," Crawford said. "But what if he thinks about it a little more? Decides the tape of his daughter could really be damaging. He's a guy who's played rough all his life so he says to Xavier, 'Hey, I don't want anyone seeing us together, so let's meet and I'll give you a check in person.' They meet at Reef Road and, pop, pop, pop. Xavier's lying there tits-up, in the immortal words of Bob Hawes."

"That could have happened with any of the fathers."

"True," Crawford said. "I just get the sense Gorman is more capable of it than the others."

"But when you think about it," Ott said. "It could be someone we don't even know about."

"What do you mean?"

"Well, let's say that Duke started doing these scams right after he retired from the porn business—"

"Five years ago, you mean?"

"Yeah, whenever it was. And for all we know he's had people wire money into the Grand Cayman or Swiss bank accounts. Or God-knows where else."

"Yeah, except my sense is Duke wasn't all that sophisticated with financial stuff."

"Why do you say that?"

"Because he had a money market at PNC paying him one percent, for starters."

"Yeah, good point, and also who uses a Day-Timer anymore?" Ott said. "So we're back to the five in the DVDs."

Crawford nodded. "We know who the first four women are," he said. "Question is, who's the fifth? And who's the boy with the girl? And another question, who's the victim...the boy or the girl?"

Ott exhaled. "I never thought of that. I just assumed it was the girl."

Crawford shrugged. "Could be," Crawford said. "But what if Duke set it up so the boy could get charged with statutory rape if the DVD ever got out there?"

Ott patted Crawford on the shoulder. "So, you mean, maybe the *girl* was working for Duke, not the boy?"

Crawford shrugged. "I don't know if either one was. But it looks like it's not just a sex tape, but a crime too."

Ott nodded. "Duke could go after a hell of a lot of money for that."

"Sure could."

"I just hope Jared's got some answers," Ott said.

"Ellis Gorman too," Crawford said. "But he's not going to be easy."

Crawford's cell phone rang. He picked it up and looked at the display.

"Rose," Crawford told Ott, then clicked on. "Hey, Rose, what's up?"

"You know how I'm always trying to solve your murders for you, Charlie?"

"Yes. Keep up the good work."

"And how I always put your livelihood ahead of my own?"

"Ah, now, you're stretching it a little."

"Okay, maybe a little," Rose said. "So anyway, last night I was at a cocktail party—"

"How unusual."

"I know, right," Rose said. "And somebody was talking about your murder—"

"Which one?"

"Carla Carton and the football player whose name I can't pronounce."

"Paul Pawlichuk, and he was a coach, not a player," Crawford said. "You mind if I put this on speaker, Rose? I'm here with Mort."

"No, no, go ahead."

Crawford hit speaker.

"Hi, Rose," Ott said. "How's tricks?"

"Good, Mortie. I miss you."

"Likewise."

"So, what was I saying?"

"About Paul Pawlichuk."

"Well, I actually have two scoops for you," Rose said. "But be forewarned: this is from a cocktail party, where people are typically well into their cups. So, what you're about to hear hasn't exactly been fact-checked."

"Understood," Crawford said. "You still got us curious."

"Okay, so here goes," Rose said. "The first one is about the skinflint and Carla."

"The skinflint? Oh, you mean Robert Polk."

"Yeah, exactly. Well, according to the rumor mill, five years ago Robert asked Carla to marry him."

"Really?"

"Wait a sec," Ott said. "He was married."

"Yes, Mort, but you don't think that the laws that apply to us mere mortals apply to billionaires, do you?"

Mort grunted his assent.

"What happened was—and this is from a pretty reliable source— twenty years ago, Polk met Carla somewhere. They had this torrid affair and Polk was ready to marry her and ditch his wife but Carla said no. Fast-forward to like a year ago, when Carla felt she was going nowhere with that soap opera and her husband Duane and she said yes."

"So it was kind of like a standing offer with Polk, you mean?" Ott asked.

"Strange, I know, but yes, something like that. My source told me Carla felt that since it wasn't happening with the soap, she might as well get filthy rich. But then, out of the blue, she gets the part in the Netflix show and starts making big bucks and decides who needs Robert."

Ott caught Crawford's eye and muttered, "Fucked-up rich people again."

"What's that?" Rose asked.

"Nah, nothin'."

"That's a hell of a story," Crawford said. "Who's your source?"

"Get this," Rose said. "Robert's wife's best friend. She said Lorinda Polk was all set to bail and get half of Robert's money. She was actually kind of disappointed it never happened."

"So, long story short," Ott said, "Polk was a pretty good prospect in Carla's soap-opera days, but not in her starlet ones?"

"Exactly," said Rose.

"Thanks, Rose, that's very helpful," Crawford said. "And what's your second scoop?"

"Oh, yes," Rose said. "Almost as good"—she caught her breath —"So, as I said, these people were gossiping about the Mar-a-Lago murders and someone mentioned the son-in-law of the football coach and how he has a gambling problem. Goes to casinos all over and loses a small fortune."

Ott eyed Crawford quizzically. "Wait? George Figueroa?"

"Yes, exactly. And this one gossip queen is yapping away about how his wife spends like she's got Robert Polk money. Goes on shopping jags to Paris and London."

Crawford sat up a little straighter. "Keep going."

"Well, that's about it. I just thought you boys would find that interesting."

"Yes, we sure do," Crawford said. "Anything else, Rose?"

"Isn't that enough?"

'It sure is," Crawford said. "Thank you very much."

"For all that intel, I'd say you both owe me dinner," Rose said.

"In a heartbeat, Rose," Ott said.

"But...you have a girlfriend, Mort?"

"I do?"

"Funny boy," Rose said. "All right, that's all for now."

"It's plenty," Ott said.

"Bye, Rose," Crawford said, clicking off.

He tapped his desk. "Isn't that interesting."

"Damn right," Ott said. "So is Polk still your lock for first place?"

Crawford thought for a second. "I don't know. We gotta take another good hard look at George and Janice."

"I still say it's Polk," Ott said. "He gets humiliated at the wedding and maybe Carla turns him down for the seventeenth time. So, he's had a bunch of drinks and goes from cranky to homicidal."

"But where'd he get a gun? I doubt he shows up at the wedding packing."

"I don't know...his car maybe."

Crawford shook his head slowly. "I'll call him. Tell him I need to have another meeting with him and this time it's going to last as long as I damn well want it to."

Ott nodded. "And Janice and George?"

"Right after we meet with Polk," Crawford said. "I have a couple of math questions for those two."

TWENTY-NINE

Jared was a huge source of information and, without question, not the murderer of Xavier Duke. He was a 26-year-old senior at Palm Beach Atlantic College, and his parents lived in Palm Beach but had kicked him out of their house the year before. That was after he came limping back home with a bad coke habit after an abortive attempt to make it as an actor in Hollywood. He said he had a walk-on part in the Amazon series *Bosch* and claimed to have had a bunch of bad breaks, but planned to head back out and give it another shot after he finished up at Palm Beach Atlantic.

Ott gave Crawford a quizzical look right after Jared said that, wondering whether he thought a sheepskin from PBA would somehow be the key to landing big parts in Hollywood. Jared had been living at Xavier Duke's house for the last five months. Duke had been paying him three thousand dollars a month, which Jared said he was more than satisfied with, along with free room and board. Duke had also agreed to help him out and paid half of his college tuition. Jared was fully aware of the cameras in Duke's bedroom that he'd lured women into and had good recall about which women had been recorded on them.

He remembered Stephanie, Natalie, Jennifer, and Olivia and was starting to get specific about them when Crawford and Ott cut him off. When they asked Jared if he knew what Duke did with the films, Jared shrugged, looked blank and said no. They believed him but had to wonder why he wasn't more curious.

Then they hit him with the question they'd been saving up: Ott showed him the pictures of the boy and young girl and asked him who they were. Jared claimed to have no idea. They pressed him. And aside from appearing more nervous, he again said he didn't know. When Crawford said they'd need to administer a lie-detector test, Jared squirmed some more but became even more adamant that he didn't know who they were. He even agreed to take the test.

Out of options and now convinced that Jared really didn't know who the two were, they asked him if he knew anyone whose intials were AC. He thought for a while and, finally, said no.

All they had left was the mysterious "Danny" to ask about. They asked Jared if he knew the man whom Duke had called multiple times per day. He did. He gave them Danny's last name and said he was a trainer at a gym in either Palm Beach or West Palm.

They thanked him and headed back to the station. When they got back to Crawford's office, they shifted the conversation to Janice and George Figeuroa.

"See, here's what I think," Crawford started out. "George has to be getting at least one percent for managing his father-in-law's account. That's five hundred thousand. That gives him a lot of money to lose, plus still have some left over for Janice's expensive tastes in jewelry and clothes."

"Yeah, but what if he was really a huge whale?" Ott said scrolling down on his iPhone. "I've heard about some of these guys losing a million at a casino in a couple of days." He pointed at his iPhone. "Okay, here you go, listen to this: 'A media tycoon by the name of Robert Maxwell lost close to two million dollars in a minute and a half at Ambassadeurs casino in England.'"

"Come on, how the hell is that possible?"

"Says he was playing multiple roulette wheels at once. Wait, that's nothing, listen to this one: "Terence Watanabe was said to have bet more than $825 million and lost nearly $127 million of it in Caesar's Palace and the Rio casinos in 2007, which is believed to be the biggest losing streak in Vegas history.""

"$127 million?"

"Yup," Ott said, "and, whoa, get this: Watanabe claimed that 'the casino was responsible for fueling his stunning streak by providing him with free drinks and intoxicants and allowing him to gamble when he was clearly intoxicated.'"

"That's not hard to believe," Crawford said. "Why don't you Google George and see if you find anything."

Ott was scrolling. "I'm one step ahead of you," he said and suddenly his eyes got big. "Oh...my...God."

"You got something?" Crawford asked, leaning across his desk to see.

"Do I ever." Ott handed his iPhone to Crawford.

It was a photo of George Figueroa. His face was colorless and he seemed to have a three-day growth. Beside him in the photo was a particularly grim-looking Janice Figueroa.

Crawford started to read the short article. "Holy shit."

"What's it say?" Ott asked.

"High-rolling American financier, George Figueroa, has been charged with refusing to pay 950,000 pounds in a line of credit at the Grosvenor Casino in London. Figueroa lost a total of two million pounds at the baccarat table over the course of two days and claimed he was unable to cover the line of credit he had established with the casino."

"Financier, huh?" Ott said, looking up at Crawford. "'Ol' George is hardly some penny-ante player. What's the rest of it say?"

"That's it. That's the end of the article."

"Well, we know he's not wasting away in some London debtors' prison—"

"Which means he must have scraped up the 950,000 pounds

somewhere," Crawford said.

"You don't suppose..."

Crawford nodded. "The guy dipped into his father-in-law's account?" he said. "Yeah, now I do. We've got to find out how much is in that account."

"But your guess is something less than fifty million?"

"Yeah, has to be," Crawford said. "And there's Janice's English thing again."

"Yeah, I know."

"The Bentley. The shopping in London."

"While George is dropping a couple mil on baccarat."

Crawford was nodding. "Want to know what I think?"

"I'm all ears."

"It's like Janice has a fantasy about wanting to be an English aristocrat. You know, like a baroness or—"

"A duchess."

Crawford nodded. "Yeah, instead of plain old Janice Pawlichuk, football coach's daughter or Mrs. George Figueroa, bean-counter's wife."

"Hey, don't forget: George is a 'financier' these days."

Crawford nodded. "Oh, right. I can just hear Janice telling the British reporter that."

"And what about that stage name?"

"Professional name, you mean," Crawford said. "Bartholomew. Lady Janice Bartholomew." Crawford slapped Ott on the shoulder. "Let's go."

"Where?"

"Pay our respects to the lord and the lady."

"And don't forget your old congressman."

"Yeah, him too," Crawford said. "So, you'll find this interesting: I looked him up and found out Gorman lives five houses down from Xavier Duke's house on North Lake Way."

"Isn't that convenient?" Ott said. "So that lot on Reef Road—"

"Would have been a short hike for both of them."

THIRTY

Crawford and Ott requisitioned six "bags," Palm Beach PD lingo for uniform cops, giving them instructions to go to all the local high schools with the pictures of the unidentified young girl and boy from what they called the "AC" tape to see if a teacher, principal, or student recognized either one.

After that, Crawford called Xavier Duke's friend, Danny, whose last name turned out to Waller. He was a trainer at a boutique gym in Palm Beach, just like Jared said.

When Crawford visited him, Danny seemed genuinely broken up about the death of Xavier Duke and in the dark about what Xavier did for a living. He said they had been friends for about a year, played croquet almost every day at the Royal & Alien Club and went out on Xavier's boat a lot. Crawford asked if he knew who Xavier had gone to see the night he was killed and Danny said he had no idea. Crawford asked him if Xavier had ever mentioned the names Samantha Kramer, Jennifer Sullivan, Natalie Drummond, Olivia Gorman or someone whose initials were AC. He said no. Crawford thought about asking Danny about the nature of his relationship with Duke, but didn't know how that knowledge would advance the case.

In both cases thus far, he and Ott had encountered a lot of non-starters. Danny Waller seemed to be yet another one.

* * *

CRAWFORD HAD LEFT THREE MESSAGES FOR ROBERT POLK AND four for Ellis Gorman.

He had decided to pay another visit to Mindy Pawlichuk, who had moved from Mar-a-Lago to the Breakers. She had explained to Crawford on the phone that she was staying in Palm Beach to resolve some issues related to her husband's death but didn't specify what they were. Crawford was surprised that Mindy hadn't simply gone to stay at her daughter's house up in Jupiter.

He drove to The Breakers, where he and Mindy had agreed to meet in an area in front of the receptionist's desk.

She was reading a magazine when Crawford approached.

"Hello, Mrs. Pawlichuk," he said and she looked up.

"Hello, Detective, please have a seat," she pointed to the chair next to her.

"Thank you," he said and sat.

He got right to it. "Mrs. Pawlichuk, I want to talk to you about your daughter and son-in-law."

The faint trace of a frown appeared on her face. "Okay," she said, "What about them?"

Crawford put his hand on his chin. "Well, it's come to my attention that George ran up large gambling debts on at least one occasion when he and Janice were in London in the past year."

Mindy sighed and moved the magazine from her lap to a table in front of her. "I'm not sure what that has to do with the death of my husband."

"Well, I'm not sure either, except that it was a substantial amount of money that he lost," Crawford said. "When we spoke to you the second time, you knew approximately what was in your account with Stoller Financial"—Mindy nodded—"so I was wondering: Do you know how much is in your account with George?"

"I'm sure we received statements," Mindy said.

"I'm sure you did too, and did you look at them?"

Mindy shook her head.

"Why not?"

"Because I don't remember Paul ever letting me see them."

Crawford paused while an older couple walked past them. "Why do you think Paul let you see the Stoller Financial statements but not the ones from George?"

Mindy shrugged. "I'm afraid I don't know the answer to that."

Crawford put his hand down on the end table next to him and thrummed his fingers. "Did Paul ever complain about how George was doing with the account?"

Mindy shook her head. "No."

"Did he ever talk about it at all?"

"No."

"Did he ever bring it up in a conversation with Janice maybe?"

"Not that I know of."

Mindy's breathing seemed to have become more labored.

"Did he ever talk about finances at all with Janice?"

Now Crawford noticed a slight tremble in Mindy's hands.

"No. Well, maybe a few times," she said, them lowering her voice to a near-whisper. "What Paul talked about mostly with Janice was about her spending. He thought she spent too much."

"On what kinds of things?"

Mindy laughed. "On every kind of thing imaginable. And he was right. But she wouldn't listen—" she put a hand on her forehead— "then he got on her about that whole Bartholomew thing."

"You mean, her professional name?"

"Is that what she told you it was?" Mindy shook her head. "She just seemed embarrassed her name was Pawlichuk. Ever since she was a little girl she was always making up these fancy-sounding WASP-y names for herself. I have no idea why."

"Going back to George's gambling," Crawford said. "I'm just going to ask you flat out: Were you ever concerned that maybe he might take money out of your and Paul's account? To pay a gambling debt, possibly."

Mindy put her hand on her chest and looked around the room. "Here's the thing, Detective: We had plenty of money, so what difference did it make, really? I mean, Janice and George were going to end up with half of it anyway."

Crawford looked around, then his eyes returned to Mindy's. "Do you think that was Paul's attitude?"

Her voice got even lower. "No. Definitely not."

"So, Paul—"

"Let's just say, Paul was not as casual about the money as I was."

Crawford nodded. "Well, thank you, Mrs. Pawlichuk. Again, I appreciate your time," he said, standing. "Have you heard from your son? How it's going on his honeymoon?"

"Oh, they didn't go after all. Rich just couldn't leave after what happened."

"I certainly understand that," Crawford said, making a mental note to call Rich.

Then he flashed to Rich's wife Addison...cranky, no doubt, about not being able to work on her tan on the Riviera.

CRAWFORD DECIDED THE HELL WITH IT, he wasn't going to wait any longer for a call that probably would never be returned. Instead, he'd go straight to Ellis Gorman's house on North Lake Way. Before heading there, he called Ott, who wouldn't want to be excluded from something which could be good and explosive.

They were on their way up North Lake Way, Ott at the wheel.

"So that Bentley of Janice Figueroa's...you ever drive one?"

Ott looked at him like he was nuts. "Oh, yeah, Charlie, my neighbor's got one. Couple other people on the block too. They let me take 'em out for spins all the time," he said. "Are you fuckin' crazy? You gotta show the Bentley dealer your bank statement before you take a test drive."

Crawford shrugged. "Just wondering."

Ott pulled into the driveway that led up to a big gray Mediterranean on the ocean.

"Christ, what are congressmen makin' these days?" Ott asked.

"You know, like two hundred thousand," Crawford said. "But Ellis has lots of side businesses."

"Like what? Bribery, extortion, bid-rigging, shit like that?"

"Yeah, exactly, shakedowns, hush money, palm-greasing and the like."

Ott snickered. "Beats workin'."

They parked and walked across the Chattahoochee pebble driveway to the front porch.

Crawford pushed the buzzer. A woman with a thick layer of make-up and fake eyelashes answered the door and gave them a puzzled look.

"Mrs. Gorman?"

"Yes."

"My name is Detective Crawford, Palm Beach Police Department, and this is Detective Ott—" Ott nodded. "We'd like to see your husband, please."

"What about?"

Crawford thought he detected a hint of Staten Island in her voice.

"It's kind of a long story."

Mrs. Gorman frowned. "Well, he's down at the pool."

Crawford nodded. "Okay, great. Is it easier to go through the house or around back?"

"Ah, I guess you can go through the house." The puzzled look hadn't left her face.

"Thanks," Crawford said, walking past her, Ott right behind him. "This way, I assume."

"Yes, straight through."

Crawford and Ott went through the living room, a TV room, a room with a pool table, then out the door of a sunroom in back.

The pool and a pool house were fifty feet ahead. A chubby man in a black Speedo sat on a chaise with a drink in his hand.

"Hey, Congressman," Crawford shouted and waved his hand.

Gorman shot him a perplexed look.

Crawford and Ott walked around the pool and up to Gorman, who had gotten to his feet.

"Who the hell are you?"

Definitely Staten Island. With a detour through Brooklyn maybe.

"Detectives Crawford and Ott. I'm the guy who left you all the messages."

"Yeah, whaddaya want?"

"We want to ask you some questions about Xavier Duke."

"Who the hell's Xavier Duke?"

Ott took a step forward. "Your ex-neighbor, just up the beach," he said. "You wrote him a check once."

Gorman nodded his head. "Oh, yeah. That schmendrick."

"What?" Ott said.

"It's like a schmuck," Crawford clued in his partner.

"What about him?" Gorman asked.

"He tried to hold you up, right?" Crawford asked.

"How do you know about that?"

"We're cops," Crawford said.

Gorman chuckled. "Yeah, I paid him off," he said. "That was right before I told him to leave me the fuck alone or I'd fuck up his life but good."

The man seemed a little profane for a public servant. But, then again, Crawford had once counted four fucks in one of Ott's sentences. So, this was kids' stuff.

"And what did he say?"

"Nothing."

"What do you mean, 'nothing?'"

"The scumbag hung up and that was the end of it."

Gorman's story sounded credible. That probably *had* been the end of it, Xavier Duke deciding—wisely—that Ellis Gorman was not a man he should mess with. There were plenty of other far less dangerous men in Palm Beach who Duke could have counted on to write him million-dollar checks to keep their daughters' privates...private.

THIRTY-ONE

They thanked Gorman and started to leave.

Gorman, who had been eyeing Crawford closely, sidled up next to him and asked if he was the "homicide dick" from New York who had come down to Palm Beach a few years back. Crawford said he was and told him he had actually voted for Gorman when he was living in New York. He didn't mention that he'd begun voting for Gorman's opponents when it became clear that Gorman was shady at best and a full-fledged crook at worst.

Gorman smiled, clapped Crawford on the back, and asked them if they wanted to "take a load off" and have a beer with him.

Crawford thanked him, said they were on the job, but maybe some other time.

They drove back to the station and went to their offices.

Still eager to get in touch with Janice and George Figueroa, Crawford decided to call Janice's brother Rich Pawlichuk, figuring Rich might be more forthcoming than his mother about George's management of the Pawlichuk portfolio.

He dialed the cell phone number that Rich had given him when they first met at Mar-a-Lago.

"Hello?"

"Rich?"

"Yeah. Who's this?"

"Detective Crawford."

"Oh, hey. What's up?"

"I have a few questions about your brother-in-law George's investment of your parents' money and also about his compensation."

"Okay, shoot," Rich said. "I know a little about that stuff, just not all the specifics."

"My understanding was that George invested in safe investments like CDs, government bonds, stuff like that. Is that correct?"

"Yeah, Arnie Stoller invested in stocks and more sophisticated things like currencies, derivatives, and international stocks and bonds. George, like you said, did the conservative stuff."

"And Stoller told me his compensation was something he referred to as 'two and twenty,' right?"

"Yeah, I have my own account with Arnie. That means he gets two percent of the total, then twenty percent of the annual profits."

"But George's compensation isn't that much, is it?"

Rich laughed. "Oh, God, no," he said. "Not even close. George makes a flat seventy-five K a year."

That was significant news. "Oh, really?"

"Yeah, I was there once when Dad was pissed off at George. Told him anybody could do what he did. Called him 'Jorge' when he got mad. Dad told him he could do it himself if he had to, but just didn't want to spend time on it."

"And what did George say?"

"Not much," Rich said. "But I remember my sister was really pissed."

"What did she say?"

"It was more the look she gave my Dad. I mean, nasty. Really nasty," Rich said. "Dad was kind of oblivious to shit like that. He just shrugged it off and said something like 'take it or leave it.' I remember Janice saying that Arnie Stoller got paid five times what George got."

"And what did your father say?"

"He said, 'No, more like ten times, but that's because he averages eighteen to twenty percent a year.'"

"What did Janice say to that?"

"Nothing. Janice just has a way of quietly seething and giving my Dad what he called 'the Janice glare.'"

"How long ago was this? When this conversation took place?"

"Oh, God, recently. The family all had breakfast together the morning of the wedding. Mom, Dad, me, Addison, Janice and George. Janice always brought money up. Always complained how she couldn't survive on how little George made."

*　*　*

CRAWFORD WENT STRAIGHT TO OTT'S CUBICLE AND TOLD HIM about his conversation with Rich.

"So, what's your thinking?" Ott asked.

"George and Janice just went from a distant third to neck and neck with Robert Polk at the final turn."

"Okay, but how do you think it could've gone down?"

"One, Paul found out that instead of fifty million plus in the account that there was—I don't know, pick a number. Say forty-five—"

"'Cause George had pissed it away on baccarat and Janice on jewelry."

"Exactly."

"And when Paul found that out, he fired George?"

Crawford nodded.

"So, if George doesn't have the family account anymore, Janice has to go hock the Bentley and half her jewelry."

"Yup," Crawford said. "Or two, Janice could have figured that if Paul was dead, she'd have a much better chance of browbeating her mother into paying George more to support her lifestyle."

"Yeah, could have been either one of those," Ott said. "So, walk me through how you see the actual murders going down. 'Cause I still see Polk as being the more likely shooter, seeing how he knows his way around guns."

"Yeah, I know what you mean," Crawford said. "But back to number two: Let's say Pawlichuk found he only had forty-five million in his account a week before the wedding."

Ott nodded. "Okay."

Crawford thought for a second. "Or maybe—for all we know—he had already found out George had been stealing from him and fired him."

"But wouldn't Rich and the other family members know about that?"

"Not necessarily. I get the sense Paul didn't confide much about financial stuff with Rich and almost nothing with Mindy. So maybe Janice realized one of two things—no, actually three: One, her father was aware they'd been looting the account and is about to fire George. Or two, it's only a matter of time until Paul finds out then fires George. Or, three, Pawlichuk's not likely to find out at all but George is still only making seventy-five K—"

"Yeah, but in that case, he could still keep looting the account.'

"True, but maybe they just decide the best solution is if Paul's dead. Then they don't need to ever worry about getting caught."

"I hear you," Ott said. "So if they did it, who do you think actually did it?"

Crawford thought for a second. "Gotta be George. Or a guy they hired," he said. "Janice might be motivated, and might be cold-blooded, and definitely is mean, but no way she takes a gun and blows away her father and Carla Carton."

"Yeah, I agree," Ott said.

"I still wouldn't rule out them hiring a hitter," Crawford said.

Ott nodded uncertainly. "And I still wouldn't rule out Polk."

"Which is where I'm going right now."

"Back to see Polk?"

"Yeah, he's probably missed me."

* * *

On the way to pay his unannounced visit to Robert Polk, Crawford worked up a good head of steam because he had lost count of how many times he had called and left messages.

He also made a call on his way, which turned out to be very productive.

He double-parked on the street near Polk's office building, put his flashers on, and took the elevator up to Polk's office on the penthouse floor. He walked into Polk's reception room and got a hostile frown from the receptionist, Jeanette.

"Can I help you?" she asked.

"I need to see Mr. Polk."

"He's in a meeting," she said. "And you don't have an appointment, sir, so he won't be able to see you."

He walked past her and back to Polk's office, the door to which was closed.

He didn't bother knocking, simply turned the knob and walked in.

Robert Polk, sitting at his conference table with a man in a suit, looked up at Crawford and glared. "What the hell are you doing, bursting in here—"

"I need to speak to you right now," Crawford said. "Not next Tuesday, not when you can spare ten minutes—" He glanced at the other man. "Sir, if you wouldn't mind, this is police business, please wait in the reception area."

The man clearly didn't know how to react.

"This is outrageous, Crawford"—Polk turned to his guest—"Max, this isn't going to take long."

Max stood.

"Actually, Max, it might," Crawford said.

Max nodded and walked past Crawford and out the door.

"Just so you know," Polk said, glowering at Crawford. "I'm going to file an official complaint with the mayor of Palm Beach. She's a close personal friend of mine."

"Do what you gotta," Crawford said, still standing. "My first question: Were you and Carla Carton having a fight at the Pawlichuk wedding related to her refusal to marry you, after previously having said 'yes.'"

Polk shook his head and huffed. "No."

"Several eyewitnesses said Carla had repeatedly embarrassed and humiliated you at the wedding. Was that enough of a reason for you to pursue her and—"

"No."

"You have a gun-carry permit, do you not, Mr. Polk?"

Ott had checked with the Florida Department of Agriculture and Consumer Services and found that Polk had registered a Walther P99 semi-automatic pistol and a Heckler & Koch VP9.

"Yes, I do," Polk said.

"And where do you keep your weapons?"

"One at home and one in the glove compartment of my car."

"And was that the car that you drove to the Pawlichuk wedding last weekend?"

"Yes, it was," Polk said, getting to his feet and shaking his head. "Look, that's enough, Crawford. If you're trying to imply that I was the murderer of Paul Pawlichuk and Carla Carton, then you've totally lost your mind and I have no intention of answering any more questions."

Crawford put up a hand. "I did what you suggested the first time we met and called your wife. We had a very nice conversation and she told me that she had no idea when you got home after the wedding because she was asleep. I asked her when she normally goes to bed and she said between ten and ten thirty. Yet you said you left the wedding at nine and, I know because I checked, your house is exactly eight minutes away from Mar-a-Lago. You see how something doesn't jibe here?"

Polk groaned and sighed at the same time.

"Okay, okay, for Christ's sake," he said walking over to his desk and picking up a pad and a pen. "Call this number"—he said as he wrote—"I was there for about an hour to an hour and a half."

Polk handed the piece of paper to Crawford.

"Whose number is this?"

Another long sigh. "Her name is Melissa."

This was something, Crawford felt, that deserved to be milked. To the max. "So, let me get this straight," he said. "You were leaving the wedding, where you had just spent a great deal of time talking to a woman who you had asked to marry you while you were, in fact, already married, to go back home to the person who you *were* married to. But along the way you decided to drop by this woman Melissa's house to...what? Ask *her* to marry you?"

If Polk's eyes could have killed, Crawford would have been dead on the carpet.

"Get...the...hell...out...of...here."

Crawford nodded as he stared into Polk's hateful, beady eyes. "I'll tell Max you're ready to resume your conversation with him," he said. "And, as the expression goes, I won't let the door hit me in the ass on my way out."

THIRTY-TWO

CRAWFORD AND OTT WERE SPENDING TWELVE TO FIFTEEN hours per day on their two cases, slaloming back and forth from one to the other.

There were so many people to talk to, it was tough to keep everybody straight. Crawford was in his office when Herb Weaver's name showed up on his cell phone caller ID. He had no idea who the man was.

"Hello."

"Hey, Charlie," the voice said. "Herb Weaver, PBPD."

Oh, yeah, big, brawny uniform cop. "Hey, Herb, what's up?"

"So, I think I found your girl. The one in the photo Ott gave me. In bed at that house on the North End."

Crawford shot up straight in his chair. "Oh, yeah. Who is she?"

"Girl by the name of Christy Lauter. Kid who dropped out of Dreyfoos School of the Arts."

"Know how old she is?"

"She'd be a senior this year. So, like eighteen or so?"

"Sure doesn't look it," Crawford said.

"I agree," Weaver said. "A friend of hers gave me an address. Want it?"

"Yeah, please."

Weaver gave him an address fifteen minutes away and Crawford went straight there.

He knocked on the door of the West Palm Beach bungalow, which was only a few blocks from where Ott lived.

The door opened and a young woman eating cereal in a bowl looked out. She was definitely the girl in the DVD.

"Hi, Christy. My name is Detective Crawford, Palm Beach Police. Can I ask you a few questions?"

She didn't look guilty of anything. "Sure, I guess. What about?"

He pulled two photos out of the breast pocket of his jacket. "This is you, right?" he asked, showing her the one of the girl in bed.

Her face suddenly turned red. "I was drunk. I didn't know..." She held up her hands and thrust the photo back at him.

Now she did look guilty.

"It's okay," he said. "I just have two more questions for you."

"Okay?"

He handed her the other photo. "Who is this?"

She leaned forward, glanced at the photo, then pulled back. "He never told me his name"—*seriously?* Crawford wanted to say—"He was even drunker than I was. I just met him that night."

"And my second question is, how old are you?"

"Eighteen," she said. "Want to see my ID?"

"I trust you. Were you eighteen at the time this video was shot?"

"Just barely."

Crawford had another thought. "Actually, I have one more question."

She looked nervous.

"Do you know who Xavier Duke is?"

"I've heard the name, I think."

"He owned that house. But you never met him?"

She shook her head.

"Okay," Crawford said with a smile. "I'll let you go back to your Cheerios."

"Fruit Loops."

Mystery solved: Christy was not AC. Instead, AC had been the boy. And whoever he was, he was off the hook for having sex with a minor.

THIRTY-THREE

CRAWFORD AND OTT DECIDED IT WAS TIME TO HAVE ANOTHER talk with the fathers who had written million-dollar checks to Duke. Crawford would pay visits to Carlton Kramer and Tommy Sullivan and Ott would meet with Tuck Drummond.

They talked through their approach at great length: This was not going to be a normal, everyday Q&A. They both felt that one of the three men might be Duke's murderer, or possibly have had hired someone to do the job. One motive to kill Duke would have been if he had gotten greedy and come back to them and hit them up for another payment. Or possibly one of them felt that, even though he'd bought Duke's silence, there was nothing quite as effective as silencing the blackmailer forever.

Ott pointed out that if he were one of the fathers, he would worry about the possibility of Duke getting drunk and blurting out to somebody, 'Oh, man, you should see this video of so-and-so I got.' Crawford agreed that was another good reason to silence him permanently.

In the end, they decided the best way to deal with the fathers was to play it straight. Say to them, in as sympathetic a voice as they could muster: *Listen, we know you paid Xavier Duke a million dollars for a film. There was nothing illegal about what you did, but there definitely was something illegal about what Duke did. But he's dead so that's the end of it. The question is, did he ever come back to you and ask for more money?* Their thinking was that if they could just get one of the fathers to say 'yes,' then they could safely assume that Duke had hit all of them up for another check.

And the best way to not have to pay him again was to kill him. The father could simply have called Duke and arranged to meet him at the vacant lot on Reef Road, purportedly to give him a check, then instead greet him with two to the face and one to the chest.

Carlton Kramer's wallet had still not turned up and he asked Crawford again to exert his influence over the burglary team at PBPD to do what they could to find it. Crawford assured him again that he would. Then he launched into his Q&A, a little stronger than he and Ott had scripted it.

They were sitting in Kramer's living room. It was not his wife's bridge day.

"Look, Mr. Kramer, I know you paid Xavier Duke a million dollars for a film your daughter was in, so don't bother denying it. I also know it had nothing to do with girls in a sorority house. Here's my question: Did Duke every come back to you and demand another million dollars or any other payment above that initial million"—and before Kramer could answer he added— "I need to know the truth, and this time there will be consequences if I don't hear it."

That was, of course, bullshit, but it sounded good.

Kramer took his time before he answered. "No. Unequivocally not. Is that good enough for you?"

"Yes, it is. If it's true."

"It is."

Crawford nodded. "And when you gave Duke the check, where did that take place?"

"I met him at his club," Kramer said. Then as if he had just caught a whiff of something foul: "That hideous Royal & Alien Club."

It was a club that, some would tell you, took in Palm Beach's outcasts and losers. Rich outcasts and losers, that is. Others, especially its members and guests, would tell you that they had more fun there than the members of any other club in Palm Beach.

"And so that was the end of it?"

"Jesus, do you want me to sign it in blood or something?" Kramer asked. "That was the last that I saw or heard from him"—his face brightened—"until the news of his untimely demise."

"Well, thank you, Mr. Kramer," Crawford said getting to his feet. "That will do it then."

"And you won't forget—"

Crawford put up a hand. "Maybe you should get a new wallet."

* * *

TEN BLOCKS AWAY, UP ON DUNBAR, OTT WAS HAVING A SIMILAR conversation with Tuck Drummond.

Drummond assured Ott that he had not heard anything more from Xavier Duke. He even went a step further and said that, if Duke had contacted him again, he was prepared to go to the cops and report him for extortion. He'd almost done it the first time, he claimed. At the end, he made a comment similar to Carlton Kramer's: "What a shame about what happened to poor Xavier."

* * *

CRAWFORD WENT STRAIGHT FROM CARLTON KRAMER'S HOUSE to meet with Judge Shanahan in West Palm Beach. His phone rang on the way.

"Hello, Dominica."

"I'm lonely, Charlie."

"Nothing I like more than a direct woman," Crawford said. "Let's figure out how we can remedy your situation."

"What we did last time worked pretty well."

"You mean, dinner and—"

"Yeah, that."

"Here's my problem—"

"Oh, God, here goes."

"I'm sorry, but I've got—well, you know—two murders that are 24/7," he said. "Make you a deal: the minute I solve one of 'em, we'll have dinner that night. Any place you want to go."

"That could be weeks."

"I don't think so. I think we're getting close on at least one," he said. "I'm on my way, right now, to get something that might help crack it."

"All right, then," Dominica said. "Just don't force me to say yes to this man who keeps calling me."

"Who's that?"

"I can't say. Just that he's devastatingly handsome, smart, funny and, most of all, *available*."

"Yeah, right, you're making this up."

"Don't make me have to prove it."

"I'll see you in a few days."

"I hope so, Charlie."

Crawford pulled up to the judge's office at 401 Clematis Street in West Palm Beach. He parked and went inside.

The judge was in golf clothes and a hurry.

He signed and handed Crawford the two pieces of paper he needed and rushed out the door, headed for a first tee somewhere.

Crawford got back in his car, drove back to the station on County Road, picked up Ott and headed up to Jupiter.

Ott had in his breast pocket a voice recorder the size of a paper clip that had ten hours of battery life and was capable of ninety hours of audio storage. Ott had jury-rigged a piece of scotch tape to it so he could stick it wherever he wanted. It came with head phones that were sitting on the center console between the detectives.

On the way there, they went over their meetings with Carlton

Kramer and Tuck Drummond and agreed that both men were likely in the clear.

A half an hour later, they pulled into the same small shopping strip in Jupiter that they had visited before. They looked around the parking lot but didn't see the Bentley with a JPF vanity plate.

They walked into the office of Figueroa & Associates and found no one at the receptionist's desk.

"Hello," Crawford shouted.

"Anybody here?" Ott asked.

"Yeah, who is it?" George Figueroa said, coming out of his office. "Oh, hello, detectives." He was clearly not thrilled to see them.

"Can we come into your office, Mr. Figueroa?"

"Sure. I don't know what you want from me but—"

"Just the truth," Ott said.

Crawford chuckled to himself. Sometimes Ott could sound like he was channeling the Detective Joe Friday from the ancient TV series *Dragnet*.

They followed Figueroa into his office. Crawford noticed that Figueroa's computer was on and a video-poker hand displayed on the screen.

Figueroa saw him looking at it and quickly went and switched off the monitor.

All three sat as Crawford pulled a piece of paper out of his jacket pocket.

"Mr. Figueroa, the is a court order from a U.S. judge for you to provide us with the records and files of Paul and Mindy Pawlichuk's account, which you manage."

Figueroa's face blanched. It was the exact same expression Crawford and Ott had seen in the unflattering photo in the online article about George's British gambling troubles.

"Let me see that," Figueroa said.

Crawford handed it to him.

He took a long time reading the simple document. Finally, he said, "I'm going to call my lawyer."

Crawford and Ott both nodded.

"Nothing he can do about it, but go ahead," Ott said.

Figueroa dialed his cell phone, his hand shaking slightly.

"Yeah, is Ed there? This is George Figueroa"—his eyes flitted from one side of the room to the other— "Okay, tell him to call me right away." He gave his number, then clicked off.

"I'm not going to just give you that file," he said. "It's private information."

"Yes, I know," Crawford said. "But private information that Judge Shanahan has ordered you to turn over to us." He had carefully explained to the judge how critical that information—particularly the balance in the Pawlichuk account—was.

"I keep all my confidential files in that safe," Figueroa said, pointing to an old-fashioned army-green safe in a corner to his right.

Crawford glanced at Ott, then back to Figueroa. "Okay, so if you would open it, please, and let us see the Pawlichuk file."

Figueroa looked like a trapped rat. "I don't understand why you need to see it. It just basically shows what the investments are and what the account balance is."

"Yeah, that's all we need to see," Crawford said. "The most recent statement."

Figueroa sighed, then stood up and took a few steps toward the safe.

As he did, Ott slipped the bug out of his pocket and stuck it under Figueroa's desk. That was the other thing Judge Shanahan had approved.

Figueroa got down in a crouch and turned the dial on the safe to the left several times, stopped, then to the right, and finally to the left again. His shakes clearly evident now, he steadied himself by putting his left hand on the wrist of his right hand. Finally, he pulled the lever down and the safe opened.

Both Crawford and Ott strained to see inside it.

Figueroa reached in quickly, pulled out a green Pendaflex file, closed the door, and turned the dial.

"Wait, was that a pistol I saw in there?" Crawford asked.

"Yeah, looked like a Glock," Ott said.

Figueroa ignored their question and opened the file. "This is what you want to see."

"Yeah, and that gun too," Crawford said

"Sorry, you've got a court order to see my records, not the gun."

"You have a problem with us seeing it?" Ott asked.

"It's all perfectly legal," Figueroa said. "Want to see the permit?"

Crawford knew he wasn't going to let them see the gun. He put out his hand. "The file, please."

Figueroa handed it to him.

Crawford took it and opened it up as Ott leaned closer.

Crawford turned the pages of the computer printout until he found what he was looking for at the bottom of page five. The balance: $51,225,341.20.

"Like I told you when you were here last time. Fifty million, give or take," Figueroa said with a smile.

Crawford eyed him "And where do you keep the assets?"

"A bank."

"Yeah, we figured," Crawford asked. "But which one?"

"Sun Trust."

"Which branch?"

"On Military Trail."

"Would you give them a call? I want to speak to the manager there and confirm that money's there."

Figueroa rolled his eyes. "Damn right I'd mind. I showed you what you asked for. That's all I'm doing. Did it occur you that I have a business to run here?"

It occurred to Crawford that today's business seemed to be online poker. He stood. "It should take us a few hours to get back here with another court order. At that time we expect to confirm that there is"— he looked down—"$51,225,341.20 in the Pawlichuk account at Sun Trust on Military Trail."

"Fine," Figueroa said. "Until then, how about leaving me alone to conduct my business."

Crawford and Ott walked toward the office door.

"Thanks for your cooperation, Mr. Figueroa," Crawford said.

Figueroa swiped the Pendaflex file up from his desk. "You're not welcome."

THIRTY-FOUR

"My guess is our visit is going to shake things up in the Figueroa household," Crawford said, sliding into the Crown Vic in Figueroa's parking lot.

Ott hit the ignition. "I've never seen a more guilty look on anyone's face in my life."

"Yeah, I know," Crawford said, putting on the headset that connected to the bug Ott had left under Figueroa's desk.

"The question is, guilty of what?"

"Well, we know—or at least are ninety-nine percent sure—that there's less in the Pawlichuk account now than when George first got his hands on it."

Ott squinted his eyes as he pulled out of the parking lot. "So you're not buying that printout?"

"No, 'cause that's all it was. A printout," Crawford said. "You gotta figure George's smart enough to at least make an attempt to cover his ass with bogus paperwork."

"I wonder how much is left."

"Well," Crawford said, "we know he had to pay back that casino in London. That was 950,000 pounds, which is over a million dollars.

Supposedly he lost another two million. He's got a rep for gambling and his wife for spending. They've got a $330,000 car. No way there's still fifty-one million in that account. Last thing George wants is to have us talk to the Sun Trust manager."

"You think the judge is going to get sick of seeing us every five minutes?" Ott asked as he took a right on Center Street.

"The problem is, he's playing golf," Crawford said. "So we've got to find out which course, scare up a golf cart, do the paperwork and track him down."

"I hope he's having a good round, We don't want to show up right after he knocked one in the water and scored a snowman," Ott said, referring to an eight.

Crawford held up his hand as he heard Figueroa speaking on the headset.

"Hey, honey," Figueroa said. "The day we talked about is here. Those Palm Beach detectives just came by the office. They wanted to see the statements on your parents' account, so I showed 'em. But now they want to talk to Sun Trust, confirm the money's there."

"So we're fucked," Crawford strained to hear Janice Figueroa say. "Come home right now."

She clicked off.

"Turn around and go back," Crawford said, "they're taking off."

"No shit," Ott said, flicking his blinker.

He executed a skidding U-turn and stomped on the accelerator.

At a red light, he looked both ways, waited for a few cars and floored it.

He had the Vic up to seventy in ten seconds. "Question is, where are they going?"

"My guess is out of the country."

Crawford was scrolling on his iPhone.

"What are you doing?"

"Looking up their home address," Crawford said. "Sounded like George left the office."

"We'll soon find out," Ott said, burning rubber as he took a corner hard.

A minute later Ott skidded up to the front of Figueroa's office. Crawford threw open his door, got out and started running before Ott had even come to a stop.

The door to Figueroa's office was open. Crawford ran inside. No one there.

He ran back out as Ott was coming in. "He didn't even bother to lock up," Crawford said. "Including the safe. Took the Glock, though."

They ran back to the car and got in. "We'll get 'em," Crawford said.

"Headed to the airport, I bet," Ott said.

"Miami's my guess. More flights out of the country," Crawford started dialing his phone.

"Who you calling?" Ott asked.

"I can't find their address. Trying Mindy Pawlichuk." A few seconds went by. "Shit. Voicemail."

Crawford looked up another number and dialed it. "Yeah, hey, Rich, Detective Crawford. Call me right away. I need your sister's address."

Crawford glanced over at Ott, who was looking extremely twitchy.

A long minute went by.

Crawford's phone rang. It was Rich Pawlichuk.

"Hey, Detective. My sister lives at 342 Eagle's Nest at Windward Farms"—Ott was plugging the address into his GPS— "off of Indiantown, a mile or two east of 95. Why do you—"

The squealing rubber of Ott accelerating drowned out Rich Pawlichuk.

"You know where it is?" Crawford asked, glancing at the speedometer.

Ott already had them up to sixty-five.

"Got a rough idea," Ott said. "Fasten your seat belt, Charlie. It's about ten minutes…fifteen if you were at the wheel."

Crawford would readily admit that there were quite a few things Ott did better than him.

One thing Ott had done was pay big money for what was billed as the "Richard Petty Experience," named after the legendary NASCAR driver. It took place at Daytona Motor Speedway, three hours north of Palm Beach. It cost more than a thousand dollars and Petty (aka "the King") was supposed to give you tips as you drove three eight-minute sessions in a real NASCAR car. But Petty was out with the flu that day so his substitute, a guy whose brother and uncle were cops, gave Ott extra time and let him get the car up to 130 MPH. Afterward, the two went and had a few beers together and the man asked Ott if he wanted to come back for another session the next day. By the time Ott headed back down to Palm Beach at the end of the next day, he felt he was ready for the Daytona 500 itself.

Windward Farms, a high-end development on Indiantown Road, had an elaborate gate house manned by a uniformed guard. Ott pulled up, jammed on his brakes, and thrust out his ID to the man at the window. "Going to the Figueroa house at 34 Eagles Nest."

"Yes, sir." The man raised the gate.

As he did, Ott looked to his left and saw George Figueroa at the wheel of his Bentley. He was about to pull out with Janice in the passenger seat. Figueroa glanced over, spotted them and floored it.

"Hey," Ott said, flicking his head, "it's them."

Crawford swiveled in his seat and saw the car pull away and go out the gate.

Ott jammed the Crown Vic into reverse, hit the brakes and floored it, but the Bentley was already a hundred yards ahead of them and picking up speed by the time they were on the road.

"Probably gonna get on 95," Crawford said, referring to the interstate that ran north and south from Maine to Florida.

"We're never gonna catch him if he does," Ott said.

"Why not?"

"That thing's got a top end of 190 miles an hour," Ott said. "Five hundred thirty horsepower. Twin-turbo V-8. Zero to sixty in five point one. That's why."

"Okay, I'll try to contact staties north and south," Crawford said, referring to state troopers who were north and south of the Indiantown Road exit to I-95.

The Bentley slowed to a stop at a light up ahead. Ott had his foot to the floor.

Figueroa, apparently seeing them catching up, thought better about stopping and blew through the light.

Ott slowed enough to be safe, saw no one coming, and sailed through. They could see the hump up ahead where Indiantown Road went over the six lanes of I-95.

They watched to see whether Figueroa was going to go north or south on 95.

Instead he went straight.

"Gotta be going a hundred," Ott said, both hands gripped tight on the wheel.

"Stay with him, man."

"No fuckin' way. Our best shot is get someone to throw down stop sticks up ahead."

Crawford got on the phone with a dispatcher to try to locate a nearby uniform who had one of the long ropes of spikes that blew out car tires.

The Bentley was now three hundred yards ahead and gaining speed. "He's losing me," Ott said.

A school bus came into sight in front of the Bentley.

"Got traffic ahead of him," Crawford said. "Both ways."

The Bentley slowed down behind the school bus as a line of cars passed coming in the opposite direction.

Ott got to within a football field of the Bentley, when, in a puff of smoke, the Bentley accelerated and roared past the school bus, just missing a UPS truck coming in the opposite direction.

"Close, man," Ott said. Seeing that nothing was coming, he floored the Vic and went flying past the bus.

Up ahead, the Bentley had another obstacle. An eighteen-wheel truck and trailer.

Figueroa nudged the Bentley over to the other lane to see if anything was coming.

Three cars were. Despite that, he gunned it and flew past the semi. The first car coming toward the Bentley pulled over to the side of the road to avoid a head-on collision. But the second one apparently hadn't seen the Bentley, and they came within 20 feet of having a head-on collision.

Figueroa yanked hard right on the Bentley wheel and the car hurtled off the road, through a barbed-wire fence, and into an open field where cows were grazing. Still going more than sixty, the Bentley clipped one of the cows then plowed into a shallow pond.

"Ho-ly shit," Ott said.

He and Crawford had watched it all play out from twenty yards behind the semi truck.

Seeing what had happened, the driver of the truck pulled over to the shoulder of the road and scrambled out.

Ott slowed down and pulled over behind the big truck.

Ott and Crawford jumped out of the Vic and ran toward the Bentley, which was smoking in water up to its bumper, stuck in a pond covered with a layer of green scum.

The truck driver, Ott and Crawford were neck-and-neck as they ran past the toppled cow. One look was all Crawford needed: it was a dead heifer.

"Never knew what hit him," the truck driver said, breathing hard as he glanced over at Crawford.

Thinking about the Glock that George Figueroa had taken with him, Crawford drew his Sig Sauer P226 pistol. Ott already had his in hand.

Off in the distance, Crawford saw Janice Figueroa push the car door open, step into the two-foot deep pond, and slosh to dry land.

Then she started to run as best as she could in a skirt and flats. But she seemed barely capable of outrunning the dead cow.

"Okay, Mrs. Figueroa," Crawford shouted to her, fifty yards ahead of him, "stop and put your hands up."

She slowed then stopped as Crawford ran past the Bentley, noticing Geoerge Figueroa pinned behind the airbag. No way he could reach his Glock, given the position he was in.

Ott and the truck driver stopped at the Bentley, waded into the pond, and approached Figueroa, while Crawford kept running toward Janice.

As he neared her, Crawford stopped and read her her rights. Then he said, "I'm placing you under arrest for suspicion of murder in the death of Paul Pawlichuk and Carla Carton."

"George did it! He killed them. Carla, just 'cause she was there," Janice couldn't rat out her husband fast enough. "I was nowhere near that pool. He stole the money from my parents' account too."

It came as no big surprise: Janice was not only a whiner and a complainer but also couldn't put her husband's head in a noose fast enough.

"Okay, let's go back to the car."

As they approached the Bentley, Crawford watched as Ott helped Geoerge Figueroa slide out from behind the airbag.

Ott read Figueroa, covered in white powder from the airbag, his rights and charged him with murder and grand larceny. Then, looking back at the dead cow, he added, "And, also, violating the Florida Cruelty to Animals Statue. Killing a...what kind is it, Charlie?"

"A black angus, I think," Crawford said looking back at the lifeless mound.

"No, man, definitely not," said the truck driver, "that's a Florida Cracker cow."

Crawford shrugged. "I could be wrong."

Ott cuffed Janice and George Figueroa, while Crawford eyed

George. "Why'd you do it?" Crawford asked as George shot Janice a nasty glance. "She told me," Crawford explained.

Figueroa shook his head. "Guy was a controlling, obnoxious son-of-a-bitch. Cheap bastard too...but Mindy put me up to it. Said she'd forgive what we took. And give us another five million."

Janice didn't deny it.

Crawford glanced at Ott, whose mouth was agape. 'No shit,' he mouthed to Crawford. Their least likely suspect.

"And did you use that pistol in the safe?" Crawford asked.

"Keep your mouth shut," Janice said.

"I have nothing more to say," Figueroa said.

Crawford and Ott led them over to the Crown Vic and put them in the back seat.

"Mild-mannered   Mindy,"   Ott   said   to   Crawford. "Who'd-a-thunk?"

The truck driver was down in a crouch in the front of the Bentley, staring admiringly at its grill.

Crawford walked up to him. "Want to have a look?" He asked. Then to Ott, "Pop the bonnet, will you?"

Ott chuckled at Crawford's use of the British name for hood. He opened the front door and hit a button. Crawford lifted the hood and the three men examined the engine.

"Holy shit," said the truck driver.

Crawford crossed his arms on his chest. "Yeah, twin turbo-charged V8 engine. Five hundred horses. Top end a hundred-ninety."

"How fast off the line?"

"If you stand on it, zero to sixty in five seconds," Crawford said, giving Ott a wink.

"Wow," the truck driver said. "You don't know shit about cows but plenty about cars."

THIRTY-FIVE

CRAWFORD WAS A MAN OF HIS WORD. IT HAD BEEN A LONG AND productive day but now it was time to kick back for the night. He'd called Dominica and apologized for it being last-minute but said he was on his way to his butcher shop to get two 3-inch steaks and he wouldn't accept no for an answer. She said yes and told him the last time he cooked for her it had been *Spaghettie alla Crawfordo* and was delicious, but this sounded even better.

Trust me, he said.

They were on his balcony, Dominica in black pants and a soft-looking, silk blouse. There was the suggestion of cleavage, but nothing brazen. Her thick, dark hair was suitably lustrous, her emerald eyes were beautiful, and her big red lips looked eminently kissable. So he put down his wine glass and did just that. For as long as it took the sound of a nearby fire engine siren to fade off into the distance.

He finally pulled back and looked out at the view of the Publix parking lot. Rows and rows of cars, people pushing shopping carts, a man with his arm around a woman walking into the main entrance.

"You have to use your imagination," he said, visualizing Rose

Clarke's ocean view. "Far off in the distance, there is a cruise ship chugging across the horizon. Off to the right, three surfers are catching six-foot waves, and on the beach a little old lady is adding to her vast collection of shark's teeth."

"Sounds like you've been to Rose's house recently, huh, Charlie?"

Caught, red-handed.

He tried to look innocent. "Nah, that's just a generic beach scene."

Dominica flashed her *I'm not buyin' it* smile. "Oh, is it now?"

"Yeah, I've got a vivid imagination," he said. "I'd really love to have that view, but I like my apartment, particularly my kitchen, so I overlook the view I...overlook."

Dominica patted his arm. "It could be worse. I like your master bath too," she leaned toward him. "Come on. More kissing."

"Don't mind if I do."

Of course, they ended up in bed and didn't get around to dinner until ten o'clock.

Crawford grilled the steaks out on the balcony with his Weber Spirit Grill and they were almost perfect—maybe just a tad too red in the center. He also grilled corn on the cob with tin foil and baked potatoes.

"I'm stuffed," Dominica said, putting down her plate and snuggling up to Crawford. "It's easier to picture the ocean and that cruise ship off in the distance when it's dark like this."

"Yeah, the surfers are all in bed now and the lady looking for shark's teeth found her quota."

They kissed again, then Dominica pulled back. "Hey, I keep meaning to ask you, how's your brother doing?"

"He's actually doing great," Crawford said. "He's completely off the sauce. Does his meetings religiously. He's got a girlfriend who's the daughter of one of the guys who was with him at the rehab place."

"What about Avril Ensor?" She was referring to the movie star who had been with Charlie's brother Cam at the same ritzy rehab facility in Connecticut.

"Yeah, he sees her a lot. They got to be good friends. She lives in New York now that she's got that hit show on Broadway. Cam told me she's got a big starring role in a movie coming up too. With Ryan Tatum or Channing Gosling, I forget which."

"I think you mean Ryan Gosling or Channing Tatum."

"Yeah, can't keep 'em straight," Crawford said. "Just a couple of pretty faces."

"What's the name of the rehab place again?"

"Clairmount. In a little town in Connecticut."

"And why was she there?"

"She had really bad bouts of depression apparently. Then throw in booze and drugs..."

"Well, I'm glad they're both doing well," Dominica said, "'cause you always hear about relapses and how hard it is to beat it."

"Yeah, I know," Crawford said. "I told you about Cam falling off the wagon when he was at the place. Ended up on a bender in New York City and almost got tossed."

"Yeah, I remember. That was pretty bad. How long's it been since he had a drink?"

"Oh, God, it's got to be close to six months," Crawford said. "He ended up leaving the firm where he used to work. I told you he and my older brother used to work together? Cam's definitely better off on his own. He started his own shop. He's the star of the three Craw-ford brothers."

"Bet he says that about you,"

"Are you kidding? Charlie the lowly cop?"

"Charlie the hero cop. Charlie the cop who always gets his man."

"Okay, enough of the Crawford family," he leaned into her and kissed her. "What's new with the McCarthy brood?"

"Well, three out of four are doing fine. My brother the dentist is still pulling teeth. My brother the fireman is still putting out fires and pumping out nieces and nephews. My sister the claims adjuster is still doing whatever the hell it is claims adjusters do."

"A wild guess...adjust claims?"

"I'll buy that," Dominica said, taking a sip of her pinot grigio. "And my sister the drug addict is still having a tough go of it."

"I'm sorry," Crawford said. "Mainly oxy, right?"

"Mainly whatever she can get her hands on," Dominica said. "Plus my poor mother is just heartsick. She thinks Carol's working for an escort service in Miami to get money. And she might be right."

Crawford put his arm around Dominica. "I'm really sorry. Your poor mother."

"Poor Carol, too." Dominica choked up, wiped her eyes with a napkin.

Crawford squeezed her shoulder.

"She just never figured out what she wanted to do," Dominica said. "I remember in high school, she was A.D.D. to the max. Did I ever tell you she had a kid?"

"No, really?"

Dominica nodded and took another long sip. "Yup, my brother James and his wife are raising him. The boy thinks they're his parents. No way in hell could Carol ever take care of a kid. His name is Dmitri"—Dominca laughed—"I mean, far be it from Carol to give him a normal Bob, Sam, Bill-type name. No, it had to be Dmitri. I remember her telling me it was between Dmitri or Nigel." Dominica threw up her hands. "I mean fuuu-ccckkk!"

Crawford leaned in and kissed her again. "Okay, that's enough family for a while. Actually, you know what? That's enough talk period."

He moved his hand around to her back and deftly unclipped her bra while unbuttoning her blouse button with the other hand. He could multi-task with the best of them.

THIRTY-SIX

CRAWFORD HAD JUST FLIPPED DOMINICA'S SWISS-CHEESE omelette. He waited a minute before he slid the spatula under it and dropped it onto her plate, right next to two, big, sweaty-looking sausages that tasted way better than they looked. He put the plate on a wicker tray that had a glass of orange juice on it, then poured her a mug of coffee. He put the mug on the tray and picked it up.

One of Dominica's favorite things was breakfast in bed.

"Hey, Charlie, check this out," he heard her say from the bedroom.

He walked in with the tray.

Dominica had her computer propped up in her lap.

"Whatcha got?" he asked.

She lifted up her MacBook Air and turned it toward him. She was on the *Access Hollywood* site.

"Carla Carton's funeral yesterday," she said. "A star-studded cast of mourners."

Crawford looked down at the screen and almost dropped the tray.

The lead pallbearer was the boy who'd been filmed in bed at Xavier Duke's house.

The boy whose initials were AC.

* * *

CRAWFORD WASTED NO TIME CALLING OTT.

"AC," Ott said. "So the C must stand for Carton?"

"Yup," Crawford said. "My guess is neither Carla or Polk wanted anyone to know. So the last thing they were going to do was name him Polk."

"Guarantee you Duke hit up Polk for way more than a million bucks."

"No doubt about it, especially since the girl looked underage," Crawford said.

"So, Polk did Xavier."

"Or hired a guy," Crawford said.

"So what do we do about Polk?"

"I don't know yet."

"Maybe it's time to pay a visit to the House of Cogitation," Ott said. "Talk things over. Come up with a plan."

"Jesus, it's ten in the morning."

The House of Cogitation was one of their nicknames for Mookie's, a downscale cop bar in West Palm Beach.

"Yeah, so? They're open."

Crawford flashed to an image of inebriated cops knocking back shots, shooting pool and rambling incoherently. "I know they're open. Too many distractions."

"Yeah, maybe you're right."

"Let's meet in my office," Crawford said, "I'll be there in half an hour. That'll give you lots of time to think about how to nail this guy."

"I'll put on my thinking cap."

* * *

Ott swung his legs off Crawford's desk and leaned toward him. "So, I had a few bad ideas, then, as usual, I had a brainstorm. Decided it's time to do one of the things we do best."

"What's that?"

"Make shit up."

Crawford chuckled. "Okay, I'm not opposed to that, but you gotta be a little more specific."

"So, I was thinking about Xavier Duke and the first time I heard his name. It was 'Xavier Duke the porn guy in bed with the mafia.' The second time it was the 'porn king and general all-around sleazebag Xavier Duke, financed by the Miami mafia.' So, I decided maybe it's about time the mafia paid a visit to Robert Polk."

"You got a friend in the mafia you haven't told me about, Mort?"

Ott pointed a finger at himself. "You're looking at him. They call me 'Squat Tony,' who's never had the privilege of meeting Polk before."

Crawford's smile was a mile wide. "Okay, Squat Tony, and what exactly did you intend to talk to Polk about?"

"Tell him I'm in possession of a video which his son is featured in, for starters."

Crawford was nodding. "And maybe you want to suggest that you're relieved that he—Polk—offed Xavier because it was something you were going to have to do and it saved you the trouble."

Ott scratched the back of his head. "Damn good idea, Charlie... but why exactly was I going to do it?"

"Simple. You were involved in financing and distributing Duke's porn flicks. Making a shitload of money at it. Then, when Duke stopped making 'em, it left you with one less income stream. And a big income stream it was."

Ott started nodding vigorously. "Yeah, so Duke told me he was sorry, but he decided he wanted to get out of the business. Retire. So, a little time goes by and I found out he hadn't retired at all, just got into a new thing: making a million bucks for each fifteen-minute film."

"And all he had to do was sell one...to the father of the girl in it."

"Exactly."

Crawford started nodding too. "So, of course, you, Squat Tony, wanted in on it. But Xavier tells you he doesn't need you to either finance or distribute them. In fact, he doesn't need you for anything, 'cause he's doing just fine by himself."

Ott was nodding. "To which, I say to him, 'Xavier, old buddy, where I come from, here's how it works. Once my partner, always my partner.'"

Crawford nodded. "So Xavier thinks for a minute and says something like, 'Tell you what, how 'bout I give you a hundred grand to go away. That's a hundred grand you don't have to do a goddamn thing for. Kinda like found money.'"

"And I tell him thanks but no thanks, I'm gonna be his 50/50 partner."

"To which, Xavier thinks 'fuck that' but doesn't say it. Meantime, he's in the process of shaking down Polk for a shitload of money. Or so he thinks. But what happens is Polk beats Squat Tony to it and caps Duke. So now you're thinking, 'Perfect, I can take over Xavier's racket now.' And that's when you go to Polk. After you find out Alex is Polk's kid and the last thing Polk wants is that DVD to go viral. So, you up the ante big-time, tell Polk it's gonna cost him ten—no, make it twenty million to burn the film."

Ott nodded. "And while all this back and forth is going on, Squat Tony gets Polk to admit he capped the X-Man."

"Wouldn't that be nice," Crawford said, shaking his head. "But that's gonna be the hard part."

"Yeah, I know," Ott said. "The reality is, none of this is gonna be easy."

Crawford sank back into his chair and thought for a second. "If we're going to go this far off of the reservation, we gotta get the okay from Rutledge."

Ott sighed, nodded, and didn't say anything.

"Except," Crawford said after a few moments, "that whole thing we ginned up with Ward Jaynes was just about as far off it as this." He was referring to a case where they had improvised on the fly. "Maybe even farther."

"Yeah, and Rutledge couldn't bust our balls since everyone was congratulating him for solving it."

"Even though he had nothing to do with it," Crawford said. "So, I guess the moral of the story is simple: We can wander off the reservation as long as we solve the crime. If we don't, we're fucked."

"Yeah. So fucked we'd be looking for a new job in the sanitation department up in Palatka County somewhere."

Crawford looked out his window as a hard rain pelted down. Then he turned to Ott and smiled. "I gotta tell you, Mort, this whole Squat Tony thing...I'm buying it hook, line, and sinker."

"Thanks, man. You see any holes?" Ott said. "Going to Polk and selling him?"

"Not if you play it right. I remember reading an article a while back about the Italian mafia in Miami and how they're still going strong there. 'Course they got competition from the Russians and Colombians and God-knows-who-else, but the story was about the bust of forty guys from the Genovese, Gambino, and Bonnano families."

"Really? Those old families are still around?"

"Yeah, article mentioned this one guy, Skinny Joey from Philly, who just got out on a $5 million bond."

"What did he do?"

"Oh, you know, the usual—racketeering, RICO, gambling, extortion, weapons charges. Article said he fancied himself the John Gotti of Philly."

"So it's not a big leap—Skinny Joey to Squat Tony?"

"Not at all, and if I'm Robert Polk and you show up with that story, you got me sold."

"I just need to smooth out a few rough edges," Ott said.

"I've been thinking about something else to throw at him," Crawford said.

"What's that?"

"You tell him you saw Duke's Day-Timer, and on the night of his murder his calendar says, 'R. Polk – lot on Reef' or something like that."

A smile appeared on Ott's face. It started out small, then ended up ear to ear. "I like it, but it's risky as hell."

"I know," Crawford said. "But look at it this way: If Polk says it's bullshit and that the meeting never existed, then he didn't kill Duke. If he doesn't deny it, then he's definitely our boy."

THIRTY-SEVEN

OTT WALKED INTO CRAWFORD'S OFFICE AT 8:00 A.M. WEARING A wide-collar burgundy shirt and dark pants.

He pointed his two forefingers at his chest. "Who am I?"

Crawford cocked his head, "Ah...my barber, maybe? He's got a shirt as ugly as that."

"Come on, Charlie...don't you remember *Scarface*?" he said referring to the old Al Pacino movie about the Mafia.

Crawford laughed as he remembered it. "You forgot the gold chain."

"I had a field day last night," Ott said. "Watched *Godfather I* and *II* and *Scarface*." He shook his head and smiled. "I've seen enough Al Pacino to last me a lifetime."

"You didn't catch *Godfather III*?"

"Nah, I just remember it really sucked," Ott said. "George Hamilton was in it...need I say more?"

"So now you're Italian? Or Cuban, like Tony Montana?"

"Italian, man. I even thought about coming up with an accent, but decided that might be pushing it," Ott said, standing up. "Well, might as well get the show on the road. Think I should just bust right into his office?"

"Worked for me. No guarantee that he'll be there, though."

"If not, I'll just come back."

"Give him hell, Tony," Crawford said.

Ott walked to the door of Crawford's office and turned around. "My favorite line was when Michael Corleone explains how the Godfather bought back Johnny Fontane's contract from the band-leader. Michael says, 'Luca Brasi held a gun to his head and my father assured him that either his brains or his signature would be on the contract.'"

Crawford smiled. "Yeah, right up there with Clemenza's immortal line to Rocco right after they popped Paulie: 'Leave the gun—'"

"'Take the cannoli.'"

* * *

IN THE ELEVATOR UP TO POLK'S OFFICE, OTT CALLED Crawford. "Okay, Charlie, I'm putting my cell phone in my pocket with the line open. You'll be able to hear every word."

"Got it. I'm recording as we speak."

"Wish me luck."

"You don't need luck."

A few moments later Ott walked into Polk's office.

He could have been Italian. Or Greek, French, Spanish, Slavic, Russian, pretty much anything but Swedish or Far Eastern.

Robert Polk's receptionist did not throw out the welcome mat for Ott, who introduced himself as Tony Colangelo. She said Polk was going to be in meetings all day long.

"Tell him it's about Alex," was all Ott said.

"Alex who?"

"He'll know."

The receptionist seemed to deem the murky reference worth bringing to Polk's attention and walked toward his office.

She came back out a few minutes later. "He'll see you after this appointment," she said. "But he won't have long."

Ott picked up a business magazine and turned the pages. Ten minutes later, a man in a suit came out and frowned at the sight of Ott in his burgundy shirt with the six-inch collar.

Ott nodded at him. He didn't nod back.

"Okay, Mr. Colangelo, please follow me," said the receptionist.

Ott followed her back to Polk's office.

Polk, unsmiling, waited behind his desk.

The receptionist walked out.

"Miss Rockwell said you mentioned a name," Polk began.

Ott smiled and held up a hand. "Let's start this all over again, Bob."

Polk frowned, apparently unsettled at being called a nickname no one used with him.

"I'm Tony Colangelo," Ott said, thrusting his hand across Polk's desk. "Pleased to meetcha."

Polk gave him a limp shake that was all fingers.

"Call that a handshake?" Ott said. "All right, let's get down to business."

"And just what business is that, Mr. Colangelo?"

Ott wondered what Carla Carton had seen in this humorless, little man. Did he somehow blossom in the presence of beautiful women?

No, it was just the checkbook, stupid.

"I gotta lot of businesses," Ott said. "Probably not nearly as many as you, but a piece here and a piece there...you know how it is."

Polk kept a solid poker face in place.

"Anyway, the business I came to talk to you about today is a business I was in with my late partner, Xavier Duke."

Polk's expression didn't change.

"You do know, Xavier, right?"

"We spoke once," Polk said.

"Recently. Correct?'

"Within the last month."

Ott nodded and let the silence hang for several moments. He'd noticed how Michael Corleone used the long-pause technique so effectively. "So," he said in a confiding manner, "you know that our business was to film couples in...intimate moments. In the heat of passion, you might say."

For the first time, Polk looked uncomfortable. He raised his hand to his forehead and rubbed it lightly a few times. "What's your point?"

"I came here for two reasons. One, to express my gratitude to you for something and the other is...well, a little different."

Polk fidgeted with a shirt button. "Okay, so go ahead," he said after a pause of his own. "Express your gratitude."

Ott reached into his battered briefcase. "Before I do, I'd like to show you two things. Let's call them Exhibit A and Exhibit B." He held up a DVD case and a Day-Timer. "Exhibit A is a recording of your son at Xavier's house. I'm sure Xavier told you what's on it, so I don't need to. Suffice it to say, it's something that couldn't be good for Alex. I don't know whether you've seen it but I am more than happy to make this copy available to you."

Ott held it out to Polk, who didn't put out his hand.

Ott dropped the DVD on the desk and leaned across. "I don't know what Xavier asked you to pay for the film and I don't care, but my price is twenty million dollars. And it is not negotiable."

Polk rolled his eyes. "You're out of your goddamn mind."

"I think it is a fair price," Ott said.

"Duke tried to extort me for $5 million dollars and I laughed at him."

Ott wasn't surprised that Duke had tried to get five times more than what the other fathers had paid. After all, Polk was worth more than five times as much as all of them put together.

Ott narrowed his eyes and leaned forward. "See, the difference is

Xavier didn't have a fourteen-year-old girl ready to testify about what she and Alex did. 'Cause the girl disappeared after that night with Alex and Xavier couldn't find her"—a big grin—"but I found her."

That knocked the color out of Polk's face.

Ott reached for the Day-Timer. "And now I'd like to express my gratitude to you," Ott said. "You saved me from doing a task I wasn't much looking forward to doing."

"Oh, yeah, what was that?"

"Putting an end to my partnership with Xavier," Ott said with a pause, "by putting an *end* to Xavier."

Ott watched Polk closely, but his expression didn't change. "Your gratitude is misplaced, Mr. Colangelo. You've got the wrong guy."

Ott played it the way he and Crawford had rehearsed it. "Well, of course, I expected you to deny it," he said. "Which is why I brought along Exhibit B"—he held up the Day-Timer—"This is Xavier's Day-Timer. He was a pretty meticulous man about appointments and meetings."

Ott thought he detected a slight change in Polk's demeanor. Like he was frantically trying to figure out where Ott was going next.

"And guess what?" Ott said. "Turns out four days ago Xavier had a date with you"—Ott held up the Day-Timer and went all-in—"says right here, 'R. Polk - Reef Road.'"

Polk was stone-faced. Dead silent.

Ott wanted to do cartwheels. "Which is exactly when and where Xavier got shot. So again, I would like to express my gratitude for you taking care of that messy job I would have had to attend to."

"No way I'm paying you twenty million dollars."

Which meant Polk had a number in mind.

Ott gave him a broad grin. "Do you think I'm fuckin' with you, Bob?"

"Don't call me Bob."

"Okay, then...do you think I'm fuckin' with you, Robert?" Ott scanned a wall of photos and saw a framed photo of Polk with a high-powered rifle slung over his shoulder. "Looks like you were quite the hunter."

"Still am," Polk said. "What of it?"

Ott shrugged. "Just curious," he said. "I went to Africa on a hunting trip once. Got a lion with a machine gun." Ott was winging it now.

Polk shook his head derisively. "That was really sporting of you."

Ott shrugged. "What can I tell ya, I tried getting him with a regular hunting rifle but kept missing."

"Why not use a bazooka?"

"Didn't have one," Ott said. "But what I *do* have is a package deal for you. I call it the *Make Tony Go Away Forever* package."

"I can't wait to hear about it."

"You pay me twenty million and I give you *both* the Day-Timer and the DVD"—he snapped his fingers—"Just like that, I become a bad memory. You don't take my package deal, the Palm Beach cops get the DVD and Duke's calendar dropped on their doorstep. They might not be the brightest guys around, but I think they'd figure it out."

Polk straightened up in his chair and pointed his finger. "I have been patiently listening to you and it occurred to me that there's another *Make Tony Go Away Forever* option."

Ott laughed. "Why, Bob, I do believe you're threatening me."

"I guess you could take it that way."

Ott leaned closer and did his version of the godfather's finger-point. "Just to let you know, I'm fourth-generation Bonanno on my mother's side. I have three psychopaths for brothers and a bunch of semi-violent uncles and cousins...you really sure you want to go there?"

THIRTY-EIGHT

THE WAY SQUAT TONY AND POLK LEFT IT WAS INCONCLUSIVE.

Ott walked out leaving his last line hanging in the air like a foul odor. "I'll be back tomorrow and if I don't get what I want you're gonna be in a world of hurt."

Crawford and Ott had spent the last thirty-five minutes listening to the recording of Ott's meeting with Robert Polk, neither of them saying a word.

At the end of it was more silence.

Ott was trying to gauge Crawford's face.

"It ain't a dagger through the heart," Crawford said finally.

Ott sighed. He'd obviously been hoping Crawford would hear something in it that he had missed.

"You did a hell of a job, though," Crawford said. "I mean, Oscar material. A little Michael Corleone, a little Sonny, even a little Tom Hagan thrown in. But there was no admission of him actually killing Duke."

"I know. I was trying. But isn't it clear he did it?"

"Oh yeah, absolutely. The fact that he didn't dispute meeting

Duke that night on Reef Road. That was the one thing that could have sunk us."

"Yeah, I was holding my breath."

"So, bottom line, not enough to convict." Crawford picked up a pen, tapped it on his desk, and smiled. "I'll tell you one thing, if we wanted to really go rogue, retire early and head down to Rio, I guarantee we could get at least 10 mil out of him."

"No question about it," Ott said. "So, what do we do?"

"I don't know." Crawford looked out his window. "He's expecting you tomorrow?"

"Yup."

"Well, the good news is he's thinking about what he's gonna have to pay or else he would have shut the door when you were there. Which gives you another crack at getting him to say he did it."

"Or maybe he's thinking about popping me?"

Crawford laughed. "Nah, not after your Bonanno thing. No way. That was brilliant."

"Yeah, I was pretty proud of it," Ott said. "You know, it's funny when you start coming up with shit like that, it kinda turns into a competition with yourself to top what you said the sentence before."

"You're a natural, man."

"Swell. A natural-born bullshitter. What a skill to be proud of." Ott shook his head and smiled, but the smile faded quickly. "There's gotta be *some* way to get him to cop."

They were silent for a few moments.

"I need a beer," Crawford said.

"I need several," Ott said.

* * *

THERE WAS A REGULAR AT MOOKIE'S WHO HADN'T MISSED A DAY there since his retirement as a detective five years back. His name was Don Scarpa and he was called "the Shoe." Crawford didn't know why they called him that, so he'd asked him one day.

Scarpa had answered, "Because Scarpa's the guinea word for shoe, numbnuts."

Scarpa had a Winston hanging off his lower lip when Crawford and Ott sat down on either side of him on bar stools at the far end of the bar. Scarpa was seated on what was called the *Donald Bruce Scarpa Memorial Barstool*, even though he remained very much alive. He was chain-smoking Winstons in open defiance of the no-smoking laws for all bars in Florida. The owner, an ex-cop and fellow *paisan* named Jack Scarsiola, had upbraided Scarpa on numerous occasions for breaking the law. "As a guy with thirty-five years in law enforcement you of all people oughta obey the damn laws." To which Scarpa always replied, "Why? I ain't in it no more," and kept on puffing.

Fact was, Scarpa had been one of the best and most respected detectives in Palm Beach and a man Crawford went to if he needed another perspective. In this case, Crawford and Ott had decided on the way over, they weren't going to give Scarpa all the details of the Polk case. They figured that if word ever leaked about what they were doing, even though Scarpa was as tight-lipped as they came, they might blow their cover, not to mention land them in big trouble with Norm Rutledge.

So they talked hypothetically, 'this guy' being Ott, 'the rich guy' or 'the suspect' being Polk.

At the end of the explanation of Ott's 35-minute meeting with Polk, Scarpa took a long pull on his beer. "Gotta up the ante, for one thing," he said, lighting another Winston off the butt of the one he had just smoked.

"What do you mean?" Crawford asked.

"Tell him you're gonna up it another twenty mil at five o'clock. Means ya ain't fuckin' around."

Crawford and Ott both nodded.

Scarpa smiled. "I like the way you used my Italian brothers to intimidate this asshole," he said, stubbing the cigarette butt out in an ashtray.

"Names that end in vowels always do the trick," Ott said.

"You gotta get under this guy's skin some more—" Scarpa exhaled a plume of smoke— "get the fucker out of his comfort zone. What's he like anyway? Besides being rich."

"An asshole," Ott said.

Scarpa chuckled. "Come on, Mort, you can do better than that. Details, man."

"A short guy with a big ego," Ott said.

"Lotta them around," Scarpa said.

"Almost a stereotype," Crawford chimed in. "Short guy making up for his size by being a big-game hunter, scoring the movie actress— though he couldn't hold onto her. Even has pictures all over his office walls of him on the Yale football team."

"Back in the days when Ivy League football sucked even worse that when you played," Ott said.

"You played college ball, Charlie?" Scarpa stubbed out his Winston.

Crawford chuckled. "Yeah, but way different from what's on TV today," he said. "So the guy's got everything, but having a cradle-robbing son—even though he wasn't—definitely wasn't part of the game plan."

Scarpa nodded, then turned to Ott. "Gotta get under his skin, Mort."

"I heard you the first time. How you suggesting I do that?"

"Gotta piss him off," Scarpa said. "I bet you're no slouch at that."

"Thanks, I take that as a compliment," Ott said.

Crawford laughed. "He's right. You got to throw everything you got at him. Insult him. Piss him off. Question his masculinity. I look at him and I see a guy who's got an explosive temper. Trick is to get him to lose it, say something he regrets."

Ott nodded and downed the rest of his beer.

"I think you got it in you, Mort," Scarpa said.

Ott turned to Crawford. "I just worry about Rutledge getting wind of it."

"Yeah, I hear you," Crawford said. "But if it works, we're good."

"And if it doesn't, we're fucked."

"Whoa, whoa, whoa," Scarpa said putting up a hand. "Haven't you guys figured out the genius of Norm Rutledge yet?"

"What the fuck you talking about?" Ott asked, raising his hand for the bartender. "Guy's as much a genius as my fuckin' goldfish."

Scarpa put his hand or Ott's shoulder. "You think Rutledge is a clueless fuck, right?"

"Most of the time," Ott said.

"Almost always," Crawford concurred.

"Well, you're wrong," Scarpa said. "You notice how he lets his good cops run with it?"

"What do you mean?" Ott asked.

"Just what I said. Like you guys. And the way he used to be with me," Scarpa said. "He figured out early on you guys know what you're doing. And gives you a lot of space."

Crawford narrowed his eyes. "I'm not so sure about that."

"He rides our asses pretty good," Ott added.

"Yeah, okay, but—trust me on this—he's got a sense when you're about to crack a case and that's when he stops asking questions and starts giving you room. I know, 'cause, like I said, that's how he played it with me. One thing about good detectives, they wander off the reservation from time to time."

"Yeah, but we wander off so far we're in fuckin' Europe."

Scarpa laughed. "Which is exactly the point. Your past cases have shown Rutledge that when you guys wander, you solve cases. And, if the whole thing blows up, then it's all on you. He can just throw up his hands and say, 'Those assholes never told me what they were up to.'"

The bartender poured them all fresh drafts.

Ott caught Crawford's eye. "Kind of makes sense."

Crawford shrugged, then nodded. "Yeah, I guess. Just something about the phrase, 'the genius of Norm Rutledge' that sticks in my craw."

THIRTY-NINE

OTT WAS DRIVING BACK TO THE STATION, CRAWFORD RIDING shotgun.

"Fuckin' Scarpa. Gotta hand it to him sometimes," Ott said.

"I know," Crawford said. "So, you gonna stay up and watch some more mafia movies tonight? Get into character?"

"I don't know. Which ones are left?"

"Plenty. You got the Boston mob in *The Departed*. Then there's *Goodfellas*. Ray Liotta and Joe Pesci. A classic."

"DeNiro's in it too."

"Yup. And *Mean Streets*."

"DeNiro again. Not a lot of mafia movies that he wasn't in, when you think about it." Ott shook his head ruefully. "But then he went off and did those fucking Focker movies."

"The what?"

"You know, *Meet the Fockers*, *Little Fockers*...there was another one."

"Yeah, what did he do that shit for?"

"Money."

"I guess."

"It's like if Meryl Streep went off and played the lead in *Spongebob Squarepants*."

"Except SpongeBob's a guy and it's a cartoon."

"Yeah, but you know what I mean."

"What else is there?" Crawford asked as they pulled into the station.

"Well, let's see, there was *Donnie Brasco*," Ott said as he turned off the ignition. "Al Pacino and that guy I can't stand."

"Who?"

"You know the guy in the pirate movies who's got all the tats and earrings and shit."

"Johnny Depp?"

"Yeah, him."

"Speaking of Al Pacino. Did you see *Carlito's Way*?"

Ott nodded. "Yeah, but that was hardly a mafia movie."

Crawford heard a door close behind him. "Sure, it was."

"Bullshit. Pacino played that little Puerto Rican dude."

"Gotta hand it to you," Crawford said. "You know your stuff."

"That other whack job I can't stand was in it too."

"Who was that?"

"Sean Penn. What did Madonna ever see in that loser?"

"What are you talkin' about, he's a good actor."

"Bullshit. The only good movie he was ever in was *Fast Times at Ridgemont High*."

"What about..."

"What?"

"That one...*Mystic River*. Or *Reservoir Dogs*?"

Ott laughed. "*Reservoir Dogs*, my misguided friend, was his brother Chris. His ex-brother, Chris, that would be. And okay, *Mystic River* was pretty good, I'll give you that."

"Thank you."

There was a tap on Crawford's window. He looked up and saw Norm Rutledge. He hit the window button. "Hello, Norm, we were just talking about you."

Rutledge chuckled. "Bet you had a lot of nice things to say."

"You'd be surprised."

"I been listening to you bozos," Rutledge said, shaking his head. "Is this what you do when you ain't got shit on a high-profile murder case? Sit around in the parking lot talking movies."

Ott ducked down so he could see Rutledge's face. "Sometimes you just gotta have a few beers, take your mind off business, Norm."

"Oh, so you been at your dive bar?"

"Yeah, we were," Ott said. "Hey, out of curiosity what do you think of Sean Penn?"

"Who?"

"Yup. Just as I expected."

FORTY

Before they went their separate ways home, Crawford and Ott agreed to meet at eight the next morning. Then Ott would head over to Robert Polk's office.

As Crawford was crossing the bridge to West Palm Beach, his cell phone rang.

It was Rose Clarke.

"Hey, Rose. What's up?"

"Hi, Charlie," Rose said. "Ready for another scoop?"

"I hope you got a good one, because we could use something," Crawford said.

"But you solved Pawlichuk."

"Yeah, but this other one's a lot tougher."

"Well, I don't know whether it will help or not. You be the judge," Rose said. "So, word is, Lorinda Polk has a thing going with the trumpet player in Peter Duchin's band."

"Who's Peter Duchin?"

"This society bandleader," Rose said. "Word is they're madly in love and she'd divorce the skinflint—that's Robert Polk, in case you forgot—in a second. Problem is she's got a bad pre-nup."

Crawford thought for a second, but didn't see much there. "Thanks, Rose, I appreciate it."

"Just trying to get another dinner out of you, Charlie."

"I already owe you one."

"I'm ready," she said. "Hope that helps."

But Crawford couldn't really see how it did.

He pulled into his condo building parking lot, turned off the ignition, then just sat there.

Twenty minutes later, he was still sitting there.

Feeling guilty, for one thing. Rose wanted something that was never going to happen. Particularly now that he had gotten serious again with Dominica. But what was he supposed to do? A few more minutes passed. Damned if he knew...he made a much better detective than boyfriend.

He grabbed his cell phone and dialed Rose.

"Hey."

"Hey. When you were hearing about Lorinda Polk, did anything come up about her kids?"

"What kids? She doesn't have any."

"Really? How 'bout...step-kids maybe?"

"No. I would have heard."

"Okay. Well, thanks."

"Sure. Sorry, I couldn't help."

"Oh, trust me, you did."

Crawford clicked off and called a friend who was a lawyer.

"Hey, Tim, sorry to call so late," he said, "but I want to ask how to break a pre-nuptial agreement."

"What? I didn't know you were married, Charlie."

* * *

Ott walked into Crawford's office the next morning with a psyched-up look on his face.

"So, coach, you got any last-minute advice for the big game?"

Crawford motioned for him to have a seat. "I had a couple of interesting conversations last night. First one was Rose. She told me Lorinda Polk has a hot and heavy thing with some musician. How she'd bail on Polk in a heartbeat if she didn't have such a shitty pre-nup."

Ott shook his head. "Jesus, these people," he said. "Does Polk know about it?"

"I don't know the answer to that," Crawford said. "But it gave me an idea. I called up Tim Sampson."

"Your lawyer friend?"

"Yeah. He filled me in on different ways to kill a pre-nup."

Ott leaned forward. "I'm not with you."

"I asked him if a guy having a child out of wedlock would do it," Crawford said. "He said yes."

Ott got it. "So you don't think Lorinda Polk knows about Alex?"

"I don't think anybody but Jaclyn Puckett, Polk, and Carla knew."

"Wow," was all Ott said.

Crawford stroked his chin. "So how do you think your friend, Mr. Polk, would feel if he had to give half his money to his wife so she could go hook up with a horn blower?"

"Uh, offhand I'd say he wouldn't be happy."

Crawford nodded. "Good. So, go make him unhappy."

* * *

OTT PARKED IN THE UNDERGROUND GARAGE OF THE PHILLIPS Point office building, took the elevator up to his Polk's office, dialed Crawford's number and put his cell phone in his pocket.

He felt a little like a boxer going back into the ring after a knock-down in the previous round. Apprehensive but pumped.

When Ott walked into the offices of Polk Global, the receptionist frowned at the sight of him. Like it was way too early in the day to deal with the likes of him.

"Not again," she muttered.

"Don't worry, Jeanette, I'm pretty sure this will be the last time you'll ever see me," he said. "Unless, of course, you'd like to go out on a date one night."

Jeanette just frowned and shook her head.

"Is that any way to start your day?" Ott. said. "That big ol' frown on your face."

"What do you want?"

"What do you think? An audience with big Bob."

She sighed and went back to Polk's office.

She came back a few minutes later. "Follow me."

"Thanks, but I know the way." Ott brushed past her and into Polk's office.

Polk, sitting in the big leather chair behind his desk, made no move to get up.

Ott sat down opposite him. "So, you got a twenty-million-dollar check for me?"

"No, I don't."

"Well, that's good, 'cause I want a lot more than that."

Polk leaned across his desk. "Look. I'm going to make this short. I'll pay you $5 million for that tape and you're getting nothing else since I had nothing to do with what happened to Xavier Duke. Take it or leave it."

Ott ignored his last statement. "What was it that Xavier said that made you shoot him? I been askin' myself that. Did he tell you he was gonna make you his bitch? Keep hittin' you up every time he needed some cash? Was that what got to you? Knowing you were gonna always be his bitch?"

Polk scowled but said nothing.

"Or was it maybe he asked if you chased little girls too. You know what they say, *like father like son*. I think the word for it is child molester. Was it something like that that pushed you over the edge—"

"All right, we're done here," said Polk, glaring with his rattlesnake eyes.

He reached into the front drawer of his desk and pulled out a three-ring binder checkbook and opened it up. He scribbled out a check, stood and flipped it in the direction of Ott.

Ott caught it in mid-air, glanced at it and tore it up into little pieces. Then he gave Polk a little chin-up nod. "Forgot to tell you something. I plan to go see Lorinda if I don't get what I want."

"What are you talking about?"

"Tell your wife about Alex. She doesn't know about him, does she? And when she does, you can kiss that pre-nup goodbye. A lawyer friend told me that having a kid out of wedlock qualifies as 'creating irreparable harm' to a marriage. Blows up even the tightest pre-nup. Oh, and if you want to deny he's your son, that's why they have DNA tests."

Polk's face blanched. He opened his mouth but nothing came out.

"So, bottom line, I'm going to be needing a check for a hundred million. Or else I go see Lorinda. Meaning she gets half your money and goes off with her musician. You do know about him, right?"

Ott held out his hand, palm up.

Polk slapped it away.

Ott smiled. "Look, man, let's recap here. I got a fourteen-year-old girl ready to get real specific about her night with Alex. And I got proof that Alex's your kid," Ott put his palm out again. "So pull that check book out again and start writing."

Polk's nasty, beady eyes drilled into Ott. Then he sighed deeply and opened the desk drawer.

He reached in, but instead of his check book, pulled out an automatic pistol. He aimed it at Ott. "You've gotten really irritating. Let's you, me and Heckler & Koch take a little walk"—Polk gestured toward a door in the far corner of his office— "to my private elevator."

Hearing Polk, Crawford sprang to his feet, grabbed his jacket from behind the door, and ran out of his office. He had no idea where he was going, just that he was.

Polk followed Ott out of the elevator into the underground

garage. "That silver Mercedes over there," Polk said, hitting the clicker in his pocket. The Mercedes's lights flickered and the door locks popped open.

"You drive," Polk said, gesturing with the pistol.

Ott opened the door and slid into the driver's seat, just hoping Crawford was tuned in.

Polk opened the back door behind Ott. He got in and put the Heckler & Koch VP9 up to Ott's head.

"Suddenly you're a lot quieter," Polk said.

Ott pushed the Mercedes ignition button. "Where we goin', chief?"

"To a secluded little spot where there's nothing but alligators and snakes," Polk said. "Take a right out of here and get on Okeechobee going west."

Crawford, listening on his cell phone, ran out of the station house, slid into the Crown Vic, and headed toward the middle bridge.

Ott pulled out of the underground parking lot and got onto Okeechobee just as Crawford hit the gas on the Crown Vic, taking the turn off of South County onto Royal Palm Way.

"So why'd you do it, Bob?"

"Why'd I do what?"

"Kill Duke."

"What difference does it make?"

"Doesn't make any difference," Ott said. "I'm just dying of curiosity."

"You're dying all right," Polk said. "But not of curiosity."

"It was because you knew he'd keep coming back, wasn't it? Be his bitch forever."

Polk sighed. "No, it was because he was a bottom-feeding, lowlife sleaze. When he came to my office it took days before the stench went away. I did the world a favor by exterminating him."

"And while you were doing the world that favor, did you use that gun?"

"Yup. German technology. Can't beat it."

Ott was approaching the Kravis Center on Okeechobee Boulevard.

"The Kravis Center," Ott said, notifying Crawford where he was. "You ever go there?"

"Just keep driving," Polk pressed the semi-automatic against Ott's head.

Ott looked in the rearview mirror for Crawford but didn't see him.

"Pick up the pace," Polk said a few minutes later. Ott was going less than the speed limit.

"What's the rush?" Ott said.

"I've got a lot more important things to do today than dumping you in a swamp," Polk said.

"Oh, yeah, like what?"

"Well, let's see, I have a golf game at three," Polk said. "Spend a little time with my girlfriend after that."

"What a life," Ott said, looking back and seeing the white Crown Vic. "Where are you planning on spending the night tonight?" Ott asked as Crawford pulled up beside them.

"What kind of half-assed question is that?" Polk said, looking through the front windshield and seeing the traffic stopped ahead.

"Because it ain't gonna be at home," Ott said, seeing five unmarked cars blocking the road.

He saw another unmarked Crown Vic pull up on the other side of him.

Polk looked to his left and saw Crawford with his gun aimed at him. Then he looked to his right and saw a man pointing a shotgun at him out the window of the back seat of an unmarked car. He swung around behind him and saw three police cars, their lights going, no sirens. Up ahead, the traffic had come to a dead halt.

"What do you think, Bob?" asked Ott. "Looks like the party's over."

FORTY-ONE

Crawford and Dominica were at Mookie's with Ott and his girlfriend Rebecca. Don Scarpa had pulled up a chair with the double-daters and, exercising great self-control, had not lit up a Winston.

"Works every time, right, Charlie?" Scarpa said.

"What's that?"

"You listen to 'the Shoe' and you get your man."

"Every time."

"Wait a minute," Dominica said. "Don't I get any credit?"

"What did you do?" Scarpa asked.

"Recon mission into the belly of the beast," Ott said. "Spotted the cameras at Xavier Duke's house."

Crawford raised his glass to Dominica. "We'd still be knockin' on doors and pounding the pavement if it wasn't for you."

Rebecca turned to Ott. "I feel kind of out of it."

"What do you mean?" Ott asked.

"All you guys arresting people and throwing 'em in jail," Rebecca said.

"Yeah, and after a few more drinks we'll be tellin' you we rounded up all the top ISIS operatives," Ott said.

Crawford leaned toward Rebecca. "Lucky you," he said. "You get to deal with dogs and cats instead of people."

Dominica turned to Rebecca. "Oh, you're a vet?"

Rebecca nodded.

"I told her," Ott said, "I'd take her mutts over our mutts any day."

"Hey, speaking of which," Crawford said to Ott. "I saw you coming out of Rutledge's office. What was that all about?"

"Oh, Christ," Ott said. "He gets me in there and he says, 'So, Ott, I heard you were running around impersonating some mafia guy.' And I get all serious and say, 'No, Norm, I don't know anything about that. Where'd you hear that?'"

"Atta boy," Crawford said. "Deny, deny, deny."

"And then he gets that stupid look on his face, you know where he's working up to one of his lame-ass jokes."

Crawford, Dominica, and Scarpa all nodded.

"Finally, he goes, 'Maybe you're just spending too much time with that dago Scarpa in your lowlife bar.' And I get all serious. 'Wait a minute, Norm, that sounds like an ethnic slur to me.' And he looks all worried like I'm going to report him to the anti-defamation league."

"Maybe I should have a little talk with human resources," Scarpa said, draining the last of his Yuengling.

Dominica turned to Crawford. "What did you ever hear from Hawes?"

Crawford and Ott both laughed. "Think he must have taken a three-day nap or something," Crawford said. "He got back to us this morning with the ballistics test results on Duke."

"What?" Dominica said.

"Yeah, I explained that we took in the killer yesterday, and he goes, 'Oh yeah, no shit?'"

"Clueless Bob," Dominica said, shaking her head. "Hey, is it true what I heard—about there being only thirty million in Pawlichuk's account? Down from, like, fifty?"

Ott nodded. "If you ever want to lose your money in a hurry, George Figueroa is your go-to guy."

"Yeah, only problem is you gotta go to a jail cell out on Gun Club Road to find him," Crawford said.

Ott leaned back in his chair. "So, I was doing some math and figured that, of Robert Polk's twenty-one billion and Mindy Pawlichuk's hundred-twenty million and whatever Janice Figueroa could hock her Bentley and jewelry for," he said, "none of 'em are ever gonna be able to spend a dime."

"I hope you're not coming up with a moral to the story," Crawford said. "Like, 'Honest and poor is the road to salvation.'"

"Jesus, Charlie, what kinda chump you take me for?" Ott said. "Honest and poor sucks. The moral of the story is—"

"Tell us, oh wise and insightful one."

Ott glanced at Dominica and Rebecca. "Cover your ears, ladies. Moral of the story is...don't ever get fuckin' caught."

THE END

AFTERWORD

I hope you liked *Palm Beach Pretenders*. If you did, I would appreciate it if you would take a few minutes and review it on Amazon by tapping this link: ***Palm Beach Pretenders***. Thank you!

In the meantime, what follows is an exclusive look at the first two chapters of my latest Charlie Crawford mystery. It is so new I haven't even given it a title yet.

To receive an email when it comes out on Amazon, be sure to sign up for my free author newsletter at **tomturnerbooks.com/news**.

Best,
Tom

CHARLIE CRAWFORD
BOOK 6 (SNEAK PEEK)

ONE

In her mind, Claudia Detwiler had already spent the commission money. For starters, she'd book a Danube River cruise on Viking, the one that started in Budapest and ended up in Prague. Someone had told her that you pronounced it *Buda-pesht,* so she planned to enunciate it properly and impress her fellow travelers right off the bat with her worldliness. Even though she lived with Jake Dawson, she'd be traveling alone. After all, everyone was always telling her that she could do better than Jake. And you never know when a handsome German industrialist or Danish count might be bunking a stateroom away.

She also needed to chic up her wardrobe a bit. She'd gotten about all the mileage she could out of her hard-shouldered Versace suit and her Herve Leger Band Aid dress, which fit fine back in her rail-thin days, but not anymore. Then she planned to take some tennis lessons from the cute pro at the Racquet Club for the dual purpose of losing a few pounds and meeting people who might eventually be looking to buy or sell a house in Palm Beach.

Speaking of which, the Donaldsons had seen the house three times already. Claudia was driving to it again because they wanted their children to see it. Kids and houses were a dicey mix, because you never knew what might come out of their spoiled little mouths. "But Mom, I can't stand that pukey carpet in my bedroom," or "How are we supposed to play ultimate frisbee on that tiny, little lawn?"

But, what could she say?

Sorry, your kids can't see the place until after you've got it under contract?

The result of all this was that Bill Donaldson was riding shotgun in her Range Rover while his wife Jessica sat in back with loudmouth Willie and princess Emma. One big, happy quintet, heading for the house on North Lake Way.

Claudia had planned ahead by dispatching her window washer Diego that morning to make sure there were no saltwater stains on the windows, thus ensuring that Bill and Jessica would once again swoon over the ocean view. It cost her a hundred dollars but was well worth it...so she hoped anyway.

"If we had a quick closing—like, say, two or three weeks— do you think we could get it for less?" Bill asked, which was the first sign that he might be considering tossing in a lowball offer.

"I know they turned down twelve five," Claudia said, meaning twelve million, five hundred thousand. She'd heard that, anyway, but wasn't absolutely sure if it was true or not. Bill chewed on that for four or five blocks until Jessica piped in.

"I know it comes with the furniture," she said, "but we're not in love with much of that stuff. In fact, we'd probably have to pay to have Goodwill come and take most of it away."

Yep. A lowball offer was definitely headed her way. It almost seemed as if the pair had practiced this tandem act of disparaging the exquisite edifice around the breakfast table that morning.

Shit, maybe paying Diego wasn't such a good investment after all.

"I don't know what they valued the furniture at," Claudia said, trying to hold things together. "Maybe not too much."

Through the rearview mirror, Claudia watched Jessica nod but not say anything. Another glance back caught Jessica concentrating hard. Like she was thinking up yet another gambit to knock the price down.

Claudia drove into the driveway, trying to think of a way to restore the Donaldson's former enthusiasm. "I just love how the driveway meanders in, then you see—ta-da!—the big reveal of this amazing house."

Bill and Jessica didn't respond despite Claudia's zealous hype job. The big house did have nice curb appeal, though it would have been a lot better if it had another fifty feet of frontage. The neighboring houses felt a little too close on both sides.

Claudia parked and all five of them got out. She pointed at the Canary Island date palm. "That's a real specimen," she said. "I've never seen one that big."

"It's nice," Bill said. He seemed to have been much more excited about it the first time they came. That is, before he lapsed into subtle negotiating mode.

They walked up the six steps to the landing. Willie was bringing up the rear, picking his nose with impunity. Emma yawned as she played a game on her iPhone. Well, at least she was preoccupied and might not bitch about the color of the carpet.

Bill smiled at Jessica as Claudia fiddled with the lock box to get the key. She took it out, pushed it in the keyhole, then turned it, opening the door. The five of them walked into the foyer, Claudia spread her arms wide, and smiled. "Wel-come to Casa...Donaldson!" she proclaimed as they all walked into the living room. It truly was a fantastic ocean view, though she noticed that Diego had missed a spot on the upper right-hand corner of a window.

"See what I mean about the furniture?" Jessica said to her husband, though the comment was clearly for Claudia's benefit.

"I wouldn't be so sure Goodwill will even take it at all," Bill said.

Claudia was beginning to hate this family of negative thinkers, nosepickers, and smartphone savants. She decided to zero in on the check-writer, Bill, as Jessica and the kids peeled off in the direction of the master bedroom.

"In analyzing the comps," Claudia said, "the price is really good on a per-square-foot basis."

Bill nodded as his eyes wandered along the crown molding.

"As you can see, they spared no expense on the details." Claudia watched Bill's eye drift over to where Diego had missed the corner.

"I've never had a place on the ocean," Bill asked. "Do you need to clean the windows all the time?"

"Oh, gosh, no," Claudia lied. "Just every once in a while."

"How often is that?" Bill asked. "Once every couple of days? Every week?"

Claudia started to answer but was interrupted by the piercing scream of Jessica in another room. Then Emma joined in. Then Willie, the little nose picker hollering louder than his mother and sister put together.

TWO

THE WOMAN'S NAKED BODY LAY FACE-UP IN A JACUZZI BATHTUB
in the spacious master bathroom, her head just below the granite tub
surround. On the surround, the words *Reclining Nude* had been
scrawled in Crest toothpaste. An empty tube lay discarded on the
floor in front of the tub.

Something in Palm Beach homicide cop Charlie Crawford's past
academic life told him that *Reclining Nude* was the name of a famous
painting. He had taken a gut course in art back at Dartmouth which
turned out to be one of his favorite classes ever. Every now and then
he'd go to the Norton Museum in West Palm or hit a gallery or two
on Worth Avenue, even though he couldn't afford to buy anything.

Crawford and his partner Mort Ott had ID'd the body, having
located her purse on a counter in the kitchen. Her name was Mimi
Taylor and the business card in her wallet said she worked at Sotheby's Real Estate at 340 Royal Poinciana Way in Palm Beach. Crawford and Ott had been joined at the scene by the medical examiner
and two women from the Palm Beach Police Department's Crime
Scene Evidence Unit.

Bob Hawes, the ME, had reached the official verdict that Taylor had been strangled to death—this, about an hour after Crawford and Ott had, unofficially, come to the same conclusion.

Crawford had Googled *Reclining Nude* and found a painting by that name by Amedeo Modigliani that had sold for $170 million three years before at a Christie's auction. It depicted a naked woman, not in a bathtub but on what appeared to be a burgundy-colored sofa.

Going back to his search results, Crawford had found another painting called *Reclining Nude*—this one painted by Picasso. The Picasso was a lot more abstract. He'd take the Modigliani over the Picasso any day, but didn't have $170 million lying around.

Crawford motioned Ott to follow him out of the bathroom so they could have a private conversation. Ott followed him out into the large master bedroom.

"So, for starters, no evidence of rape," Crawford began.

"But obviously she didn't walk in here with no clothes on," Ott said.

"So the killer either had her strip while she was still alive, or took her clothes off after he killed her," Crawford said. "I'm guessing it was either someone she was showing the house to or else the suspect was already here."

"Well, if it was someone she showed the house to, he wouldn't have been stupid enough to have called her on his own phone. Or given her his real name."

"Exactly. So he'd have used a burner and a fake name."

Ott nodded. "Or could have met her here," he said. "Called her on the burner and told her he saw her name and number on the sign and wanted to see it right away. She might have been in her office or car and came right over."

"Yeah," Crawford said. "Could be. I was also thinking he could have been a burglar she caught in the act. Except if he was, he would have taken her cash and credit cards—" he had a second thought— "Plus that whole thing with the toothpaste and staging her body...it's gotta be premeditated."

"So you're ruling out burglary?" Ott asked.

"I'm not ruling out anything yet. Let's just call it unlikely."

"I agree."

"There are two other things," Crawford said, glancing around the room. "The vic's car isn't here, neither are her clothes."

"So maybe the suspect took her car. Clothes, too."

"Which means he didn't drive here."

"Or... maybe there were two of them?"

Crawford cocked his head. "Yeah, but I'm not getting that vibe."

One of the CSEU techs walked into the master bedroom. Her name was Dominica McCarthy, and she and Crawford had a history.

"What's your take?" Ott asked her.

"Hell if I know, Mort," Dominica said. "I'm just the hair, prints, and DNA girl."

Ott chuckled. "You're a lot more than that," he said. "Whatcha got so far?"

"I got lots of everything," Dominica said. "Which tells me one of two things: either the house has been shown a lot lately, or else the cleaners haven't come around in a while. Or maybe both."

"A lot is better than nothing, right?" Crawford smiled at her. "So what are you zeroing in on?"

"The hair and DNA in the tub and that toothpaste tube."

"Think you might lift a print off the tube?" Crawford asked.

"Maybe," Dominica said. "A partial anyway. What do you guys have?"

Ott smiled. "Being the art connoisseur I am, I know that both Picasso and Mogigliano did paintings called *Reclining Nude*."

Dominica chuckled. "I believe it's pronounced Modigliani," she said.

"Close enough," Ott said.

"Other than that, we're just tossing things around," Crawford said.

"Where it all starts, right?" Dominica said.

Crawford nodded.

"All right then, boys," Dominica said, walking toward the door. "Wrap it up by the weekend, will you?"

"Do our best," Crawford said as Ott nodded.

* * *

BACK IN HIS OFFICE AT THE POLICE STATION ON COUNTY ROAD, Crawford called the Sotheby's office, identified himself, and asked to speak to the manager, whose name he had just learned from the receptionist was Arthur Lang.

"Yes, hello, detective, this is Arthur Lang."

Crawford could tell by his tone Lang knew about what had happened to Mimi Taylor.

"Hi, Mr. Lang, I'm calling about the death of your agent, Mimi Taylor."

"So horrible," Lang said. "I—well, I just can't even comprehend it."

"I know and I'm very sorry," Crawford said. "I'd like to ask you some questions."

"Of course," Lang said. "Ask me anything."

"Thank you," Crawford said. "First, I need to know who her next of kin are, if you know."

"Yes, I looked that up shortly after I heard what happened. Her mother's name is Mrs. Andrew Taylor and she lives up in Vero Beach."

"So Ms. Taylor was never married?" Either that or she had been married and kept her maiden name. Or had been divorced and had taken it back.

"As far as I know," Lang said.

"And do you have her mother's phone number?"

Lang said yes and gave him the number. "I also suggest that you speak to another agent here named Carrie Nyquist. Mimi and Carrie were best friends."

"Is she in the office now?" Crawford said.

"I think so. I saw her a little while ago," Lang said. "I can transfer you, if you'd like."

"Before you do," Crawford said, "I assume you have Ms. Taylor's address?"

"I do," Lang said. "She lived down at one of those condo buildings at the south end. Address is 2500 South Ocean Boulevard. Just south of the Par Three."

"You don't happen to have a key to her condo, do you?"

"No, but Carrie might."

"Okay, thanks. If you could transfer me over to Ms. Nyquist now..." Crawford said. "Oh, and Mr. Lang, I'd like to come to your office tomorrow morning and speak to all your agents if that's possible."

"Sure, I understand," Lang said. "How is ten o'clock?"

"That's good."

"I'll send out an email and tell my agents it's a mandatory meeting."

"Thank you again," Crawford said. "Now, if you could transfer me, please?"

"You're welcome. Here goes."

Crawford waited a few seconds.

"This is Carrie," said the voice.

"Hello, Ms. Nyquist, my name is Detective Crawford, Palm Beach Police. I am very sorry about the loss of your friend, Ms. Taylor. Would you mind if I asked you some questions?"

The woman sighed deeply. "Oh, God. I just can't believe it. She was the best..." And with that she began to cry.

"I'll make this brief, Ms. Nyquist. Was Ms. Taylor ever married?"

"No, but she had been living with a man until recently. For almost three years. Lowell Grey is his name."

"And had she been seeing anybody else since then?"

"Yes, but she wouldn't tell me who."

"Why not? Do you know?"

"I could guess."

"Because the other man's married?"

Nyquist didn't respond.

"Ms. Nyquist?"

"I think he might have been," she said

Crawford tapped his desk with his fingers. "Did Ms. Taylor ever mention anyone she was...scared of, maybe? Anyone who ever threatened her? Or who may have physically assaulted her?"

Carrie Nyquist sniffled. "No. She never mentioned anyone. I mean, Mimi was a woman who worked very hard but had a pretty simple life. She wasn't a party girl or a social butterfly like a lot of the women in this business."

"Mr. Lang told me about her mother up in Vero Beach. Do you know whether she had any other immediate family?"

"No. She was an only child."

"One more thing. Do you happen to have a key to her apartment?"

"Yes, I actually do, she gave it to me because she used to have a dog," Nyquist said. "Sometimes she'd go out of town for a day or two and I'd go feed and walk it."

"I understand," Crawford said. "Could I stop by and get that key from you? I'm going to need to go inspect her apartment."

"Sure," Nyquist said. "I'll be in and out the rest of the day. I'll leave it with the receptionist, who's here until six."

"Sounds good. Thank you very much. Oh, also, Mr. Lang's going to ask all of you agents to come in tomorrow morning to meet with me and my partner, so I hope to see you then. I may have some more questions at that point. Thanks again."

"You're welcome," Nyquist said. "See you tomorrow morning."

Crawford clicked off and thought about what he'd say to Mimi Taylor's mother. It was pretty much the same script every time, just a different name. He and Ott alternated making the calls. It was a job no one wanted.

* * *

CLAUDIA DETWILER WAS IN A FOUL MOOD. THE *RECLINING Nude* murder had probably killed her sale of the house on North Lake Way and now Jessica Donaldson wasn't returning her calls. The drive back to her office after they found the body of Mimi Taylor had been a quiet one. Except for that little pain-in-the-ass Willie, who'd whimpered all the way home, as if he'd just crashed his Luke Skywalker Landspeeder into a bridge abutment.

The Palm Beach EMS team had gotten there ten minutes after Claudia put in the 911 call and an EMT had paid particular attention to Jessica Donaldson, who seemed to be in shock. He'd offered to take her to Good Samaritan Hospital, just over the north bridge in West Palm, but she said she was okay. Her daughter and husband were doing fine and her son...well, Willie was Willie.

Crawford and Ott had come to Claudia's office to interview her and the three now sat together in the real estate agency's conference room.

"During the entire time you were at the house on North Lake Way, Ms. Detwiler," Ott was asking, "did you see anyone else there?"

"No," Claudia said. "No one."

Unlike his short, stout, balding partner, Charlie Crawford looked nothing like a cop. He looked more like a male model who'd just popped out of a GQ ad (minus the snappy threads.) "So, you and your clients walked into the house and were going through it when Mrs. Donaldson and her son and daughter walked into the master bathroom?" Crawford asked.

"That's pretty much it," Claudia said. "I was with the husband when the wife and two kids went into the master and master bath. I ran in when I heard the screaming."

"Did you ever go up to the second story?" Ott asked.

Crawford knew what Ott was thinking. Maybe the killer had gone up there to hide if he heard Detwiler and the Donaldsons come into the house.

"No, we never got that far," Claudia said. "The police came, then the paramedics. We left a little while after that."

"Did you make an appointment with Mimi Taylor, the listing agent, before going to the house?" Crawford asked.

"Yes, I did," Claudia said. "She was going to show the house to my customers. I thought it was odd she wasn't there, because she's normally so prompt."

"So you've worked with her before?"

"Oh, yes, quite a bit," Claudia said.

"Was anyone else around?" Crawford asked. "Like a landscaper maybe, or a pool man or a caretaker?"

"Nobody that I saw," Claudia said. "Oh, wait a minute, I forgot. I sent over my window cleaner in the morning. Maybe he saw something."

Ott noted that in his well-worn notebook, then looked up. "What's his name? And number if you have it."

Claudia scrolled down on her iPhone. "His name is Diego. I don't remember his last name...wait a minute, here it is Diego Andujar." She read Ott his phone number.

"And, Ms. Detwiler, just so we're clear," Crawford said, "you were with the husband, Mr. Donaldson, when you heard Mrs. Donaldson screaming. Correct?"

"Yes."

"And where were you?"

"In the living room. He was admiring the view of the ocean and the beach."

Crawford nodded. "Did you happen to notice anybody walking away from the house toward the beach when you were looking out?"

"No, sorry, I didn't."

"You mentioned having worked with Ms. Taylor fairly frequently. Did you know her pretty well?"

"Not that well," Claudia said. "I just knew her as a good agent. I sold another listing of hers last year."

"What do you know about her?" Ott asked.

"What do you mean? I just told you."

Crawford hadn't had a chance to catch Ott up on his conversations with Arthur Lang and Carrie Nyquist.

"I just wondered what you know about her relationships with men or her personal life in general?" Ott said.

Claudia exhaled and glanced out the window. "I remember hearing that she had a longstanding relationship with a man, but I think they may have broken up."

"Do you know any more about it?" Ott asked.

Claudia shrugged. "Sorry."

Crawford nodded and glanced over at Ott. "I can't think of any more questions, for now."

"Me either," Ott said, standing up. "Could we get your card in case we need to get back in touch with you."

"Sure," she said, then she reached into her purse and pulled out two cards. She gave one to each of them.

Crawford and Ott stood up, across the conference table from Detwiler.

"Oh, one last thing," Crawford said. "Could you give us the cell phone numbers of Mr. or Mrs. Donaldson, please. Just in case we need to talk to them."

Claudia gave them Jessica Donaldson's number. "Be my guest. I think my conversations with those two are fini."

* * *

On the way back to the station house, Crawford put in a call to Diego Andujar. It went to voicemail, so he left a message. "Mr. Andujar, my name in Detective Crawford, Palm Beach Police Department. Please call me as soon as possible." He left his number.

"Why does that name sound familiar?" Ott asked

"I don't know," Crawford said. "Third baseman for the Yankees? Except it's Miguel."

Ott shook his head. "The guy I'm thinking of boosted cars."

"Really?" Crawford said. "Wonder if he boosted Mimi's Taylors'?"

"Let's find the little beaner," Ott said, never one you'd call politically correct. "Meanwhile I'll check him out on FDLE."

Ott was referring to a website that contained a database of individual criminal records.

"While you're at it, see about getting a search warrant for Mimi Taylor's place?" Crawford said. "If you're right about Andujar having a record, he wouldn't be a guy I'd give access to a twelve-million-dollar house."

Ott smiled. "*If* I'm right."

"You were once back in 2016."

Ott shook his head and rolled his eyes. "Funny fuck, Chuck."

END OF EXCERPT

To receive an email when the sixth Charlie Crawford Palm Beach Mystery is released, sign up for Tom's free newsletter at tomturnerbooks.com/news.

ABOUT THE AUTHOR

A native New Englander, Tom dropped out of college and ran a bar in Vermont...into the ground. Limping back to get his sheepskin, he then landed in New York where he spent time as an award-winning copywriter at several Manhattan advertising agencies. After years of post-Mad Men life, he made a radical change and got a job in commercial real estate. A few years later he ended up in Palm Beach, buying, renovating and selling houses while getting material for his novels. On the side, he wrote *Palm Beach Nasty*, its sequel, *Palm Beach Poison*, and a screenplay, *Underwater*.

While at a wedding, he fell for the charm of Charleston, South Carolina. He spent six years there and completed a yet-to-be-published series set in Charleston. A year ago, Tom headed down the road to Savannah, where he just finished a novel about lust and murder among his neighbors.

Learn more about Tom's books at:
www.tomturnerbooks.com

 facebook.com/tomturner.books